Thomas McMurray

Temperance Lectures

With Autobiography

Thomas McMurray

Temperance Lectures
With Autobiography

ISBN/EAN: 9783337117849

Printed in Europe, USA, Canada, Australia, Japan

Cover: Foto ©Raphael Reischuk / pixelio.de

More available books at **www.hansebooks.com**

IPERANCE LECTURES.

BY

THOMAS McMURRAY.

WITH AUTOBIOGRAPHY.

TORONTO
HUNTER, ROSE & COMPANY.
1873.

◀

HUNTER, ROSE & Co.,
Printers and Binders,
Toronto

Dedication.

THIS VOLUME IS RESPECTFULLY DEDICATED

TO THE

Honourable Malcolm Cameron,

IN CONSIDERATION OF HIS

UNFLINCHING ADHERENCE TO TOTAL ABSTINENCE PRINCIPLES,

AND AS A MARK OF

APPRECIATION OF THE DISTINGUISHED SERVICES

HE HAS

RENDERED THE TEMPERANCE CAUSE IN CANADA

DURING THE PAST FORTY YEARS,

BY HIS SINCERE FRIEND,

The Author.

CONTENTS.

AUTOBIOGRAPHY.

LECTURES.

LECTURE I.

PROHIBITION.

LECTURE II.

DANGER.

LECTURE III.

OUR DUTY.

LECTURE IV.

THE TEMPERANCE ENTERPRISE.

LECTURE V.

OBJECTIONS CONSIDERED.

LECTURE VI.

INTEMPERANCE.

LECTURE VII.

THE LIQUOR TRAFFIC.

LECTURE VIII.

THE EFFECTS OF ALCOHOL.

LECTURE IX.

THE ASPECT OF THE QUESTION.

LECTURE X.

THE MEDICINAL USE OF ALCOHOLIC STIMULANTS.

ADDENDA.

MISCELLANEOUS.

TEMPERANCE BALLADS.

INTRODUCTION.

IN presenting this volume to the public, I lay no claim to originality or literary ability. The delivery of those Lectures, however, have not been without results in the past, and numerous friends having urged that they should appear in this form, I have complied. More willingly have I consented, as it is no longer possible for me to make my periodical visits to advocate the claims of Temperance as in days gone by. I deeply regret that other business engagements have prevented me from having sufficient time at my disposal to prepare them as I would have desired for the press. I trust that critics will look mildly upon my humble production, and that it may in some measure tend to prepare the public mind for the entire prohibition of the Liquor Traffic.

I have to acknowledge my indebtedness to Mr. John Parkhill for much of the information regarding my native place, which is taken from his excellent work entitled "The History of Paisley."

THOMAS McMURRAY.

AUTOBIOGRAPHY.

I WAS born on the 7th of May, 1831, at Paisley, Scotland. As disputes have arisen at the close of some of my meetings as to my nationality, I desire to state that my father is a native of County Armagh, Ireland; my mother (whose maiden name was Jane Baxter) was born at Alloa, Scotland. Paisley, including its suburbs, is spread over a tract of ground comprising an area of about two and a half miles. Its main street runs from east to west nearly two miles, and forms part of the road from Glasgow to Beith, and the towns on the coast of Ayrshire. Various have been the opinions held respecting Paisley. Rowland Hill pronounced it the Paradise of Scotland, while others have circulated very different views. Of late years its appearance has been improved. The streets are well paved and lighted with gas. The town is also plentifully supplied with very superior water, brought from the Braes of Gleniffer by means of reservoirs. Amongst the attractions are the John Nelson Endowment, for educating, clothing, and outfitting young persons who have acquired a three years' residence in town, and whose parents have died without leaving funds for that purpose. The building, which is erected on the highest point of ground, is one of the greatest attractions of the place. It is of Ita-

lian architecture, with four fronts 120 feet in length, sur-
mounted by a central dome 90 feet high, from the balcony
of which ten counties may be seen. The magnificent Abbey
Church, which existed at the Reformation, was built in
the reigns of James I. and II., and was nearly completed
by Abbot Thomas in 1459. It was after the model of a
cathedral, in the form of a cross, with a lofty steeple finished after the Abbot's death. The spacious building of
this monastery, with its extensive orchards and gardens,
and a small park for fallow-deer, were surrounded by a
magnificent wall of cut stone, upwards of a mile in cir-
cumference, which was built in the reign of James III, in
1485, by George Shaw, Abbot of Paisley. The nave of
the monastery, now the Abbey Church of Paisley, forms a
most interesting surviving specimen of Gothic architecture. It is the only part which now remains of this once
splendid building. The Abbey of Paisley was the family
burying-place of the Stuarts before their accession to
the throne, and even after that period; Euphemie, Queen
of Robert II., and Robert III. were buried at Paisley—
the first in 1387, and the second in 1406. In 1847 an
Athenæum was instituted, also an Artizans' Institution,
and a Government School of Design was likewise opened.
The Grammar School is a royal foundation, having been
established by James VI. in 1576. Some years ago, a
public cemetery was formed. It is beautifully situated
on a rising ground to the west of the town, and is taste-
fully ornamented; here my dear mother, who departed
this life on the 13th day of April, 1859, is buried. Hope
Temple Gardens is a lovely spot, adorned with the

choicest selection of plants and flowers, and trees of the rarest kind. It is acknowledged one of the finest in Scotland.

Paisley has attained the eminence of being one of the first manufacturing towns in the world. The manufacture of silk was first introduced in Maxwelton, Paisley, in the year 1759, and started a new era in the prosperity of the place. The shawl trade, for which Paisley has become so noted, commenced in the early part of the present century.

Paisley has long been celebrated for the manufacture of thread, which forms the most generally prosperous branch of trade. At first it was made from linen yarn, and originated with a Miss Shaw, daughter of the Laird of Bargarran. The two largest factories are the Seedhills (J. & P. Clark), and Ferguslie (J. & P. Coats). The thread is made of the best cotton yarn, and the machinery used is of the most ingenious description. It is a grand sight to view the process of thread-making, and see the hundreds of handsome, healthy-looking young women, all clad with drugget petticoats and light-coloured *jupes*, busy as bees in a hive. Paisley thread was exhibited in Paris, in the Universal Exhibition of 1855, by all the manufacturers, and the jury awarded a medal to each exhibitor, and expressed their opinion strongly in favour of its excellence.

Paisley has become noted as the birthplace of eminent men. Mr. John Henning, the celebrated modeller, was a native of Paisley ; Fillans, the sculptor, spent his boyhood days in this ancient town ; Mr. Morrison, Jacquard machine maker, whose inventions have won for him a high place in manufacturing circles, was born here. John Wilson—the celebrated Christopher North, of world-wide celebrity—was a Paisley man ; Robert Tannahill, the sweet lyrical poet, was the son of a Paisley weaver ; to which I may add William Finlay and Alexander Wilson, the ornithologist and poet.

At Elderslie, about two miles west of Paisley, stands the venerable old house where the renowned Sir William Wallace was born. The tree under which the hero took shelter when pursued by his enemies, stood about the centre of the village, and was an object of great admiration. A small portion of it I have now in my possession, and value it highly as a relic of the past.

The Braes of Gleniffer—braes rendered classic by the muse of Tannahill—have always been a favourite place of resort by Paisley folks. The view from various points on these hills is scarcely to be equalled in Scotland. The fine vale of Renfrewshire lies before you like a map, with its towns and villages, railways and rivers ; whilst beyond this is seen the Clyde, with steamers constantly plying on it. Dumbarton Castle, and beyond this the mountains of Argyleshire, rise in majestic grandeur, with beautiful Loch Lomond to complete the view, forming one of the most magnificent landscapes that the eye ever witnessed.

The Romans invaded Britain under Julius Cæsar fifty-five years before the Christian era, but it was not till one hundred and thirty-five years later, in the reign of the Emperor Vespasian, that Agricola, with the Roman army, advanced into the northern parts of the country.

The Romans occupied Britain to a certain extent for nearly five hundred years, during two hundred of which Paisley was an important Roman military station. No doubt the natives gained a knowledge and practice of the useful arts by coming in contact with the warriors of Rome, and as there were many Christian soldiers in the Roman army, this little colony was soon instructed in the new faith. During the eventful years that followed, the people of Paisley stood steadfast to their Presbyterian integrity, and during the civil wars had a sad struggle. The restoration of the unprincipled Charles II. was the restoration of unprincipled tyranny. There is one episode, however, which cannot be omitted: James Algie and John Park, farmers in Kinneshead, in the parish of Eastwood, were charged with Covenanting principles. On private information they were arrested and brought to Paisley Jail. Hamilton of Orbiston, a commissioner for the trial of Covenanting rebels, came to Paisley to superintend the trial. On the 3rd of February, 1685, they were charged with refusing the oath of abjuration. They were found guilty at 10 A.M., executed at 2 P.M., and buried at the foot of the gallows in Gallow Green. On their gravestone was placed the following inscription: "Here lie the corpses of James Algie and John Park, who suffered at the Cross of Paisley, for refusing the oath of abjuration, February 3, 1685." This stone, with part of the dust and bones of the martyrs, was removed from the common place of execution to a new burying-ground in Broomlands, adjoining the cemetery, by order of John Storie, John Pattison, and John Cochrane, magistrates in Paisley. A few years since, an elegant monument, from a design by Mr. Drummond, was erected to their memory. The horrid state of things indicated came to an end, and the twenty-eight years of cruel persecution which Scotland suffered for conscience sake were finished by the flight of the detestable James II., and putting William, Prince of Orange, of glorious memory, in his place as King of Scotland, England, and Ireland.

Paisley was constituted into a free burgh in barony on the 19th day of August, 1488, and in the first year of the reign of James IV.

My father was a weaver. When only seven years of age I was employed as a draw-boy, at which I continued until I was eleven years old; then I commenced weaving, but not being content with driving the shuttle, I afterwards was engaged to Mr. John Spence, butter and egg merchant, with whom I stayed for three years. During my apprenticeship with that gentleman, I attended a night school, where I acquired a limited education. On the 9th of September, 1845, the first juvenile Total Abstinence Society was formed in the town, when my name was enrolled as its fifth member, and before I was sixteen years of age I was elected president, and frequently addressed meetings in my native town, Ayr and other places.

And here I cannot help expressing how deeply I am obligated to Mr. John Spence, to whose wise head, kind heart and Christian example I owe much, and as a mark of my lasting gratitude I have given one of my sons his name, praying that he may emulate his many virtues.

I remember being told by my mother, that my grand-father—while plying his vocation as a stocking weaver—on one occasion during a thunder storm, near a window, had his hair instantly turned from black to white, the silver-washed buttons on his knee-breeches tarnished, and yet felt nothing beyond a strange sensation pass over his whole frame.

From having read stories of life at sea, I acquired a strong desire to become a sailor, and on June 23rd, 1846, I sailed from Glasgow as an apprentice ; but the voyage from Liverpool to New York more than satisfied me that I had not the wisdom of Solomon. One or two little inci-dents of the voyage I have never forgotten. The first mate frequently employed me to wash for him. On one occa-sion I tied a rope's end to a pair of pants and flung them overboard to rinse, when the action of the water quickly severed the connection, and away went the pants. Know-ing by past experience that if they were not forthcoming when demanded a sound flogging would be the result, I instantly ran to the ship's stern and leaped overboard, and succeeded in regaining the inexpressibles, throwing them over my left shoulder, and made my way back to the ship. Fortunately the sailors observed my impulsive act, and sounded "'bout ship," so that a rope was thrown over, which I greedily seized, and once more stood upon the deck of the *Ellerslie* of Glasgow. While lying at anchor at the Quarantine in New York harbour I observed three men making ready to abandon the ship. While they were dropping their hammocks into the boat, I ran down to the forecastle, and, unlocking my chest, seized the Bible

which had been presented to me by my mother on leaving
home, and made for the boat. While descending the cable
chain the sailors objected, but I said I would sound the
alarm unless they would allow me to enter, to which they
reluctantly complied. Off we rowed in a straight line
ahead of the ship, then we steered for Red Hook Point.
On our arrival at Long Island, the boat was pulled on
shore; here the three sailors went into a tavern. Whilst
drinking, they stated that there was an apprentice out on
the beach, and expressed their regret at being obliged to
leave him, but as he was the property of the ship, they
were afraid to do otherwise. Fortunately for me, Mr.
Henry Beardall was painting at this place, and overheard
what passed. During this conversation I was sitting on
the shore, without a cent in my pocket or one friend on
this side of the broad Altantic, my entire stock in trade
consisting of a pair of canvas trousers, blue flannel shirt,
and the Bible before alluded to. While lamenting the
bitter fruit of my past folly, Mr. Beardall approached, and
kindly invited me home, an offer which I gladly accepted,
and for which I shall ever feel deeply thankful. After
spending some days at his hospitable dwelling, he suggested that I should go to the place where the long-boat
had been left and inquire if the ship had sailed. On entering the tavern, I was surprised to find the first and second
mates, boatswain and others sitting round a table enjoying their grog. Quick as thought, I turned round and
ran with more than ordinary speed, never stopping until
I had placed myself in a concealed place beyond their
reach; and thus I escaped. When Mr. Beardall was satis-

fied that the ship had sailed, he began to exert himself in order to find employment for me; this he continued without success for about two weeks, when, accompanied by his son, I proceeded to New York to apply for a situation. On leaving, I resolved that I would not return to be a further burden upon his generosity, no matter what the consequences might be, as I could not bear the thought of remaining longer when I had no prospect of remunerating him for his kindness. Many were the attempts I made to find work, but failure awaited me on every hand; at last, wearied and downcast, I stood upon the side-walk, not knowing what to do: the young man who was with me all the while doing his best to persuade me to return home with him to Brooklyn. While in this dilemma, a man who had been observing my movements came up and said, " My brave young fellow, will you go to sea ?" to which I replied, " Yes, I'll go anywhere," when he invited me into an adjoining tavern to have dinner, whereupon young Beardall ran home and informed his father that one of the men-catchers who got so many dollars per head for entrapping young men to go to Greenland on whaling voyages had taken me. Mr. Beardall on hearing this news left his work and came over to where I was, and lifting me in his arms—while the tears ran down his face —he never let me go until he placed me down upon the deck of the ferry-boat plying between New York and Brooklyn. The stern men-catchers refused to let me go, stating that the ship would sail in an hour, but my benefactor wept and pleaded so that at last they allowed him to carry out his purpose; thus was I again delivered, and brought once more beneath the roof of my genuine friend.

Some days afterwards the following advertisement appeared in the morning papers :—" WANTED, Men to work on the 63rd and 64th sections of the New York and Erie Railroad," &c. &c., in response to which I took my departure.

My friend accompanied me to the boat and paid my fare as far as Ottisville, and as the advertisement stated that teams would be waiting there to convey parties to the works, I refused to accept of anything saving my bare passage money. On leaving Mr. Beardall, it was a trying scene ; I was deeply conscious of my obligations, and yet had not the ability to make any compensation. All I possessed was the Bible before referred to, and just as the boat was moving off I placed it in his hand, although I prized it beyond gold, and requested him to keep it until he should hear from me again. At length I arrived at Ottisville, but no teams were in waiting, so I was obliged to take shelter for the night in the freight shed. Next morning, feeling hungry and being destitute of means, I entered a house and asked for help, but was roughly refused. Thus without money, food, or friends, I was left to reflect on the folly of leaving home contrary to the entreaties and tears of loving parents. At length my eye caught a wild apple tree in a field near the station, which I ascended, and gladly did I partake of the *sour* fruit to allay the cravings of hunger. Again the shades of evening gathered over me, and I took refuge in the freight shed. After spending a restless night the long-looked-for morning came, and as I sauntered forth I met a navvy going to his work with a piece of bread in his hand. Stepping up to him I said, "Friend, I'm very hungry; will you give me a bite of bread?" to which he replied, "Here, take it all, and I will go and bring you more," which he did, and for which to this day I feel truly thankful. It is utterly impossible for me to convey even the faintest idea of the bitter remorse which I felt. At last despair seized me, and I began to contemplate taking away my life by hanging or drowning, when the long-looked-for team arrived, and off I started to my new field of labour. Arrived at the shanty and partaken of a hearty meal, I retired to rest; next morning at sunrise I arose with the other men, and after breakfast began work as a common navvy; but being only 16 years old, and never having been accustomed to outdoor labour, I found it hard work to wield the heavy pick, as I undermined the stiff embankment. The contractor (Bevere Depuy) coming along soon perceived that the work was more than I could manage, and kindly promised to look out for something lighter. Shortly afterwards I was appointed carter, but not being accustomed to horses I drove too near the edge and precipitated horse and cart down the steep embankment, a distance of 60 feet; but, fortunately for the owner, no serious injury resulted. The cook having taken sick I was requested to fill that important office which, I occupied during my stay at the Shewangunk mountains. Thus the time passed. Every month the roll was called, and the men appeared and received their wages; but as it was my intention to return home, I left my wages in the hands of my employers until

I would have sufficient to enable me to accomplish this. But imagine the disappointment I experienced when one morning the news spread along the line that Bevere Depuy had failed, and, although he had near eighteen months' wages of mine, it was with difficulty that I procured a coat and pair of boots out of the store, and sufficient money to carry me back to New York. What was I now to do ? Whether would I proceed further into the country and attempt to earn enough to take me home, or make for New York and try to work my passage back ? Love of home predominated. On my arrival at New York I waited upon several captains, related my circumstances, and asked permission to work my passage home ; but was refused in every instance. Making the acquaintance of a ship carpenter on board a homeward-bound vessel, I seized the opportunity, and just before the ship left her moorings stepped on board. After the pilot had left, and I learned that we were out at sea, I left my hiding place ; the news soon spread, and the captain demanded that the stowaway should appear in his presence. Never shall I forget that introduction ; his first act was to kick me across the deck, and then I had to go aloft, where I was exposed to the cold for hours. The weather was exceedingly stormy ; for 48 hours the sailors did not retire to rest, their only food being biscuits and water. The galley and one of the anchors were swept away, and two of the sailors were washed overboard. I well remember that while the ship was going at the rate of 13 or 14 knots an hour, the captain, maddened with brandy, would pace the deck and would alternately whistle and exclaim, "Blow, ye d—d winds, blow." After a voyage of 19 days we arrived at Liverpool, with only the mainsail on board, all the rest having been shattered to pieces. Though in Liverpool, the next difficulty was how to get home. Gladly did I deposit the boots and coat with the steam-boat agents in pledge for a passage from Liverpool to Greenock, which occupied 24 hours, during which I only ate once. Then I had 18 miles to walk to Paisley; hungry and fatigued I journeyed on, glad to beg a raw turnip from a farmer's boy. When within two miles of home, overcome with weakness I entered a house and asked for a morsel of bread, to which the servant replied, "The maister and mistress are awa at the kirk, and I hae naething tae gie ye." Coming out I sat down upon a ditch and reasoned thus: "Here am I within two miles of home, and, after all my fatigue, shall I die before I see my parents, or will I try to proceed? O, how I long to see my father's face! and how I wish that my dear mother's tender hands would close these eyelids! I'll try it again, if I should crawl on my hands and feet." At length my father's house appeared in sight (this was on Sabbath evening, March 12th, 1848). No sooner did I enter the close than my dear mother recognized my step, and said: "There's Thomas," and for nine days she never spoke another word. O, the depth of a mother's love! it is firm as a rock and stronger than death. "If there be one thing pure, where all beside is sullied, that can endure when all else pass away—if there be aught surpassing human word or deed or thought, it is a mother's love."

The fever had been raging in Paisley; every member of

my family, excepting my father, had been afflicted by it, and the hardships through which I had just passed made me an easy victim to the disease ; consequently I took ill, and my life for some weeks was despaired of, but God in his mercy restored me again.   After my recovery I removed to Glasgow, where I was employed as salesman in a large grocery establishment.   On 10th June, 1850, although not 20 years of age, I got married to my second cousin, and commenced business on my own account in my native town.   In 1852 I removed to Belfast, and for several years followed the occupation of commercial traveller, and in 1858 became identified with the "Irish Temperance League."   In 1861 I emigrated to the district of Muskoka, in the Province of Ontario, where I have resided ever since.

It is with pain that I am obliged to state, that when I became a young man I began to indulge in the drinking usages, and my position as a commercial traveller greatly exposed me to the seductive influences of strong drink ; but I am glad to add that, through the exertions of Mr. James H. Beatty, a zealous Temperance man, I was induced to identify myself with the good cause, and from that time to the present I have endeavoured to do my utmost to advance its interests.   I look upon it as the cause of humanity and the cause of God.

LECTURE I.

PROHIBITION.

THE all-absorbing topic of the day is the Prohibition of the Liquor Traffic; nor is this to be wondered at, when we consider that the greatest evil of the present day is the use of alcoholic stimulants as common beverages. And still the demon flaunts before the youth of our land, in gilded saloons and taverns, at the corner of almost every one of the streets in our various towns and cities—there with the words "Licensed to sell," instead of, "Beware, young men, this is the way to hell." With glittering decanters and smiling decoys, the youth of our land are in danger of being led to acquire an appetite for strong drink, whereby they become ruined for time and ruined for all eternity. Now, would you save the flower of the age from a drunkard's grave and from a burning hell, you must arise and strike for freedom, because this blighting curse is sweeping over our land like a mighty wave, killing and threatening destruction to tens of thousands of the most promising young men to be found upon this vast continent.

It has been asked, What is the panacea for this gigantic

c

evil ? to which we reply, It is just what the blessed Redeemer taught over eighteen hundred years ago, when He
said, "Lead us not into temptation ;" for if the bar-room
be not a temptation to the youth of the land, then there
is no temptation to which they are exposed.

An Irishman once went to a magistrate and said, "Your
honour, Denis O'Brien has sworn that he'll take my life."
" Well, Pat," said the squire, "go home and make your
mind easy, and if he kills you, Pat, I'll hang him." " But
sure, your honour," replied Pat, " wouldn't it be better to
hang him before he takes my life ?" Pat thought that
prevention was better than cure. He wanted to save one
precious life at least, and that was his own. So we want
to prevent, as far as possible, the recurrence of the sad
effects of intemperance ; and oh ! surely drink has done
enough of harm in the past to cause every man and woman
in the realm to set themselves for ever against it.

" It were better," said a poor condemned criminal to
the judges, dressed in their long robes, after they had
passed sentence upon him, " it were better for you to close
the whisky shops than punish the crimes they lead to."

John Knox said—"Pull down the rookery, and the
rooks will leave it."

If you would get rid of wasps, you must not only kill
the wasp that stings you, but you must destroy the wasp's
nest. So with drink ; we must destroy the taverns, which
are moral pest-houses.

If you would give the drunkard a chance to reform,
this is indispensable ; for often his strongest resolutions
of amendment become as threads of wax in the presence

of a hot furnace of fire, as he comes in contact with a liquor shop.

The celebrated Dr. ——, of Simcoe, was addicted to intemperance. The doctor told Elder Slaght, of Waterford, that nothing less than Total Prohibition would save him. He often contemplated going to Maine to escape the temptations to drink. He was often seized with *delirium tremens*, and in the last stage he experienced a very offensive smell, and recovered. The doctor told the Elder that if he took it again, death was inevitable; for he had attended scores of cases, and never knew a single instance where the patient had manifested this symptom, but the next time he was attacked he died. Alas! the doctor was again seized, and died, as he had predicted. Thus passed away one of the most gifted of men, a scholar and a gentleman—one who was an honour to the medical profession.

It has been proved that seventeen cases out of every twenty brought before our J. P.'s, coroners and quarter sessions, have their origin in, or are the result of, this traffic.

But what would become of the revenue only for this traffic? We believe the Licensed Liquor Traffic, from beginning to end, to be a Royal mistake. Take, for example, the statistics of this Province for the year 1851.

According to a Government report, there was in 1851 imported 536,040 galls. of spirits of different kinds, valued at £120,523 3s. 11d.; and in bond, 268,383 galls., valued at £66,908 5s. 11d. In addition to which there was made

and reported, by 149 stills, 2,269,141 galls., valued at
£141,821 6s. 3d., besides an immense quantity made and
not reported to the Government ; making the cost for the
liquor alone £329,252 16s. 1d. ; in addition to which must
be recognised—because we have to pay the enormous *bill*
—the cost of the administration of justice in the Province,
which burdensome expense is, to a very great extent, in-
curred to punish crime.   According to the report of the
Hon. F. Hincks for 1852, the administration of justice
cost, directly and indirectly, the tremendous sum of
£127,161 4s. 9d.   In addition to which amount ought to be
placed the cost of our police, bailiffs and other public officers of the peace not included in the above sum, which,
added to the cost of the prolific source of the crime punished, presents the sum of £456,414 0s. 10d. paid for a
traffic the history of which is written in crime and blood,
and for which the Government has received a revenue of
£67,981 6s. 6d., leaving the people to pay £388,432 14s.
4d.   *One million four hundred and forty-three thous-
and seven hundred and thirty dollars* for the privilege
of getting as a revenue £67,981 6s. 6d.! to which enormous *loss* might be added the cost of the time lost, litiga-
tion. caused by, and bad debts the result of, intemperance.

The Ontario Parliament in 1868 voted as follows :

For the Administration of Justice........$206,580 26.
For Hospitals and Charities............... 169,488 50.
For Penetanguishene Reformatory........ 23,013 37.

                                        $399,082 13.

While the entire revenue from tavern and *other* licenses

only amounted to $22,250.00. I think all must admit that three-fourths of the above expenditure is caused by strong drink, so that in this Province alone there was a loss of $376,832.13. If you add to this the money expended for liquor, and the time wasted in the drinking usages, together with the loss of life and property caused by intemperance, what a fearful aggregate is presented!

Some time ago a friend in Toronto published a tract, entitled "Begin Right; or, Facts in Figures for the People," from which I submit the following :—

"There were three thousand five hundred and sixty-six arrests in the City of Toronto for the police year eighteen hundred and sixty-four, each of which cost, on an average, seven dollars, for their mere arrest and police court trial. Two thousand five hundred and forty-four of them cost fourteen dollars each for their prosecution and imprisonment. Two thousand two hundred and sixteen of the above were taken up for being drunk and disorderly, and for illicit selling. Now, if three-fourths of the remainder of the arrests were caused by drink, then three thousand two hundred and twenty-nine out of the three thousand five hundred and sixty-six originated with drink, or only three hundred and thirty-seven cases in the whole but what resulted from the traffic."

I also find that the expense to the public of keeping up the Houses of Providence and Industry, and the Boys', Girls' and Orphans' Homes amounted to thirty-four thousand four hundred and twenty-eight dollars. That no less than four thousand eight hundred persons were brought to the House of Correction, or the Houses of Charity named, through drink. That while the liquor traffic from all sources only brought in a revenue to the city of twenty-one thousand five hundred and seventy-three dollars, it cost in the punishment of the crime caused thereby seventy-five thousand three hundred and forty-nine dollars; producing a direct loss to the ratepayers of fifty-three thousand seven hundred and seventy-six.

During one of my visits to Barrie, I found that out of 160 committals to gaol, 132 were for drunkenness; the other 28 were accounted for as follows :—

4 habitual drunkards,
1 insane person,
2 Indians,
1 Idiot.

Twenty said they could take it or let it alone ; but the jailer said they could let it alone best when in jail.

Judge Hagarty stated at the assizes held in London, Ont., in October, 1864, that "It was well known to every Judge on the Bench that the great mass of the crime committed in the country was occasioned by tippling in these abominable nests or dens which infested every part of the country."

"That's the end!" said a distiller to a visitor as he pointed to the product of the still as it flowed out at the completion of the manufacturing process; "That's the end," said the distiller exultingly. No! my friends, that's not the end; it's only the beginning of the work of death, and instead of it being the end, it is the commencement of poverty, misery, wretchedness, crime and death. It fills our jails, our poor-houses, our lunatic asylums and our graveyards; and it will take eternity itself to exhaust the end of the mischief this traffic is causing. Distilleries have been called the Devil's tea-kettles; and if anything would clothe the Devil and his imps with mourning, it would be the destruction of the liquor traffic.

I hold that what is morally wrong cannot be politically right. Now, here is a traffic which, according to the testimony of judges, jailers, magistrates, and all who are competent to give an opinion, is proved to be immoral in its tendency.

The Government has committed a ˙grand mistake in throwing the sanction of law around the liquor traffic; and we fully endorse the following platform laid down by the United Kingdom Alliance:—

"I. That it is neither right nor politic for the State to afford legal protection and sanction to any traffic or system that tends to increase crime, to waste the national resources, to corrupt the social habits and to destroy the health and lives of the people.

"II. That the traffic in Intoxicating Liquors, as common beverages, is inimical to the true interests of individuals, and destructive of the order and welfare of society, and ought therefore to be prohibited.

"III. That the history and results of all past legislation in regard to the Liquor Traffic abundantly prove that it is impossible satisfactorily to limit or regulate a system so essentially mischievous in its tendencies.

"IV. That no consideration of private gain or public revenue can justify the upholding of a system so utterly wrong in principle, suicidal in policy, and disastrous in results, as the Traffic in Intoxicating Liquors.

"V. That the Legislative Prohibition of the Liquor Traffic is perfectly compatible with national liberty, and with the claims of justice and legitimate commerce.

"VI. That rising above sectarian and party considerations, all good citizens should combine to procure an enactment prohibiting the manufacture and sale of intoxicating beverages, as affording most efficient aid in removing the appalling evil of Intemperance."

Government has legalized the traffic in strong drink, which it ought not to have done, as it is the cause of three-fourths of all the crime that floods the land, and for which all Prohibitory statutes are professedly in force. Crime, disease, poverty and death are the direct results of this traffic. Let us refer to Scotland for an example. The *Edinburgh Review* for April, 1838, states that in Scotland the use of liquors has trebled during the past fifteen years (that is, up to 1838). In Glasgow there is one spirit shop for every ten dwelling-houses, and while the increase in the property had only been sixty-six per centum, the consumption of spirituous liquors had increased five hundred per centum; fever, sixteen hundred per centum; crimes, four hundred per centum; deaths, three hundred per cent.; and the chances of human life had diminished forty-four per cent. And yet the Government have licensed men to sell this drink! And what are they licensed to do? They are—

> " Licensed to make the strong man weak,
> Licensed to lay the good man low,

> Licensed the wife's fond heart to break,
> And cause her children's tears to flow.

> " Licensed, where peace and comfort dwell,
> To bring disease and want and woe ;
> Licensed to make this earth a hell,
> And fit men for a hell below."

The tavern-keeper is—

Licensed "to inveigle and kill, to rob and enslave, to ruin and destroy, without any respect to sex or age, to rank or condition. Too well it does its nefarious work, as is shown by the ghastly annals of our jails and gallows, our poor-houses and mad-houses, our hospitals and cemeteries, our penitentiaries and reformatories, our brothels and other dens of vice, not to mention the countless victims whose sad career, though not exposed to public view, bring unutterable lamentation and woe and sorrow to the domestic hearth."

A revenue is for the purpose of maintaining good government, but this traffic is weakening and ruining our country; it would therefore be much wiser to seek to prevent crime than to punish that which law sanctions; but, unfortunately, the Government has been more anxious to punish than to prevent crime.

Too long have we been punishing the drunkard; instead of imposing on him a fine, or confining him, the day has arrived when the drunkard-maker should be stopped in his work of death.

I believe in Prohibition—total Prohibition. Nothing less will do. But I have been told that Prohibition is a new thing. Once an M.P. remarked to me, " If you

would confine yourself to moral suasion I would join
you, but Prohibition is a new thing." I replied, " I beg
to differ with you, sir; I hold that Prohibition is as old as
man." " Prove it," he said. " Have you a Bible ?" I
asked. One having been procured, I called his attention
to the 2nd chapter of Genesis, 16th and 17th verses.
Again, turning over to the 20th chapter of Exodus, I
pointed to the ten commandments and said, " You will
find that nine of these are prohibitory in their nature."
And if you turn from the book of God to our statute
book, you will find that the Government of our country
has recognized and acted upon the principle of Prohibition with reference to the liquor traffic up to this hour
with this distinction, with legalized exceptions. Why, I
ask, is there a monopoly of the liquor traffic ? Why allow one man to sell, and prohibit another from selling ?

If the thing be right, why not be logical and go on
that principle ? The law says it is wrong for you to sell
unless under certain conditions ; but subject to those conditions, and for so much money, we will permit you to do
this wrong. God says, " Thou shalt not kill." Law
says, for so much money you may kill : not with sword,
spear, pistol, dagger ; no! but with intoxicating drinks:
that is, provided you have the necessary accommodation,
and are of good moral character. Now, if you may do
one thing that is palpably wrong for a consideration,
why not another ? Don't hold up one sin by the sanction
of the law, and bear the sword of justice against every
other.

If the reform we propose is a sound and safe reform,

you will find it to correspond and to work well with all that is progressive and true in other reforms. If the principle of Prohibition, as applied to public evils and nuisances, be a sound principle of political science—which all precedent and practice affirm it to be—there is no solid reason why it should not be applied to this greatest evil and nuisance of our time—the Liquor Traffic. And its application in that way would assuredly not be in conflict with any other principle of true political science, but would most certainly result in the development of higher progress, and the increase of social comfort and real liberty for the masses of the people.

This traffic cannot properly be called a trade. A trade benefits both sides, and a transaction left a blessing on its track, but this traffic leaves nothing but ruin and misery.

For five hundred years Government has been legislating with a view to regulating this traffic, and still intemperance deluges the land. They have been regulating as to the character of the men who shall engage in this business, the rental of the premises where drink is to be sold, and the number of letters to be painted on the sign-board; but they have overlooked the very thing itself—that is, the drink. Strictly speaking, it is the drink that does the mischief; it is the drink that does the harm; the drink is the only agent; intemperance is a mere abstraction. It is a result, not the cause; it is the drink that produces it. It is not the rent paid for the premises where it is sold that does the harm—it is the drink. It may be sold in premises of one hundred pounds per annum rental, or so many dollars; under the sign of the

" Queen's Hotel" or the " Monkey Shaving the Goat;" it
may be sold by a professedly Christian man or an infidel,
by a Jew or a Turk, by a white man or a coloured gentleman; but it matters not where it is sold, by whom it
is sold, nor at what price it is sold. It is the drink that
does the harm.

The license system has been tried and has failed; with
all the restrictions which have been placed upon the traffic, drunkenness is rife.

This drink traffic is an injury to us personally. .

Take a practical experiment. Let a drinker propose to
insure his life ; let him set down, opposite to habits, this
answer: " Takes wine and spirits freely," and either his
proposal is declined, or an extra premium is demanded.

Some Insurance Companies have two branches—one
solely for abstainers, the other for ordinary business—
and the result is nineteen per cent. in favour of the
former.

It is amazing the amount of money that some men spend
upon intoxicating liquors. They seem to have forgotten
the maxim, " Take care of the pence and the pounds will
take care of themselves ;" and if the sum total, with interest added, was summed up, which some men spend
upon these drinks, they would be as much surprised as a
country squire was with the figures of a horse-dealer.
The squire was very fond of a good horse, and this horse-
dealer had a very fine animal which he took to the
squire. " What do you want for him ?" asked the squire.
" Three hundred pounds," replied the horse-dealer. " Do
you think I'm a fool ?" said the squire ; " I like a good

horse as well as any man, but I ain't a-going to pay two prices for him." "Well, I see you like the horse," returned the dealer, "and suppose you buy the nails in his shoes; now, will you consent to give me one farthing for the first, one halfpenny for the second, one penny for the third, twopence for the fourth, and so on, doubling the sum every time for every nail—there are thirty-two nails in all?" "Done!" said the squire. So the horse-dealer took out his pencil and added up the figures and showed them to the squire. "What! two million two hundred and thirty-six thousand nine hundred and sixty-two pounds two shillings and eightpence! Nonsense!" "Well, add them up yourself, and I guess you'll find them quite correct;" and so he did, and was glad to give the price first asked to settle the affair. So with some people who drink. If the sums thus spent were added up, with interest, it would mightily astonish them—the amount they put into the tavern-keeper's till, while they thus empty their own.

I know one who, some years ago, owned 1,200 acres of excellent land, but who, by drinking at a tavern adjoining his residence, acquired intemperate habits, whereby he has lost all his property, and now he does not own a foot of soil in Ontario; his wife and children, who a few years ago moved in the first society, have been scattered to the four winds of heaven.

If you will accompany me up Yonge Street, I will point you to farm after farm—some of the best on Yonge Street—which have changed hands not only once but even twice, and some of them have been actually lost three times through drink, until it has become a proverb that a man has swallowed so many hundred acres of land.

A farmer once asked a doctor to look down his throat. "I can see nothing the matter," replied the doctor. "Why, that's strange," replied the farmer; "for I have swallowed three farms, and I'm dry still."

It is an injury to us commercially.

The principle of political economy, which lies at the root of commercial prosperity, is the employment of the industry and capital of the country in that which produces wealth and prosperity in the community.

Hundreds of thousands of dollars are annually wasted upon drink, which would, only for the drinking customs of society, go into legitimate trade and enrich the nation; besides, thousands of persons are so reduced by their intemperate habits, that they are incapable of paying their just debts, and merchants and others suffer immensely in this way.

Four years ago last winter, passing along · through one of our villages in company with a merchant, we met a farmer. The merchant asked him for payment of a certain account which had been a long time due, to which he replied that the times were hard and the crops had been light, and he did not feel able to discharge the debt just then, but would do so as soon as possible. The merchant pointed to a tavern, and said, "Do you see that tavern?" "I do," was the indignant reply, as he muttered, "What about that?" "Well," said the merchant, "If you had put past, towards paying my account, the money which you have foolishly expended for liquor in that house, my account would have been settled long ago." "Oh," said the farmer, "it is not all the money I spend for drink that does it; it is the hard times and the bad crops; but don't be uneasy—you'll be paid, and that sooner than you think." A few hours later, on my way to my appointment, I observed a man very much intoxicated, seated upon a home-made jumper, with reins in one hand and whip in the other, as he tugged away, muttering rather indistinctly, "Get up! get up, I say!" He had, however, neglected to hitch the traces to the sleigh, and, dropping the reins, the horse walked off, leaving the poor inebriate sitting, yet all the while he fancied he was guiding and whipping the animal, which was rods ahead of him. The onlookers were doffing their caps and making great sport at the stupidity of the drunken man. Now, that was the same person who said in my hearing, hours before, that it was not what he expended for liquor that prevented him from paying his debts, but it was the bad crops, &c. But here is the secret: It goes out in little dribs—a quarter now and a quarter again, or it may be from one to five dollars of a night—and they do not observe it; but if they were to sit down and add up the amount of money that they have foolishly wasted upon drink, many of them would find that they had squandered fortunes. I know several persons in the decline of life who are obliged to toil and labour under a burning sun to earn a scanty subsistence, who expended as much money in the drinking usages as would have kept them comfortable in their old age.

All political science teaches this one great truth, that the true way to enrich a nation and to benefit a people is by the employment of the capital and industry of the people in such a way as to promote the health, wealth and happiness of the inhabitants ; but such is not the case with reference to the drink traffic.

I find that, just in proportion as the tavern-keeper gets rich and increases in wealth, those poor unfortunate victims who frequent his bar become impoverished and reduced. Now, this is not the case with the miller who grists your wheat, or the blacksmith that shoes your horse. It has been estimated that for every pound that is expended upon liquors, only from 9d. to 1s. 3d. returns back into the pockets of the working men ; whereas every pound that is expended upon dry goods, boots and shoes, etc., causes from 6s. to 12s. to return into the pockets of the working classes. '

It is certain that the money invested in the manufacture of liquor is not so reproductive as is money invested in legitimate trade. For instance, sixty millions sterling of capital invested in the manufacture of cotton will give employment to over 400,000 men, whereas the same amount invested in the manufacture of liquor will only employ 60,000 ; so, by the investment of sixty million pounds sterling in the manufacture of liquor, instead of in the cotton trade, there is a direct loss to the labour market and the working population of 340,000, at, say, one pound sterling per week the whole year round.

The man who spends twenty shillings on liquor gives less than one shilling to the working man ; but if he had spent his twenty shillings on useful articles, he would have put from six shillings to fifteen shillings in the pocket of the labourer. If the money now paid for liquor was expended on other articles, it would greatly increase the demand for mechanics, etc.; besides, it would advance materially the wages of the working classes.

One of the largest employers in the Province, near Richmond Hill, said to ———, " I could not do business if I lived in ——— or ———. I must be away from taverns; I must have sober men that I can rely upon, or give up business."

"The Low Moor Iron Company" send an omnibus round every morning for the purpose of collecting their men; they thus escape being decoyed into taverns. If the plan succeeds, more omnibuses are to be started.

No trade will be injured by Prohibition but the liquor traffic, while every legitimate branch of business will gain by the change, for it is indisputable that the drink traffic thrives at the expense of every other interest.

Prohibition will elevate the race and ameliorate the condition of suffering humanity.

It is an injury to us nationally. " Political economy is to the State what domestic economy is to the family." Temperance will add to our national wealth and prosperity. The liquor traffic is a gigantic folly. The term manufacturer as applied to the liquor maker is a misnomer : the manufacturer takes things of little value and makes them more valuable, but the distiller does the reverse—he takes the precious grain, which has been given by a beneficent Providence to be food for man, and con-

D

verts it into a curse, and sends the poisonous liquor
streaming through the veins of the social system sowing
the seeds of pauperism, disease, crime and death throughout the length and breadth of the land. It is high time
that political economists would look into this matter, for
Temperance will certainly add to our national wealth and
prosperity. Canada is not the richer for its criminals
and paupers, though they give employment to a few
turnkeys and officials ; neither is it wealthier for maintaining in affluence and ease those men who are engaged
in dealing out that which is producing three-fourths of
all the vice and crime that afflicts our country. We are
informed that no less than fifteen hundred persons died
in Canada through intemperance in one year, and no
doubt as the country is settling up the deaths annually
far exceed that number. Well did Sir John Carr say
that the argument in defence of the Government permitting the use of alcoholic stimulants for the sake of increasing the revenue, was as if the Legislature were to im-
pose a tax upon coffins, and then inoculate its subjects
with the plague. It would be a happy day for Great Britain and our beloved Canada if Her Most Gracious Majesty
Queen Victoria would say as did the sovereign of the Chi-
nese people. He was waited upon by one of his ministers,
who told him that if he would legalize the trade in opium
he would avert all danger of a war with Great Britain,
besides he would greatly increase his revenue ; to which
he replied nobly, "I will never consent to raise my revenue on the ruins and vices of my people." O noble, heroic
and glorious reply ! Would to God that our beloved

Queen would also say so in reference to the traffic in strong drink !

It has been proved that one-sixth of the effective strength of the navy, and a much greater proportion of the army, is as much destroyed by that most powerful ally of death, intoxicating drinks, as if the men were slain in battle.

During the British and American war, a British cruiser took an American ship, and was returning to England with the prize, but the Americans drugged the rum which the British sailors drank, and they became incapable. The Yankee captain then went to the British officer and asked him to surrender. "No!" was the indignant reply. As the British captain drew his sword, the American took his revolver, told him that there was no use in resisting—that his men were all unconscious. The British officer called his men, but they were disabled by drink, and he lost his own life in the encounter. The American captain took command of both ships, turned them round, and returned to America. Would a crew of Teetotalers have acted thus ? No, verily.

What is the tendency of this traffic in the eyes of one of England's greatest statesmen ? Lord Palmerston, when addressing the "Labourers' Encouragement Society," warned them "to shun the beer-shop and the public-house," adding, "They ruin the health, lead to all kinds of disease, degradation, poverty and crime, and tend to place man in the condition of a convict and a felon."

The noblest product of a Christian nation is its men. Whatever improves or elevates men, increases the power of the nation. Whatever weakens or debases men, casts down the commonwealth.

The preservation and cultivation of the mind is the first grand duty of the Legislature, and it is their business to protect as far as possible the lives and property of all.

One has said, "But you are going too fast with your Prohibition." The same was said when Lady Mary Montague, in the face of an adverse public opinion, would have her children vaccinated. She had to bear considerable ignominy : she was preached against, and even hooted at in the streets by the unthinking rabble, while some learned divines denounced her course as "an impious interference with the behests of an all-wise Providence." Yet what does an enlightened public say now? Lady Mary Montague was only a little ahead of the times, —that was all. It is no uncommon thing for those who strike out a new course to be subjected to opposition and even persecution.

Luther went too fast in the estimation of some, and yet the glorious Reformation followed; and had not our blessed Saviour gone faster than our ideas, the world would not have been redeemed. Instead of us going too fast, our objectors are going too slowly. I hold that Prohibition is one of the pivot-points upon which the welfare of this vast Dominion depends to a very great extent.

When John P. Roblin, Esq., late M. P. P., proposed to prevent liquor from being sold on the show grounds at the Provincial Fair, there was only one man that would support his motion, and he was much abused by at least one hon. gentleman for taking such action; and yet what is the fact?—why, that which Mr. Roblin fought for has now become the law of the land, and he has lived to see it come to pass.

According to the present state of things, if I steal from or murder my neighbour, the law will punish me; but if I, under the ban of the law, sell that which will cause my neighbour to steal or to kill and murder, I escape. Are we to have law to punish crime, and no law for that which originates crime? Shall we seize upon the man possessed of a demon, or seize upon the demon before it enters into a man?

The distiller makes it by law.

The tavern-keeper sells it by law.

A man buys it by law,

And drinks it by law.

He then goes home and murders his wife.

The constable arrests him by law.

He is tried by law,

And he is hanged by law.

And who is to blame for all this?

Not the constable for arresting,

Nor the judge for condemning,

But the people for sanctioning so infernal a system. It is terrible that a man is licensed to sell for a "Yorker" to his fellow that which will rob him of his reason, and send him out of his tavern to stab his wife, butcher his children, and set fire to his neighbour's house, and yet the seller of spirituous liquors gets off free.

It has been raised as an objection that Prohibition is

anti-British,—that it is unconstitutional. Now, those
persons who say that it is unconstitutional to prohibit
forget that the mass of the people at present are prohibited from selling; only a few (comparatively) have
licenses and dare sell; and yet they rave about it being
anti-British to prohibit.

According to the fundamental principles of the British
Constitution, the people by majority appoint their representatives, and they by their major representative power
make the laws. Hence all power is vested in the hands
of the majority, and Prohibition cannot become the law
of the land without the consent of the majority.

"But you deny us the right of Free Trade with your
Prohibition." I think, before any one can claim the right
of "Free Trade," he must not only be anxious to embark
in a business, and convinced that it is an easy way of
making money, but the people have a right to enquire,
"Is the traffic in which this man is anxious to embark
injurious to society or no?" John Stuart Mill, one of the
most profound thinkers of the present age and a great
writer on Political Economy, has said that "any trade
that tends to produce pauperism and crime is an evil
against society, and society has a perfect right to deal
with it." Every member of society should be employed
in some useful calling, not in dealing out death and
damnation, for

"Wherever has flowed the crimson flood,
  It is swollen with tears—it is stained with blood."

All civilization depends on the concession of individual
rights, but all civilization will be careful not to abridge

any individual right unless imperatively demanded by the public good.

To maintain freedom, all that fires the passions and robs men of self-control must, like other incendiaries and robbers, be coerced, that all innocent trades may enjoy their freedom. This, which is not innocent—which inflicts a wound on every other—which destroys health and reason, and all that gives security to trade, must no longer be permitted a licence for spoliation.

The basis, the foundation of all freedom is virtue and morality; and what is so injurious to these as the Liquor Traffic?

PROHIBITION IS AN INFRINGEMENT OF OUR LIBERTY.

Upon no ear doth the music of this word sound more sweetly than on ours; but the liberty we love is not liberty to do what we like, but liberty to do what is right. That is not worthy of the name of liberty which enslaves and enthrals mankind.

At thy sound, sweet liberty, the slave leaps from his manacles and breathes the salubrious air of freedom.

For thee, O liberty, our fathers have fought and our ancestors have bled, and even now, to maintain thy sacred sway, a crimson Potomac flows.

For liberty the prisoner pants and sighs and writhes and groans, and at thy presence his chains become a rope of sand.

Liberty brings up the prisoner from the cold, damp, dark cell, to behold and enjoy the glorious light of day.

Liberty !—with thee this earth is a Paradise, but without thee it is a very Hell.

O, ye winds, carry the glorious sound of liberty o'er hill and dale, o'er land and sea, till every man can sing, " I'm free."

O, ye lightnings of heaven, fly and let your message be of liberty.

O, ye thunders, with your dreadful organ pipes, proclaim in every ear the heaven-born sound of liberty, in its highest, truest, holiest sense, till man, freed from the awful slavery of intemperance and every form of vice, shall bask in the unsullied sunshine of Divine favour, and delight himself in the perfect law of liberty ; for "whom the Son makes free, he is free indeed."

The British Parliament passed an Act placing the sale of arsenic under very stringent regulations, and it has been followed by the best results ; and if the sale of arsenic is thus forbidden, which only killed a few annually, should intoxicating liquors be tolerated, which are killing thousands annually ?

Gambling houses have been closed, lest our sons should get ruined ; yet taverns are licensed, where the youth of our land are corrupted.

Meat diseased is seized upon. Why ? Because it is injurious and unhealthful. And what is the tendency and often the results of the liquor business ? It is to promote and spread misery.

TALK ABOUT DRINK GIVING LIBERTY.

" When I began to drink," said a reformed drunkard,

"I had liberty. Yes, my elbows had liberty to go out of the sleeves of my coat, my toes had liberty to look out of the windows of my boots, I had liberty to run my fingers through my hair without taking off my hat, and as I passed along the crown of my hat went flipperty-flap, as the wind whistled, 'How do you do, sir?'"

Others argue that they may do as they like with their own. Well, you may do as you like with your own, if you do right; but no man should have a private right to do a public wrong.

There is a law preventing parties from keeping on their premises more than a limited quantity of gunpowder; and why? Because it is dangerous, and to guard against an explosion; and yet, although intoxicating drinks are dangerous, and exposes people to accidents, death, &c., still tavern-keepers may keep and sell as much as they please. Paul's view of the law was, that it was "a terror to evil-doers and a praise to them that do well;" but the licensed liquor system inverts this maxim, and makes it a temptation to evil-doing and a burthen to them that do well.

There was a time when the African Slave Trade was a lawful one—now it is severely punishable; and methinks the day is dawning when the traffic in alcoholic stimulants too will be pronounced illegal and will be severely punishable. At present it requires strict magisterial regulations to keep it in anything like check, and in this it differs from every other department of business. What would you think of a law forbidding you to sell flour or pork to Indians on any terms, or the same articles to white men without a licence? And yet the law prohibits the sale of liquors to Indians, while it sanctions the sale of the same article to white men; and while there is no law to prevent you selling these necessary articles to white men, you require a licence to sell them spirits— so that the very law acknowledges that it is a dangerous traffic.

It is intended to establish an Inebriate Asylum for the care and cure of habitual drunkards.   Mr. Langmuir in his report says, "When the State is benefited by the receipt of money from the use of intoxicating liquors, it ought to try its best to counteract the effects of the abuse of these drinks."

It is highly commendable to erect asylums for those unfortunate inebriates who have lost all self-control, but why not go a step further and remove the cause ?

If there was a broken bridge in your neighbourhood, through which persons were constantly falling, would it be considered sufficient to build an hospital, and keep it furnished with nurses and doctors, where the wounded might be cared for ?   Nay, the bridge would have to be repaired to prevent future accidents.   Then why not apply the same remedy to the injury caused by drink ?

For generations it has been tried to regulate the traffic by legislation, but all past legislation goes to prove that such cannot be done.   Still, although the drink traffic is so mischievous in its tendencies that it cannot be regulated by legislation, it has been demonstrated that it can be stopped.

Our battle-cry is Total Abstinence for the individual, and Prohibition for the State.

Now, what has been the results of Prohibition where it has been tried ?

Mr. James Gray, Chairman of the Edinburgh Parochial Board, said at a meeting of the Town Council, October 23, 1849 :—" There are thirty-four parishes in Scotland without a public-house, and the effect upon the parishioners is, that they have not a penny of poor rate in one of them. *Before I came to Edinburgh I lived eight years in a parish where there was no public-house, and during all that period I never saw a person the worse for drink. There were no poor rates in the parish then ; but now there are five public-houses, and a poor rate of* 1s. 8d. *in the pound.* In a foot-note the following significant statement occurs : " It may not be out of place to state here, for the edification of our ratepayers, that in the two neighbouring parishes—*viz., Mertoun on the one hand, and Leagerwood on the other—not a penny of poor rate is required ; and why ? The reasn is quite obvious—not a whisky shop is in either parish ; while Earlston, with eight such houses, has in round numbers £450 to pay annually in supporting a class, three-fourths of whom have been directly or indirectly pauperized through the liquor traffic.*"

Squire Tener, County Tyrone, says there are forty-seven and a half square miles, or thirty thousand four hundred statute acres, with a population of nine thousand five hundred souls, without a single public-house or policeman or any crime whatever. Besides, the rates here were formerly one shilling and fourpence in the pound, now they are reduced to sixpence in the pound.

On February 18th, 1869, I visited Garden Island, containing eighty acres—it is two miles distant from, and opposite to, Kingston—the property of D. D. Calvin, Esq., M. P. P. Shipbuilding is carried on in this place; it contains seven hundred inhabitants. A Prohibitory Law has been in force for 34 years, and there is not a drunkard on the island; besides, the people are all comfortable, which demonstrates that temperance and prosperity go together. Drunkenness and misery are inseparable. Mr. Calvin occupied the chair, and made a powerful speech on the Temperance cause; he stated that four-fifths of all the inhabitants had grown up under his care, and not one of all the hundreds raised upon the island had turnèd out a drunkard. "Temperance has been a mutual benefit; you have prospered, and I have succeeded. I can trust you, I can send you wherever required, and you do your duty like men.

"When the bell rings on Monday morning, you are always at hand, ready to play your part. Can the employers of Kingston say so? No; they cannot.

"Here you are all well dressed, and some of you have saved by honest industry over two thousand dollars.

"Here are some reformed drunkards, men who can live nowhere else but here, and your families have everything they require, and are happy here; and why? Because the demon Drink is not allowed upon Garden Island. Thirty-four years ago I put my foot upon it, and have kept my foot upon it. I would not take ten thousand dollars for half an acre of land on this island; and why? Lest a grog-shop should be started to injure my business and curse my people." At the close of the meeting seventy-five persons signed the pledge, some from Kingston.

On returning to Kingston, which is just opposite, what a contrast met my gaze!

First, the Penitentiary, with eight hundred souls, some of them fine-looking men, sitting down to dinner guarded by soldiers with fixed bayonets.

Second, three Lunatic Asylums, six-sevenths of the inmates of which were brought there through drink.

Third, the Orphans' Home, the matron of which said that nearly all were brought there through the same seductive influence.

Fourth, the Distillery—the great feeder of the institutions first named, and the chief cause of the vice and crime which abound in our land.

The results of Prohibition are shown in the following letter, which was written during my engagement with the United Canadian Alliance :—" I have just visited the teetotal village of Bridgewater, the property of the Hon. B. Flint, one of the Vice-Presidents of our Society, where I have been confirmed in my views as regards Prohibition. This village has been in existence for about seven years. It contains 400 inhabitants,—not a rowdy amongst the number. No liquor has been sold here since the place was first started. It can boast of a white marble Wesleyan church ; a hotel, the largest and most elegantly furnished to be found between Toronto and Kingston ; here you will find in full operation a saw-mill, grist-mill, oatmeal-mill, pearl-barley-mill, axe factory, hammer factory, edge-tool factory, chair factory, foundry, tannery, six gold mines, crushing machine, store, &c., all without the aid of whisky. And what of the people? Why, they are, in my humble opinion, the most happy, contented, prosperous and pious that I have met with on this side the Atlantic. Let those who have doubts regarding Prohibition visit Bridgewater : I can promise them a kind reception from my warm friend Dr. Higginbotham, or Squire Harrison. Happy Bridgewater! Would to God that every village, town and city in Canada were, like thee, free from the curse of a legalized Liquor Traffic.

"Talk about 'Inebriate Asylums ;' here is one. When I last lectured in Belleville, Dr. Rufus Holden, who presided at my meeting, stated in his opening address that a short time since a first-class mechanic asked him if he thought he could find employment at Bridgewater ; that he had been trying to reform his life, but the temptations were so numerous about Belleville that it was impossible, and that unless he was removed from those temptations he was a ruined man.

"I shall henceforth designate the. Hon. B. Flint the distinguished Canadian philanthropist, and one of the warmest friends of the Temperance cause to be found upon the continent of America.".

Certain depreciatory statements having been made in the British House of Commons respecting the operations of the Maine Law, called forth a reply from the Hon. Neal Dow, together with certificates from prominent public men, the whole of which appeared in the London "Times."

The following is the testimony of the Governor and Executive Council of the State :—

" To give a full and accurate account of the operations of the Maine Law in Maine, and its effect upon the liquor traffic, and upon poverty, pauperism, and crime, would require much more time than we can devote to the subject, and we therefore confine ourselves to a very brief statement of the facts.

" At the time of the enactment of the Maine Law the liquor traffic was carried on in Maine extensively and openly, as it is now in States where the trade is licensed. The effect of the law in diminishing the trade in intoxicating drinks was immediate and very great.

" In many parts of Maine the liquor trade has absolutely ceased to exist, liquor shops are unknown, and wherever within the State the trade exists at all, it is carried on secretly and with caution, as other unlawful things are done. One effect of the law has been to render the liquor trade disreputable, and no person who knew Maine as it was before the Maine Law, and has been acquainted with it down to the present time, can doubt that the effect of the law has been most marked and salutary. Poverty, pauperism and crime have been greatly diminished by it, because vastly less money has been wasted in strong drink.

" In some places and at some times the execution of the law has been fitful and capricious, yet, with these exceptions, the law has been as well enforced as our criminal laws generally are. "

Another certificate, signed by three members of Congress from Maine, Messrs. Hamlin, Morrill and Frye, has these words:—

" The immediate effect of the statute was to outlaw the

trade, declaring it to be inconsistent with the general welfare, and reducing it to very small proportions.

"In many parts of the State it is now nearly or quite
unknown. There are large districts of country where
liquor shops are unknown; and everywhere within our
border, and where the trade exists at all, it is carried on
secretly and in a very small way. The favourable effects
of this change are great, and everywhere apparent to the
most casual observer who has any knowledge of the State
prior to the year 1851. We do not believe the people of
Maine, for any consideration, would again sanction the
policy of licence to drinking houses and tippling shops."

It must be remembered that a law does nothing. Black-
stone says the law is a rule, not an agent. Law is that
which governs agents; so when the Bill is carried your
work only commences, for a law does nothing good or bad.

The prospect of obtaining an entire Prohibitory Law
is cheering, and at no distant date the people will be
called upon to decide this matter for themselves. At
Ottawa, April 10th, 1873, the Speaker read a memorial
from the Legislative Assembly of Ontario, stating that that
body had received 369 petitions, signed by upwards of
28,000 persons, and petitions from thirty-nine municipal
bodies, praying for legislation to prevent the manufacture
and sale of intoxicating liquors; and that as the Legislature of Ontario had no power to grant the prayers of such
petitions, the Parliament of the Dominion should take the
necessary steps to pass such a law as would prohibit the
manufacture and sale of alcoholic liquors as a beverage.

Let us seek to create a public sentiment in favour of

Prohibition—there is wonderful power in an enlightened public opinion.

Daniel Webster has remarked, "The earthquake hath power and the tornado hath power, but greater than these is the power of public opinion ;" and if we are to move and create a public opinion in favour of this enterprise, we must be united while we give no quarter to the enemy.

We oppose with all our might the three great causes of intemperance, namely :

> Personal use,
> Social example,
> Legal temptation ;

and we implore you, because of the multitudes who have by the personal use of these drinks been ruined, to abstain. We entreat you, in the name of myriads who by social example have been led to indulge in the use of those drinks that have blasted their hopes in time and paved for them a miserable eternity, to refrain from setting a dangerous example ; and we beseech you, in the name of common justice, to try and obtain the passing of a Prohibitory Law—to prevent the sale and remove the temptations out of the way.

There are four great difficulties in carrying Prohibition, namely :

> Ignorance,
> Custom,
> Taste and
> Self-interest,

but it is a fixed principle in the Divine government that

all violations of moral duty can only be satisfactorily met
by the offender returning to the first point of divergence
from duty.   Now, I look upon distillation as the reservoir,
so to speak, from whence flow those streams of vice and evil
which abound in our land on account of intemperance,
and if you would stop the evil, you must remove the
cause by preventing the importation, manufacture and
sale of spirituous liquors.

"Up, patriots, citizens, saints,
    Strike a blow at Iniquity's throne;
Strike for justice, for virtue, for God,
    Strike often, strike hard and strike home."

LECTURE II.

DANGER.

THE DANGER OF THE DRINKING USAGES.

DANGER! "What! with the United States?" No; ten thousand times, no. God forbid that two Christian nations should imbrue their hands in each other's blood. May that dark day never come, but rather let us live in peace until the world shall be converted to God, and all mankind shall speak one language. Danger! "Are the Fenians coming to invade our country?" They had better not. It is a dangerous thing to trample on the tail of the "Old Lion." "Why then do you sound the alarm and cry of danger?" Ah! there is danger—great danger; not from a foreign foe, but from an enemy, nevertheless, more to be dreaded a thousandfold than American gunboats or Fenian bullets.

The foe we fear is drunkenness, and night and day it is doing its work of devastation and death. This formidable evil rests chiefly upon two pillars, namely, traffic and custom, and these are supported by the people and fostered by the State. Therefore we consider it to be the duty of all philanthropists and Christians to endeavour as far as possible to mitigate, at least, if they cannot altogether suppress, the evils of intemperance. It is to be regretted that, on account of the prevalency of this vice, many have become familiarized to its baneful effects, and never make the slightest exertion to counteract the evil.

The author did not always consider that there was danger connected with the drinking usages. Once he thought it was both safe and fashionable to drink; but sad experience and careful observation have led him to change his views upon the subject, and now he would sound the alarm, and O that all the young men on this vast continent might catch the sound and shun the seductive wine-cup. Young men, beware! there is danger connected with the use of spirituous liquors as common beverages. The longer I live and the more I study the nature and effects of alcohol upon the human system, the stronger are my impressions of the necessity of total abstinence.

" But there are other things which are dangerous as well as alcoholic stimulants, and is it right to give up their use simply because there is danger connected with them ? It is dangerous to erect tall chimneys in our manufacturing towns and cities; and it is dangerous for the sailor to plough the stormy ocean ; and would you discontinue these because there is danger connected with them ?" These are not parallel cases. The one is necessary, the other is not. We have the testimony of over 2,000 of the most distinguished physicians both in Europe and America who have affixed their names to the following :

"We, the undersigned, are of opinion that the most perfect health is compatible with total abstinence from all such intoxicating beverages, whether in the form of ardent spirits or as wine, beer, ale, porter, cider, &c." And not only have we the testimony of these eminent medical men, but we have thousands of other witnesses who can come forward and prove that as great an amount of physical labour and intellectual effort can be performed without stimulants as with them. Total abstinence has been tested in hot climates and in cold regions by travellers and mariners—in the mine, in the harvest field and on the battle field, and universal testimony is on the side of temperance.

In addition to the foregoing testimony, the highest physiological authority will bear me out in this, that intoxicating drinks are positively injurious to persons in a normal state.

All men acknowledge intemperance to be an evil. The tavern-keepers themselves admit this, and yet they continue in the traffic, while some who speak most harshly of the inebriate, plead for and practise what they call the moderate use of the drunkard's drink. I would not cry down moderation, but I go for moderation in lawful things. Who would advocate the moderate use of strychnine or prussic acid? Now, alcohol is a poison; if alcohol be not a poison then prussic acid is no poison.

Sir Astley Cooper has said, "I never suffer ardent spirits in my house, knowing them to be evil spirits. If the poor could see the white livers and shattered nervous systems which I have seen as the consequences of drink-

ing, they would be aware that spirits and poison mean
the same thing." Science stigmatizes alcohol as a poison,
and consigns it to its proper place upon the shelf of the
apothecary. The great danger of the liquor traffic, in
my opinion, lurks in this, that the tavern-keeper wields
his fatal power chiefly through the seductiveness of the
drink which he sells. It must not be forgotten that there
is something in the very nature of alcohol to create a
craving, a thirst, an appetite, a desire for more, such as is
not the case with water or food. When you feel thirsty
and take a glass of water your thirst is quenched, or
when hungry if you partake of a meal of victuals you are
satisfied, but on the other hand the more you indulge in
the intoxicating cup, the greater the appetite that is created thereby, and thus men are led on, step by step, from
what is called moderate to immoderate drinking.

That the so called moderate use of spirituous liquors
tends to promote intemperate habits is abundantly proved,
and it is now an established fact that those sailors who
partake of grog allowance when at sea, thereby acquire
an appetite for liquor by which they are unconsciously
impelled to rush to greater excess when they come on
shore.

I assert that moderate drinking is the school where all
drunkards are trained. The greatest drunkard of your
acquaintance was once a moderate drinker. Little did
he think when he commenced to imbibe that in a few
years he would be a slave to this vile habit, but as he
continued to indulge in the intoxicating glass, the habit
was being formed ; the appetite was being acquired and

the serpent drink had been coiling itself around him, and at length the poor man found that at last "It biteth like a serpent and stingeth like an adder," just as

> "A pebble in the streamlet scant,
> Hath turned the course of many a river,
> A dewdrop on the baby-plant,
> Hath warped the giant oak for ever."

As drops of water form the ocean, as grains of sand compose the shore, as one brick raised upon another rears the colossal pile on which you gaze with wonder and astonishment, so it is by little and by little that the thirst for drink is formed.

I remember hearing Bevere Depuy speak upon the subject of Temperance, in New York State, in eighteen hundred and forty-seven. He said: "Now here on my left is a moderate drinker, and on my right a cold-water man, and before me is the drunkard. Now, from which of these two classes is the drunkard made ? Not from that of Total Abstinence, for if a man never tastes he can never become a drunkard; hence you see it is from the ranks of the moderate drinkers that drunkards are supplied. Moderate drinking is the devil's railroad leading down a steep incline to the depot of destruction, and so long as effect follows cause, so surely does moderate drinking lead to Intemperance. O this cursed moderate drinking—it is this that binds those hands and fetters those feet. It is by this that men who begin freemen are made slaves. It is this that will make drunkards of what are now called moderate drinkers. There is an Arab proverb, 'Beware of the camel's nose':—

'Once in a shop a workman wrought,
With languid hand and listless thought,
When, through an open window space,
Behold, a Camel thrust his face,
" My nose is cold," he meekly said ;
"O let me warm it by thy side."

'Since no denial word was said,
In came the nose, in came the head ;
As sure as sermon follows text,
The long excursive neck came next ;
And then, as falls the threatening storm,
In leaped the whole ungainly form.

' Aghast the owner gazed around,
And on the rude invader frowned ;
Convinced as closer still he pressed
There was no room for such a guest.
Yet more astonished heard him say,
"If incommoded go thy way,
For in this place I choose to stay."

' O youthful heart to gladness born,
Treat not the Arab lore with scorn ;
To evil habit's earliest wile
Lend neither ear, nor glance, nor smile ;
Check the dark fountain ere it flows,
Nor even admit the camel's nose.'

A child may unchain a lion, but the strength of many
strong men may not bind him ; so a bad habit may be
easily formed, but O how hard to break off such. What
seems to be a small affair will soon become fixed, and
hold upon you with the strength of a cable ; that cable is
formed by spinning and twisting one thread at a time,
but when once completed the proudest ship turns and
owns its power.

The writer well remembers when he first began to indulge, and what induced him to tamper with strong drink.
He was serving his time to the grocery business in the
City of Glasgow ; his employer (who was an Elder in the
P. Church) would often sit with his merchants in his office, adjoining the shop, enjoying their whisky toddy ;
frequently he had to enter to inquire about the payment
of certain accounts, &c., and was met by the odour of the
whisky toddy, heated up with loaf sugar and hot water,
and he thought it smelt good ; besides, when the merchants
imbibed they became jolly and would appear so happy. So
he thought "what was sauce for the goose would be
sauce for the gander," and suggested to his companions
that after shop was closed they would go to some respectable public-house (this is where most respectable
young men begin to learn the art of drinking; at first they
will only frequent first-class hotels and drink with the
upper ten, but does it end there ?) and get some toddy ; so
after business was at a close, off we started. We were
ushered into a neat little room; the bell was pulled; a beautiful Scotch lass entered, covered with smiles, and asked
" What will you have ?" "Some pure Islay whisky, beat
up with loaf sugar and hot water," we replied ; "and see
you do it up in the most scientific manner" was added
with a laugh. Presently the liquor was served upon a neat
tray, and then it was who would pay for it ; and here I
would remark that I have often seen persons ready to
knock each other down, so anxious were they to pay for

the treat, while I have never seen any act so in their anxiety to subscribe to the Bible Society or any other Christian object. Well, at first a table spoonful or so of the toddy was pleasant, but more than that was disagreeable and offensive, and often I have wished, when it came to my turn to drink that I could have emptied my share out. I drank because it was fashionable, and for the sake of the company. I loved a good story and could sing a good song; and though at first I drank for the sake of the society, by continuing to sip I got to be so fond of it that at last I drank the drink for the drink's sake. Young men, there is danger. Drinking may begin with "a feast of reason and a flow of soul," but of all the dangerous paths that the foot of young man ever trod, that of moderate drinking is the most dangerous. Pray be admonished, admonished by one who, in the good providence of God, has been plucked "as a brand from the burning." You need not expect to ascend one single step in the ladder of fame or usefulness by following the drinking usages.

Would you be great ?

Would you be good ?

Would you be eminent ?

Would you be useful ?

Would you make your mark in the world and leave it better than you found it ? Remember you are not to find the elements of success in life by lounging around the tavern, or by following the drinking customs of society; every step in the damnable ladder of drinking leads downwards. There was a young man of my acquaintance; he occupied one of the first situations in the City of Glasgow as a commercial traveller; for years he filled it honourably; but by treating his customers, and by being treated in return by them, he gradually acquired a love for drink. At length his employers found fault. Once they said, " John, we observed you the worse for liquor; now we wish to warn you, if we find you the worse for drink again, we will be under the painful necessity of dismissing you from our employment; we cannot entrust you with large sums of our money if you are going to drink in this way." John thought that he would be more careful; that if he did drink, he would do so on the sly; but once, while under the influence of drink, he lost a large sum of money which he could not replace. The truth came out—he was dismissed. After a time he got another situation, inferior to the former. From that he was dismissed also on account of his intemperate habits; and then he got another situation, and yet another, until he became so dissipated in his habits that no merchant would have him in his employment, although he was one of the best salesmen in the West of Scotland. About twelve years ago, just as I was leaving the Old Country, one of the last sights on which I gazed was that once noble man, but O how changed! He came to me without a coat on his back or a hat on his head, and with bent form and palsied hand, looking pitifully in my face, said, " Thomas, give me sixpence." Never till death shall I forget that look or those words. Now, who is that young man ? His father is a retired merchant in Belfast, Ireland; his brother is one of the most influential merchants in that prosperous commercial town ; and were John ——— to go to his father's or brother's door and knock for admittance, he dare not enter, but would be taken by the collar and hurled from their door-steps. Now, what is it that has caused that father to bar his door against his son ? nay, what is ten thousand times worse, what has caused that father to bolt the door of his heart against his own son ?—nothing but this debasing, demoralising, body-destroying and soul-damning drink, which is laying its foul hand upon some of the most intelligent and promising young men to be found in almost every village, town and city in the land.

The wife of one of the greatest drunkards of my acquaintance told me that she was painfully aware of her husband becoming addicted to intemperate habits; that she warned him of his danger, and pleaded with him to give up the use of strong drink ; but he was indignant, and said, " Am I a dog that I should do this ?" The thought of being a drunkard never entered his mind, and the very idea, when hinted at by his loving wife, filled him with anger ; and yet he fell, and how great and how sad the fall ! Once he was the leading man in the place, the largest merchant in the village, one of Her Majesty's Justices of the Peace, active in his habits, useful to society, a pillar in the church ; kind, generous and noble, his purse was ever open to relieve the distressed and aid every good movement, and his house was a home for the minister and the moral reformer ; but, alas ! drink has mastered him : now he is a wreck—physically, morally and intellectually ; loathsome to look upon, the indirect murderer of his wife, his children's sorrow and the neighbourhood's pest.

A sin so terrific in its consequences should be traced to

its origin and strangled in the very cradle. Now it is this moderate drinking that is the great feeder of this parent vice—it oils the hinges of the gate leading to excess. It might be compared to a steep incline leading down to the depot of destruction; therefore,

> " On reason build resolve,
>   That column of true majesty in man,"

and shun the tempter.

Were all the drunkards that now inhabit our world swept away and not one left, how long do you think it would take before another army as great as the present would arise from the ranks of the moderate drinkers? Only a few years at most. During the past winter quite a number of persons met with their death from exposure to the cold, and chiefly on account of their intemperate habits; and as I read of one poor victim after another who had met with his or her death through drink, I thought that I heard a voice saying,"March forward, moderate drinker;" and there stepped forward, from the ranks of the moderate drinkers, others to fill up the blanks, and in no other way can you account for the fact that the army of drunkards is constantly kept up. Were it not for this, as a natural consequence they would die off and pass away. But although they are dying rapidly and numerously, the multitude of drunkards is constantly kept up; and why?—because there is being schooled, there is being educated in this school of moderate drinking, thousands of unsuspecting persons who come forward and fill up the vacancies as fast as they are made; and so long as moderate drinking is continued drunkenness will be the result, for it is daily supplying us with a fresh crop of drunkards.

I have sometimes asked the advocates of moderate drinking for a definition of moderation; but it has not been better defined than from a glass of wine to a hogshead of brandy. Some of those who have tried moderation found it to be a great botheration.

A minister is reported to have said to a man once, " John, you're drunk again." "Yes, minister, I'm drunk again." " Well, John, you're just gaun tae hell as fast as ye can gang." " What, minister, hae you turned teetotaller ? " " No, I'm nae teetotaller, ye ken; I tak it in moderation, John." " Weel, what dae ye ca' moderation, minister?" "Well, I tak a wee drap in the mornin' when I get up; then I tak a glass before dinner to sharpen my appetite, and for some years back I hae been in the habit o' takin' a wee drap o' whisky toddy gaun tae bed, tae mak me sleep." "And that's what you ca' moderation, minister ?" " Yes, John, that's the use, no the abuse, o' the guid creatures o' God." " Weel, minister, I'm paid every three months ye ken, and when I get my quarter's pay I gang on the spree and tak a fuddle. Now, I drank three glasses to-day, and you say I'm drunk and that I'm gaun tae hell as fast as I can gang on my three glasses in the three months or twelve glasses in the year, and you fancy that you're gaun tae heaven in a han' basket on your, at least, 365 glasses in the year."

See the full-grown cucumber in the window of the pickle merchant; how it has been trained to grow into its glass prison. How like the poor drunkard ! See the green youth insinuated into the bottle's mouth ; see it grows and swells until it becomes too large to be withdrawn, and has to be cut off and separated from the vine that cherished it. So with the drunkard ; habit makes him swell until he is cut off from the general world, and has no home but the bottle. " Bacchus," like a pickle merchant, has his bottled cucumbers in the shape of poor drunkards ; once good-looking, now they are sign-boards.

Following the drinking customs of society might be compared to the meanderings of the mountain's rill. You see that little stream descending the mountain's brow as it sparkles in the sunbeam ; it is insignificant in itself, but as you follow it on its course it increases, other streams become tributary to it, and at length it forms a mighty river, and becomes a mighty torrent, raging and foaming and sweeping all within its course into the yawning abyss of desolate despair. So many men who begin in the placid stream of moderation become drawn into the vortex, and are at last engulphed in the awful whirlpool of intemperance.

It is worthy of remark that men have not to be reasoned into drunkenness. You have not to argue with men to show them that it is desirable to become addicted to intemperate habits ; nay, they know that it is far otherwise : and yet, although they are conscious of the evil, alas ! they not unfrequently fall victims to this vice ; while, on the other hand, if you would have men relinquish the cup, and make sober men of drunkards, it is through the intellect (not the appetite) you approach them, and then appeal to their conscience and judgment in the matter.

Young men, the hope of our country, we appeal to you.
Would'st thou escape being drawn into the fearful whirlpool of intemperance ? then avoid moderate drinking.
Would'st thou save thyself from remorse and sorrow of
the keenest sort ? then avoid moderate drinking. Would'st
thou save thy sisters and brothers from burning tears of
shame and sorrow ? avoid moderate drinking. Would'st
thou dread bringing thy parents' grey hairs with sorrow
to the grave ? then avoid moderate drinking. Would'st
thou save thy soul, O young man ? then avoid, we pray
thee, moderate drinking, which has led so many into the
drunkard's misery.

How many parents' hearts are breaking to-day because
of this evil !—parents who have toiled late and early to
earn wherewith to provide for their families ; parents who
have spent thousands of dollars in educating their children and preparing them for the active duties of life, and
whose hearts beat high with hope that they would leave
their mark in the world; but, alas! no sooner did they
leave the parental roof than companions gathered around
them, and they have been enticed to frequent the hotel
and the saloon, and step by step they are being led away
from paths of virtue, sobriety and happiness, until around
ten times ten thousand hearths, to-day, parents' hearts
are breaking and mourning because of drink. The drinking customs of society are so prevalent, and the temptations to drink so numerous, that young men, especially,
require to be well fortified if they would avoid being
shipwrecked upon the sea of life. See two ships at sea :
one observes a dark cloud arising in the western horizon,

and furls her sails in preparation for the coming storm. She weathers the gale. The other, heedless of the danger, is overtaken—the sea begins to roll, the squall rises, the wind blows, the thunder peals, the lightning plays in the rigging—a perfect hurricane rages ; the sails are torn to shivers, the ship is dismasted, and at length she becomes a total wreck. So with two young men : one acts cautiously, becomes a pledged abstainer, outweathers many a fierce gale of storm and temptation ; the other, heedless of consequences, shuns the warning and is overtaken ; and hence thousands of our bravest young men have been led away and ruined by the drinking customs of society.

Parents, there is danger.

What parent would wish his children to become drunkards ? No one having natural affection could desire so sad a result, and yet how many parents, both by precept and example, do what they can to bring about this sad consequence. I know it is not designedly, but the effect is produced as perfectly as if it were intended on their part : they favour the drinking customs of society, and imbibe in the presence of their offspring, and thus the young look upon such as innocent and harmless, instead of shunning the drink as they would a rattlesnake. It has been remarked that example is more powerful than precept. We are creatures of imitation, and children will as a rule follow in the footsteps of their parents. Our children should be taught that, to abstain from drunkenness, they must abstain from intoxicating drinks.

" Never take more than two or three glasses at most, my boy," said a father to his son. "I have been a member

F

of a church for over twenty years, and no one ever saw me drunk in my life, my boy; follow your father's example, and you'll never be a drunkard; steer after me, my boy, and I'll show you how to avoid drunkenness. This is the clear stream of Moderation; yonder is the rock of Intemperance. Sail after me, my boy." The father mans his oars, and the son follows after. All goes well for a time. But see! the father nears the rock, and with wonderful nicety he rounds the point and escapes as with the skin of his teeth; but the son is less fortunate. "Sail after me, my boy," shouts the father. The son strives hard, but, notwithstanding all his efforts, his frail barque strikes against the rock, is upset, and, commingling with the moaning of the waves, the father hears the last cry of his boy, uttering the terrible words, Lost! Lost!! Lost!!! Ah, well might that father exclaim, with bitter anguish of soul, "O Absalom, my son, my son Absalom; would God I had died for thee, O Absalom, my son, my son Absalom;" and oh! how often has it happened that the father, of a sedate temperament, while he has drank moderately for years and never became a drunkard, yet his own son, of a sanguine temperament, has been overcome, and laid in the most awful of all graves— that of the poor unfortunate drunkard, made so by the example of his father and the ruinous drinking customs of society.

How often retribution follows wrong-doing, and how terrible the blow. I have seen the son of one of our Judges, while attending school, turned out on account of his intemperate habits; I have seen him dragged to the Police Court a bloated wreck before he was out of his teens; and all the while the father was indulging in the use of that which had ruined his son, blasted his own hopes, and whitened his hair. When will parents be wise, and warn their children of the danger connected with the use of spirituous liquors ?

Hannibal, when a child, was taken by his father, and there, upon the altar, the father made his boy swear eternal vengeance against Rome; and, as the result of such training, we find him, at the age of twenty-four, leading the armies of Carthage over the everlasting and untrodden Alps and thundering at the gates of Rome. So parents should ask their children, in the morning of life, to promise them that they would "neither taste, touch, nor handle the unclean thing."

What do you think of yourself now?

A young man of respectable birth was convicted and sentenced to transportation. What disgrace upon the family! The mother wept. The father visited him in prison—he enters—the door creaks on its hinges—father and son confront each other—they look, and the son says, "What do you think of yourself now?" "Think of myself!—what do you mean, Robert?" "Father," continued the son, "the half glass of toddy did it, and your hand mixed it. But for the practice you taught me, I would have shrunk from the tavern; but what harm could I see there, when I saw the same practices at my father's table?"

On the morning that he left the prison, both father and mother were at the cell early, and as he entered the prison van, the son addressed his father thus: "Farewell, father; there rests on me the brand of villain, and you affixed it there."

Awful position for a parent to be placed in !!!

Reformed drunkards, there is danger. "Let him that thinketh he standeth take heed lest he fall." I honour the men who have conquered this desperate appetite, and pronounce them true heroes, but still I would have them watch and pray, for there is danger. There is a twofold enemy to fight against—the enemy within, an appetite which may be roused at any moment; then there is the enemy without, in the shape of a legalized liquor traffic, and the drinking usages of society—all of which admonish you to be ever on your guard. There is really no safety for the reformed drunkard other than total abstinence.

Ah! there is danger even in one glass.

A sea captain who had once been greatly addicted to drink, became an abstainer, and for a considerable time held fast. But on returning home after a long voyage, as the vessel came near land, one of the passengers exerted much of his persuasive eloquence and induced the captain to take one glass; but, oh! it was an unfortunate glass. It flew to his brain, and under its maddening influence he leaped overboard and was drowned. The first mate took charge of the vessel until it reached the port. As the ship neared the wharf, a female figure was seen waving a white handkerchief. She knew the vessel, and in an ecstacy of joy she waved it high in the air; her heart was glad that, amongst so many casualties, once more her beloved husband had been brought in safety home. But now she becomes restless; how uneasy she seems. Where can he be? Is it possible that he is at his log-book? Why does he not come on deck? Surely he expects me. At last the ship is made fast to her moorings, and she leaps on board and rushes down to the cabin and inquires for her husband. One of the passengers informed her of how her husband came by his death, and oh! what grief, what anguish, what heart-rending sorrow wrung that poor woman's spirit as she wept and mourned the death of her beloved husband—a death made ten thousand times more painful by having been caused by drink.

See that ship at sea. Hark! how the storm rages! The winds blow, the waves rise mountains high, the thunders roll and the lightning plays amongst the rigging; but amidst it all she is fast at anchor. But one link in her cable gives way, and you see her driven with tremendous fury against the rocks, and you hear the groaning of the dying commingled with the moaning of the waves. What caused this disaster? Only one link gave way. So, reformed one, if you take but one drop of the liquor, your resolution becomes broken, and it may awaken that old appetite, which creates a greater storm in the soul than ever was produced by the elements during a storm at sea. And yet some will be so thoughtless, nay wicked, as to induce such men to drink.

I can point to farm after farm that has been squandered away through intemperance, and there are multitudes to-day who are reduced to want and poverty by over-indulgence in this fearful habit of drinking.

Health is in danger. We have known men of naturally
strong constitutions, to have them broken down, long before they arrived at the prime of manhood, by indulgence
in drink. We have also known persons to improve by totally abstaining, who were in the habit of only drinking
but moderately, and some even who were using it medicinally—as in the case of Mrs. Wightman, the authoress
of "Haste to the Rescue"—have been greatly benefited
by totally abstaining.

Character is in danger. What is so valuable to a man
as a good character ? Let a man possess never so much of
this world's goods, let him boast that he is a millionaire,
and be destitute of a good character, and we despise him ;
but let him be never so poor, if he possess a good character he has that which is beyond all price ; he is, in the
true sense of the word, rich. Shakspeare said, "Who
steals my purse steals trash; 'twas mine, 'tis his, and
has been slave to thousands ; but he who filches from me
my good name, robs me of that which not enriches
him, and makes me poor indeed." Some men begin to
drink with a good character, but by indulging in it they
lose not only their health and their property, but many of
them their character also.

Life is in danger. That habits of intemperance tend
to shorten the span of human existence, none will dare to
dispute. Not only do frequent and sudden deaths occur
daily from the excessive use of alcoholic drinks, but this
practice is constantly sending numbers to a premature
grave.

I appeal to the moderate drinker, and ask, what ad-

vantage have you moderate drinkers over those who abstain ? Surely, if you lend your influence to these customs, you must derive some advantage over us who totally abstain. It surely cannot be possible that you will
countenance this evil without you gain some wonderful
advantage over those who do not countenance it ; and if
you do, what are the advantages ? Do you live longer,
do you enjoy life better, is your muscle firmer, is your
complexion more healthy, is your breath less offensive,
can you endure the summer's heat or withstand the winter's cold better, are you more exempt from sickness, or,
when it comes, less liable to death ? Have you a clearer
intellect, a serener frame of mind, a less irritable temper,
or a more approving conscience? Is there one joy of
earth, or one hope of Heaven, over which the moderate
drinker has the advantage of the "Total Abstainer ?" Not
one ! Then, in the name of God, dash the poisoned cup
away !

If, on returning home and entering your bed-chamber,
a serpent met you rising on his tail, opening his horrible
jaws, with his deadly fang ready to plunge it into your
vitals, would you stand and admire its fantastic colours ;
would you stroke it and say, "Oh, pretty creature, what
varied hues; how lovely you are ?" No ! you would seek
some weapon by which you could deal it a deadly blow
on the head, and you would do right; but with reference
to the serpent Drink, although from the glass that contains the liquid fire there may be audibly heard the serpent's hiss, and visibly seen the adder's sting, yet people
admire it as it giveth its colour in the cup while the mon-

ster is coiling itself around its victim, and thus unconsciously chains of habit are being forged more difficult to
be broken than bands of iron.

Mr. Pollard, of Manchester, has said :—

"Let it stick in your head
    What friend Pollard once said,
For a long-headed fellow he's reckoned ;
  Never quaff the first pot,
    And the devil cannot
Compel you to swallow a second."

LECTURE III.

OUR DUTY.

IN this Temperance movement you have a duty to perform. The Rev. John Fletcher remarked, "A man may do your work, but none can do your duty."

The great Duke of Luxembourg declared upon his deathbed, "He would rather have it to reflect upon that he gave a cup of cold water to some worthy object in distress, than to have gained a thousand battles."

Now the question arises, if I can follow a safe course without any violation of principle, without bringing any guilt upon my conscience, or without injuring my fellows, am I not bound to do it? Now, I am certain that each of you will admit, that it is safer and there is not so much likelihood of my ever becoming a drunkard if I never "touch, taste nor handle the unclean thing," than if I were to tamper with drink and begin to follow the drinking customs of society. Well, then, if it be safer for me to abstain, and if my abstaining entails no guilt upon my own head nor any injury upon my neighbours, am I not bound in all conscience to do so? Besides, above mere personal grounds, my example will be safer and not so dangerous, and none can say that it was calculated to lead them to indulge in this vice.

When Dr. Edgar, of Belfast, first saw the necessity of suppressing the evils of intemperance, he put down the drink and said any that wanted it might help themselves, but that he would not offer it. The result was not one would drink, and next morning he took out the decanters and smashed them against the lamp-post, and the ducks were seen lying with their heels up opposite his residence.

A meeting was held in the west of Scotland to form a Total Abstinence Society. When several speakers had addressed the meeting, the parish minister rose, and stated that he saw no need for pledging themselves; that each for himself should use and not abuse these gifts; when a drunken weaver rose and exclaimed, "That's right, that's right; you're on our side—you're a man after my ain heart." The minister turned pale and replied, "If I'm on your side, I'm wrong." That was his turning point. Go thou and do likewise.

If the drunkard only is to abstain, how can he? A poor inebriate once waited upon a dry goods merchant and asked him, "Mr. Y., will you save a lost soul?" "What do you mean?" "Why, sir, you know I've been a poor degraded drunkard for so many years, and it breaks my heart to think of the misery that I have brought upon my poor wife and my innocent children, and I come to you to see if you will take the pledge with me; and if you will, I will. There's room on earth for another man, and by God's help I'll be that man." "It's the very best thing you can do," responded Mr. Y., "but I have no occasion; I never was drunk in my life; I have perfect command

of myself; but it's the very best thing you can do. I recommend you to join." "But," replied the poor drunkard,
"if none but drunkards would join, they would be pointed out and derided; but if Christian men like you will
join, then there will be protection and help for the likes of
me. Will you join with me, Mr. Y.?" "No; I have no
occasion, but I recommend you to join." The poor man
left. That night sleep forsook Mr. Y.; he tossed in his
bed, first on one side, then to the other; now he would
pull down his night-cap over his ears; but it was his conscience, not his night-cap, which troubled him. And,
friends, if we have a troubled conscience we cannot expect
to enjoy sweet sleep or calm repose, no matter how thick our
night-cap or how far we pull it over our ears. At last he
touches his wife with his elbow and said, "Betsy, I cannot sleep." "What's the matter?" replied the guidwife.
"Oh," responded Mr. Y., "Duncan McLean called at the
store this afternoon, and asked me if I would save a lost
soul. He wanted me to join teetotal with him and I
would not, and the words, 'Mr. Y., will you save a lost
soul?' are constantly ringing in my ear, and I can't sleep,
Betsy." She replied, "Weel, toots dinna bother me about
it. If you canna sleep, let me sleep mysel, wull ye?"
But sleep he could not, and early next morning he was
seen approaching the miserable home of poor Duncan, and
they both went to the secretary of the Temperance Society
and took the pledge, and Mr. Y. has been one of the best
friends of the good cause in that village since. So we
want you not to wait till you are forced like Mr. Y. to
join our ranks, but spontaneously and cheerfully to come
forward and join our noble cause.

We want your assistance in order to remove this great
curse from our land. "Greater love hath no man than this
—that a man lay down his life for his friends." We do
not ask you to lay down your life, but we do implore and
entreat of you to give up the use of alcoholic stimulants, ·
and for the sake of thy brother, thy weak brother, to
deny thyself the gratification which the cup affords thee,
in order that thou mayest stop this awful source of misery
and sin.

Dr. Johnson has quaintly said that he who waits and
expects to do a great deal all at once will never accomplish anything. "Life is made up of small things; let us
then do what we can and when we can."

Do not be like Belzoni's toad, which lived in the rock
three thousand years and did nothing, but rather come
forward nobly and help in this great moral reform.

"England expects that every man this day will do his
duty." Lord Nelson could exclaim, "I thank God I
have done my duty," and happy are those who can say
so in reference to the temperance question. "To him that
knoweth to do good and doeth it not, to him it is sin." If
you saw a vessel dashed to pieces against the rocks, or a
house on fire, you are bound to try and save the lives en-
dangered; but if you were asleep and in a state of uncon-
sciousness you would not be guilty of sin. Drunkards
are dying around you; are you trying to save them? It ·
was one of the shortest and yet most eloquent lectures
that ever was delivered upon this subject, when the late
Moderator of the General Assembly of the Church of
Scotland stated, "If all Skye should perish through intem-

perance, I thank God my skirts are clear of their blood."
Would to God that all ministers and professing Christians
could say the same, and like the great Apostle to the
Gentiles exclaim : " I take you to record that I am pure
of the blood of all men." May not one drop of the blood
of the ruined drunkard be found spotting our garments!
" Judge this rather, that no man put a stumbling block in
his brother's way."

It is astonishing what may be done in reclaiming inebriates where persons are earnestly desirous of doing
good. Once I had the pleasure of lecturing in the Parish of —————, and while there I was a guest at the
vicar's. Dinner was served up in real Irish style. There
the waiters, in patent slippers, white stockings, velvet
breeches, and all the livery requisite to adorn an Irish
nobleman's mansion, brought in dish after dish of the
good things provided. Then came the decanters with
wine, brandy and whisky; then porter, ale and every
variety of choice and rare drinks. In due time they were
passed to myself, but as I was a total abstainer I dare not
even touch them, and contented myself with a glass of cold
water, and allowed the waiter to pass them to the other
members of the vicar's family.

After dinner the vicar said to me that he would be
much obliged if I would go and visit some drunkards in
his parish. I replied that I would be glad to do anything in my power to reclaim such, but that if he were to
join our ranks he would exert a much greater influence
than I, a stranger, could possibly have. But, said the
vicar, "I have been accustomed to my glass of wine at

stated times daily for upwards of forty years, and I feel that as the time arrives when I have been accustomed to take it, nature demands it; besides, I fear if I were to give it up that my health would give way under it." I told him that the distinguished authoress of " Haste to the Rescue " had feared a similar result, but she saw so many injured by drink, that she resolved to give up her daily allowance of wine, although her medical advisers considered it essentially necessary; and instead of her suffering thereby, her health became very much improved. Besides, although he would be likely to feel the want of it for a time, still every day as he continued to abstain he would feel less inconvenience, and by abstaining he would be more likely to win over those who were confirmed drunkards. The vicar considered a little, and then decided that he would abstain ffor six months, and if, at the end of that time, his system was not injured by abstaining, he would become a member of the Society in that place; and now the vicar is an out-and-out teetotaller, and President of the ——— Total Abstinence Society.

There is abundant work for each and all to do. Sir Fowell Buxton placed more dependence upon ordinary powers and extraordinary exertion, than upon extraordinary powers and ordinary exertion. Let each, therefore, endeavour to do his duty, and success is certain.

Let the golden rule have its effect—"Do unto others as you would that they should do unto you." O man! if thou wert a poor drunkard enslaved, would'st thou not be glad that some one would endeavour to save thee? O woman! if it had fallen to thy lot to get a drunken husband, would'st thou not have welcomed the Temperance Reformer in his endeavours to reclaim thy poor husband? O son! if thy father had been an inebriate, would'st thou not have been thankful to see efforts being put forth to save him? O daughter! if thy mother, on whose kind lap thou hast lain, on whose breast thou hast hung, whose gentle voice hath oft hushed thee to sleep, and whose prayers hath oft ascended to Heaven on thy behalf—if she were a drunkard, would'st thou not appreciate the efforts of those who would visit thy mother and endeavour to win her back from her awful position? O fathers and mothers! if your children were treading the downward path—if they were victims to horrid intemperance,— would'st thou not love the men who were striving to reform them? And there are thousands suffering from, the sad, sad effect of this fearful vice; and if thou art not, be thankful to God for it, and put forth every effort in thy power to counteract these terrible evils.

We should pity and feel for the poor drunkard.

Many there are who spurn and pass by the drunkard, while they love and countenance that which has made him such. A lady once said in my hearing, "I hate a drunkard." "Pray, madam," I inquired, "are you a teetotaler?" "No, I am not; why do you ask me that question?" "Because, madam, all the total abstainers I have known, have pitied the poor drunkard, but hated the drunkard's drink." Instead of passing by the poor drunkard as an object beneath our notice, we should feel for him as a brother; and instead of despising him, we should stoop down and say, Here, brother, here's my

hand; I will try, both by precept and example, to bring
you up out of the horrible pit and miry clay of Intemperance; for howsoever low the poor drunkard has fallen,
still he is a brother, and only for drink he would be as
good or perhaps a better man than those who loathe him.

O, my friend, would'st thou have compassion for poor
suffering humanity? Then go visit the drunkard's home.
See his poverty-stricken dwelling; listen to the tale of
sorrow from the lips of his poor heart-broken wife; behold the squalid looks and tattered garments of his poor
children. Mark the wretchedness and misery of that
place known as a drunkard's home, and if thy heart be
not very marble, thou canst not but feel for the inmates
of that habitation.

The Rev. John Newton remarked:—"In the world I
observe two heaps—one little heap of happiness, and one
large heap of misery; and if I can take but the smallest
bit from the large heap of misery and place it upon the
small heap of happiness, I have gained a point. If, on my
way home, I meet a child crying who has lost a penny,
and if, by my putting my hand in my pocket and giving
it another, I can bring joy to the little one's heart, I have
done something. I should like to do more, but I will not
even neglect to do this little." This is the feeling that
ought to actuate every man. No doubt but there is a
large heap of misery in the world, and who will dispute
that that heap is largely increased by intemperance? In
fact, it is this one parent vice that fosters and feeds it to
a great extent.

Let us try and imbibe more of the spirit of love and

true sympathy for mankind. Would that we were actuated by the same spirit that actuated a good lady near Tower Hill, London. During the winter months there is much danger in horses walking at this place, when the ground is frozen, and many poor horses ofttimes fall as they ascend the hill; and this good lady, during the winter mornings, is seen out with her ash-bucket, spreading the ashes on the ice, in order to protect the poor horses, and as far as possible prevent them from slipping and falling. This is doing what is within her power.

> " O, this old world would be better
> If each hand would break a fetter ;
> If each one would do his part
> To bind up one broken heart."

If you had been present at the great fire at Chili, would you not have made an effort to save the unfortunate inmates? Would you not have broken in those doors, and endeavoured to extricate those inside ? You would! Every one of you would have done your best to rescue those within that building. When you see your neighbour's house or stable on fire, how you fly to render every assistance in your power to save the furniture, the horses, and whatever you can from the flames ; and if you will put forth such efforts to save chattels and cattle, will you not try to save the thousands who are being destroyed, body and soul, by drink ?

> " Drunkards are dying day by day ;
> Thousands on thousands pass away.
> O Christians, to their rescue fly,
> And seek to save them ere they die."

ALL HAVE INFLUENCE.

A gentleman lecturing upon individual influence, pointed to a man in front of him with a child on his knee and
said, "Even that little girl has influence." "That's true,
sir," cried the man. "I was an awful drunkard; my
eldest daughter, a girl of nineteen years, caught cold while
waiting at the public-house door to take me home in the
evenings, lest I should fall into pits, and when she died I
would take this child to the tavern for company, but she
caught me by the skirts of my coat, and with tears in her
eyes cried, 'Father, don't go.' I turned home, and have
never tasted drink since."

Then there is woman's influence; who can withstand her
power—who can withstand her eloquence ?

When she takes up the cause of the oppressed and enslaved, the fetters fall off and the joyous notes of freedom
are heard; twenty millions of beings are liberated.

When she espouses a cause nothing can daunt her courage, but she rises above every difficulty, and the world
acknowledges the power of woman's influence.

It is said of the immortal George Washington (a name
that will be green in the history of the world when that
of Cæsar, Alexander and Bonaparte shall have been forgotten), that on one occasion when passing through the
city a negro took off his hat as he approached the great
general. Washington returned the compliment, and one
of his generals observed this and remarked rather tauntingly, "Do you take off your hat to a nigger ?" "I would
not be outdone in politeness by a negro," said the immor-

tal Washington. I love that name; it is one of the purest,
one of the kindest, and one of the best that history has
recorded in this or any other land. Speak kindly, then,
we say, to the drunkard; never beat a cripple with his
own crutches. The poor drunkard feels deeply and keenly
his deplorable condition, and instead of scolding he needs
words of hope, words of comfort, words of encouragement. Remember,

> " Kind words can never die,
>   Heaven gave them birth ;
>   Winged with a smile they fly
>   All o'er the earth.
> Kind words the angels brought,
> Kind words our Saviour taught,
> Sweet melodies of thought,
>   Who knows their worth !
>   Kind words can never die, never die, never die ;
>   Kind words can never die ; no, never die."

Byron has one beautiful passage in his writings, which
is :

" There is more glory in drying the tears of sorrow from
the cheek, than in shedding oceans of blood."

O, wouldst thou dry ten thousand tears, try then to reclaim the drunkard, and thou shalt not lose thy reward.

I know something of what the poor drunkard feels ; I
know something of the remorse that goads him; and I
implore you, if you would try to rescue such, don't scold
nor abuse. Experience is said to be a good teacher. I
remember well when I was regardless of everything that
pertained to my spiritual well-being. I enjoyed company
very much. I desecrated God's Sabbath. I, in fact, nei-

ther feared God nor regarded man.   While in that state I
was visited by a pious young man; had he taunted me, I
would have spat in his face; had he scolded me, I would,
if in my power, have kicked him out of doors; but he
pitied me.

I saw he loved me; I observed in his entreaties and in
his tears proofs of his sincerity and affection; and by
exercising kindness I permitted him after many efforts to
search for my boots, and when he had found them I
allowed him to pull them on, and I complied with his
wishes and accompanied him to the house of God, where
I became convinced of the error of my ways, and was led
to seek and find mercy, and to my last breath I shall bless
and respect the name of James H. Beatty.

It is possible to do a right thing, and yet do it in a
wrong way.   If we could hope to benefit the drunkard,
we must not scold and abuse him, but speak kindly and
softly to him. Civility is very cheap, and yet how beautiful
to behold. If you look at those men who have been most
successful in the world, you will find that they have generally possessed a large share of this quality; and those
persons who have been most useful in reforming drunkards
have been men who are remarkable for civility, kindness
and strong affections.   Some seem to pride themselves in
giving offence and manifesting their want of common
civility.   In the Old Country we have first, second and
third-class carriages on the railways, and when the guard
enters the first-class he says, " Tickets, please, ladies and
gentlemen ;" the second-class, " Tickets, please ;" the third
class, "Tickets." Let a careful observer enter some of our

banks. A gentleman enters, hands his cheque, and is courteously asked, " Shall I give you large bills or small ones ?" and bows gracefully as he hands the needful. Immediately there follows him a poor but honest farmer with home-spun coat; he lays down his cheque, the price of a load of grain or pork which he has brought to market for sale; the cashier picks it up quite hastily, and, without consultation or ceremony, puts down such bills as he has a mind to give, and the poor farmer may either take them or let them alone. Now, this man with his home-spun coat may be an honest son of toil, and perhaps a child of God, related to the Blood Royal of Heaven; while the man dressed in broad-cloth, who received most attention, may have been one of the vilest of characters, and one who has cheated and defrauded his creditors of thousands of dollars. We must learn to value men by their moral worth, not by the texture of the cloth they wear. On one occasion Robert Burns, Scotia's own noble and immortal bard, was observed by a noble Earl talking to a Highland Scotsman with a broad blue bonnet and large strong boots. " Well, Burns," said the Earl, " is that the kind of company you keep?" " Toots, you gommeral," said Burns, " it's no the man's bonnet I'm talking to, it's the man's sel'." So when we see a drunkard, let us pity him; let us not be ashamed to be seen speaking to him; words of kindness let us speak; let us ever remember that it is the drink that has laid him so low—that only for it he might be great, good, and respectable.

There are thousands lost to themselves, lost to society, lost to everything that's good, lost to God, and, if not reclaimed from drunkenness, lost, lost! soul and body, for all eternity; and will you not try to reclaim them? There are thousands who have nothing to lighten up the darkness of their gloom; they have no friend to speak to them. "No man careth for their soul," is their bitter lament. Will you try and save such lost ones? I know we shall yet conquer, for—

> " Right is right since God is God,
> And Right the day must win ;
> To doubt would be disloyalty,
> To falter would be sin."

The Rev. Benjamin Cutler was stopped on his way home by a poor woman, and asked if he would please accept a present of two fat chickens. He refused, saying he had never done anything to merit such kindness. She replied, "If you do not take them you will offend me much. I have fattened them for you for weeks." "But I never did anything to deserve them." "Yes, you looked so sad when my husband would be drinking, and spoke so kindly, that he could not withstand it, and he has joined, and is now sober; so you will please take the chickens, sir."

One of the most touching instances of gratitude that perhaps ever was witnessed was in the case of the great trial in Dublin of Major and Mrs. Yelverton, in 1860. Mr. Whiteside conducted the case for Mrs. Yelverton; and at the close of that powerful and brilliant address he remarked, that "the only fault Mrs. Yelverton had was, that she loved Major Yelverton too well; that if she had a crown, she would have placed it upon his brow; if she had all the gold of Ophir or the wealth of the Indies, she would have cast them at his feet." The trial being over, and judgment having been given in favour of Mrs. Yelverton, the fact was made known to her; and as Mr. Whiteside entered the room where she sat with some of her lady friends, she sprang upon her feet, and rushing forward caught hold of him by both hands, as she with streaming eyes lifted her face to heaven, while the warm tears of gratitude flowed in copious streams down upon his hands, as she exclaimed, "May Heaven reward you for how you have pleaded the cause of the innocent this day! I can never repay you, but Heaven will." So if you engage in the good work of endeavouring to reclaim the fallen, you shall be rewarded; the poor drunkard himself will bless you; his wife and children will bless you—not perhaps so eloquently as the accomplished Mrs. Yelverton. It may be something after the manner of an old beggar-woman in Ireland, who, when a young gentleman would drop a copper into her lap, would lift both her hands up as high as possible and exclaim, "Arrah, arrah, that your soul may be in heaven a fortnight before the devil knows you are dead." It may, I say, not be in so touching, pathetic, or eloquent a strain as the educated and accomplished Mrs. Yelverton; it may be only in the illiterate style of the poor beggar-woman, but if you engage in the work of Temperance Reform and put forth all your effort, verily you shall not lose your reward.

On one occasion Her Most Gracious Majesty Queen Victoria visited Paris, to pay her respects to Napoleon, the Emperor of the French. The French soldiery were drawn up in lines in the principal streets of the city;

their trappings and bayonets glistened in the sunbeam as
the royal carriage passed with Her Majesty, the Prince
Consort, the Emperor and Empress Eugenie. Presently
the carriage reached one of the principal thoroughfares,
where there stood a man with a great portion of his face
carried away, and minus an arm and a leg. As soon as
the carriage arrived opposite this man, the Emperor gave
orders to halt, and going up to one of the chief officers in
command he inquired how it was that he allowed a miserable object like that to stand right in front of one of
the principal thoroughfares while Her Majesty was passing. "Oh, sire," replied the officer, "that is one of
France's bravest sons. It was while fighting for Her
Majesty on the heights of Alma that he was struck with
a shell and received those wounds, and he came to me
with tears in his eyes, and implored, as the only reward
to be given to an old veteran, that he might be permitted
to gaze upon that queen for whom he fought, suffered,
and bled, and the appeal was so eloquent I could not
withstand it. The fault is mine, sire." The Emperor
was pleased. He went to the carriage and gave orders to
drive on, and then related the circumstance to Her Majesty the Queen. Her tender heart was touched, and she
requested that the carriage would return, that once more
she might get a sight of the devoted soldier. The order
was given to halt, and the Emperor alighted from the carriage and stepping forward to the man, took the star of
the legion of honour from his own breast, and with his
own fingers pinned it upon the breast of the old veteran
soldier, amidst the most vociferous shouts of "Long live

the Emperor!" That was honor—honor paid to a faithful old veteran who had fought nobly for his country; and will not those who engage in this struggle receive honour? We seek in this crusade not to destroy men's lives, but to save them; not to make many hearts sad by the shedding of blood, but to make many hearts glad by the reclaiming of those poor unfortunates who have become addicted to intemperance.

Ladies, we ask you to help us in this work. Truly your sex has suffered enough by this evil to cause every woman in the land to set their face for ever against it, and depend upon it, if ever this world is to become better and happier, woman, properly educated and truly benevolent, sensible of her mighty influence and wise enough to exert it aright, must move in this great and important movement.

LECTURE IV.

THE TEMPERANCE ENTERPRISE.

IT is gratifying, notwithstanding the coldness, the selfishness and the indifference of many of the professed friends of this enterprise, to mark the progress and success which have crowned the efforts of those engaged in this mighty reform.

When we look abroad upon the multiplicity and magnitude of the Temperance organizations which now cover the land and spread their healing and blessed influences upon society, we are bound to thank God and take courage; but let us never forget the men who first buckled on their armour and went forth to do valiant service in this great, good and glorious cause. It has been remarked that "fame is the reward of the dead, not of the living."

> "They sleep in secret, and their sod,
> Unknown to man, is marked by God."

But the early pioneers of this godlike enterprise shall never die; such men as Dr. Rush, Dr. Justin Edwards, Dr. Lyman Beecher and Rev. Joseph S. Christmas, and a host of others, are deserving to be held in everlasting remembrance. Let their noble example stimulate us to greater exertions, so that we may be worthy followers of such noble heroes, and that we may speed the glorious consummation of that work which they so nobly commenced.

Now Temperance occupies a prominent place in the land ; it numbers amongst its members millions of all rank[s] and classes in the community. We have now enrolled upon our pledge book the name of the peer as well as the peasant, the rich as well as the poor, and the noble as well as the mean. Our principles are now practised in the gorgeous mansion as well as in the humble log cabin. Ministers of the ever-blessed gospel and senators of state ; men of the most gigantic intellect and the brightest genius—all give evidence in favour of the soundness of our heaven-born cause. We have a Garibaldi, the purest of patriots ; the late President Lincoln, of the United States; Lord Shaftesbury and others who dine at the table of our most gracious Queen, who are not ashamed to practise and preach the principles of Total Abstinence.

At first when this cause was agitated there were some who were afraid to move either tongue or pen until they would see whether it would become popular or not, while there were others, more daring than they, who did everything in their power in order to crush the seed of Temperance in the bud ; but their opposition only increased the zeal of the friends of the cause, and instead of it dying, it revived and prospered and spread. Just like two boys who were playing in an avenue on one occasion—one of them picked up something, and closing his hand upon it, he exclaimed, " O, Jamie, I have found something."

" What hae ye found, Tom ? let's see it."   " No, you would take it."   " Honour bright, Tom, I'll no take it."   With that he opened his hand and exposed his treasure.   "Toots, man, that's an acorn," replied his companion.   " What's an acorn ? " inquired Tom.   " The seed of one of them big trees there," replied Jamie ; and with that Tom flung it down, and stamping his foot upon it he sank it into the ground.   " That's right, Tom, that's right ; just where it ought to be, in its native soil." Time rolled silently past; by-and-by it sent forth its tiny shoots ; every year added to its strength and importance, until it became a giant oak in the branches of which the fowls of heaven could lodge, and became material out of which proud England built her navy, and became mistress of the seas.

" O, the wooden walls of England,
    Her sailors and her seas ;
    Hurrah for Nelson, Trafalgar,
    The battle and the breeze."

Little did Tom think when he stamped in anger upon that acorn that he was planting the seed of a giant oak that would flourish when his poor body would be mouldering in the silent graveyard, and yet it was so ; and as little did those who opposed the Temperance enterprise imagine that they were by their very resistance planting the seed of Temperance ; for as

" The oak strikes deeper as its boughs
    By furious blasts are driven,"

so the more opposition we have had, the more zealously we've striven ; and just as the limpet clings tenaciously to

yonder rock, so have the true friends of this glorious cause
stuck most firmly to their principles, when they have
been most fiercely and most bitterly assailed.

Some thought the Temperance movement wild and
ridiculous, and although we were not compelled to swear
a recantation like Galileo, yet we were branded as fan-
atics and enthusiasts; but, notwithstanding all this (as
the great Tuscan philosopher said to one who was
standing by as he rose from his knees after swearing to
a series of propositions, "It moves for all that"), our
glorious cause, in spite of bitter foes and trembling
friends, "moves for all that."

It was called a Utopian scheme—an impossibility. But
so it ever has been. When Stephenson proposed to run a
steam coach between Manchester and Liverpool, they
said it would set fire to the houses on the line, that the
hens would lay no more eggs, and that the cows would
give no more milk, but he persevered until the land has
at length been belted with railways.

A great work is yet to be done if we would suppress
the evils of intemperance and stay the further ravages of
this Hydra. Wherever we go, the demon Drink stares
us in the face, and opposes us in every step we take in
order to elevate society; and if statesmen were to sit down
calmly and ask themselves the question, "What measures
if adopted would tend most to the physical, social, mental,
moral and religious advantage of the people?" I fancy
the response would be to mitigate, if not entirely do away
with, this injurious traffic. Lord Brougham has remarked that "the philanthropist has no more sacred duty to

perform than to mitigate, if not altogether suppress, this traffic." The Temperance enterprise commends itself to every man, no matter to what shade of politics or religious denomination he may belong, and I consider this one of the beauties of this movement. Just as the various colours constitute the rainbow and make it lovely and attractive to the eye, so is the fact that all persons, howsoever they may differ in their political or religious views, here can meet upon one broad common platform to fight against one common foe. This I look upon as one of the most grand and distinguishing glories of our movement. Rally then, friends, around the Temperance flag. The people in the Old Country are putting forth mighty effort, and never was the cause so warmly sustained and zealously promoted as at this present moment. In eighteen hundred and sixty-three, five hundred ministers of the Established Church subscribed their names to the Temperance pledge, and are putting forth great effort to crush this monster evil. Upwards of eight hundred ministers in Scotland are devoted advocates of the cause; and in Ireland, according to the report of the Irish Temperance League for 1863, the ministers are joining by hundreds, and public opinion is becoming vastly changed in favour of Total Abstinence.

Scotland can boast of one of the greatest Temperance organizations in the world, the world-renowed "Scottish Temperance League," an organization which, both by its able advocates and splendid publications, has done more for Scotland than the most sanguine amongst us could have expected. And why is it that such success has crowned this cause ? It is because the smile of God rests upon this enterprise, and he has blessed the efforts which have been put forth on behalf of suffering humanity ; and we may rest assured that if we labour in this good work the God of heaven will own our humble efforts.

Nor is Canada lagging in this grand movement ; never in the history of the cause was there so much zeal and earnestness manifested as at the present time. The various Temperance Societies throughout the Dominion are doing a good work in their own spheres, while at the same time every indication gives promise that united action will be taken in order to obtain the complete overthrow of the liquor traffic at no far distant date.

This happy state of things is largely owing to the strenuous efforts put forth by the " Ontario Temperance and Prohibitory League," which is destined, with the co-operation of the other Temperance Societies throughout the country, to accomplish a glorious victory.

It gladdens our hearts to take any humble part in this glorious enterprise ; and when we review its wonderful success and bloodless triumphs, we are proud to be found on the side of virtue and sobriety, giving no quarter to, but taking a decided stand against, this deadly enemy of man.

It gladdens our hearts to see misery replaced by comfort, to see the home once desolated by the demon Drink now a peaceful and happy abode. It gladdens our hearts to see the father who was once cruel and unfeeling (made so through drink) now a kind and loving parent, giving his children the best legacy a poor man can bequeath them

—the benefits of a liberal education and a virtuous example. It gladdens our hearts to see the drunkard's wife, who
was once sad, sorrowful and careworn, now cheerful, blythe
and gay, and to see her dear children, who were once ragged, tattered and torn, now comfortably clothed and fed.

Temperance is the friend of all, the enemy of none ; it
is the handmaid of religion ; and one of its distinguishing
glories is this, that it blends in and beautifully har-
monizes with every Christian and philanthropic effort in
which we engage. As an evidence of this I might mention
the case of Rev. Hugh Hanna, of Belfast. I was careful to
observe as far as possible, during the Ulster revival in
eighteen hundred and fifty-nine, the connection between
Temperance and Religion, and I am bold to assert that, as
far as my observation went, I invariably found that those
ministers who were total abstainers were much more
successful in gaining and retaining converts than those
who opposed or stood aloof from temperance. As the result
of that revival, the Rev. Mr. Hanna got a fine large brick
church erected, the former one being quite too small to
hold his congregation. He had a Temperance Society in
connection with his church, and special pains were taken
to watch over reformed drunkards, and his labours were
abundantly owned of God ; while some that I could name,
who took no interest in the Temperance movement, derived but little advantage, and the falling off in the latter
case was much greater than in the former.

Dr. Marsh, on the laying of the Atlantic cable, states,
" To Temperance is the world not a little indebted for this
mighty achievement. Who brought the lightning from the

skies ?—Franklin, a teetotaler. Who made it the ready communicator of thought?—Morse, a teetotaler. Who sunk it in the ocean's depths and made one of distant peoples ? —Field, a teetotaler. Who stood at the helm of the noble *Niagara*, which bore the cable to our shores ?—Capt. Wm. Hudson, another firm teetotaler."

O, ye moderate drinkers, we ask you for your trophies ! Show us those who have been reclaimed from intemperance by following your moderate example. We can point here and there and yonder to persons now kind parents, useful members of society, and many of them ornaments of the Church of Christ, who, through this Temperance enterprise, have, by the blessing of God, been raised from the depths of degradation into which drink had plunged them, and now are loving husbands, kind parents, useful members of society, and active in every good word and work.

We are impelled by a noble philanthropy, a true patriotism and a Christ-like charity.

Thank God, philanthropists still live though good old John Howard is no more, and men are to be found who are willing to sacrifice personal interests for the public good.

When this agitation was first commenced, the object aimed at was the reformation of the drunkard, and through those efforts the following indirect results have flowed, viz.:

1st. The present state of public opinion.

2nd. A sense of moral danger in the use of drink.

3rd. The evil is more thoroughly understood.

H

4th. A change in the social customs.

5th. A desire to train up the young in temperance.

6th. A disposition to limit the facilities for drinking.

7th. Tipple, and your credit is suspected.

Our thanks are due to the press and the editors; those men who spend heart and brain for the better future of the world. Few know the consuming fever of the toil which supplies them with their paper, or they would more highly appreciate it, and would know that there are battle-fields more destructive than that of war. But while papers and editors can do much, what can I do by my small efforts? Look at the tiny rain-drop; it falls upon the sturdy granite, makes its way into the crevice, and finally succeeds in splitting the monster rock; so your small efforts may do much. Only do what you can; the greatest archangel in heaven cannot do more; but you must not wish and sigh—you must gird up your loins, and go to work like Hannibal scaling the Alps, who at the age of twenty-four led the armies of Carthage over the ever-lasting and untrodden Alps, and thundered at the gates of Rome.

It is cause for thankfulness to Almighty God, that the press, hitherto so indifferent in this matter—a matter of such vital interest to humanity at large—is beginning to do good service in this noble work. There are some news-papers that fearlessly expose the evils and accidents re-sulting from this fearful habit; and when we consider the influence, the power, the omnipotence of the press, we hail this as a delightful feature of the "signs of the times." Could we, with supernatural power, call from the dreary charnel-house the inhabitants of the antediluvian world, and conduct them into one of our large printing establishments, where, amid the everlasting clinking of type and clatter of presses, broad sheets are thrown off at the rate of thousands per hour, affording at a single glance information that at one time would have cost a lifetime of labour, surely they would think that we live in the "golden age" of which philosophers dreamed and poets sung; or could those Athenians who, on Mars Hill, listened to the burning eloquence of Paul, see that discourse bound up in morocco in the Book of Books, or were they permitted to enter into one of our large book-rooms, where thousands of volumes, in almost every language under heaven, make the very shelves groan with the mass of literature they bear, how amazed would they feel, and what a mighty contrast to the old rolls of parchment stored up in the Areopagus.

A few years since I met with J. J. E. Linton, Esq., of Stratford, who was the first Secretary to the first Temperance Society in England or Scotland; it was formed in eighteen hundred and twenty-nine, at Greenock, and Rev. Dr. Edgar was the man who delivered the first lecture in connection therewith. But how mightily has the cause grown! The little one has become a thousand, and the great secret lies in this, that the smile of God rests upon the cause, and we have thousands of living witnesses to prove that God has owned the efforts which have been put forth.

The Temperance tide is flowing; it is reaching the enemy in his stronghold; its foundations are being undermined; and the cry will soon be heard, "Babylon isfal len."

Blessed be God, there are a noble and goodly number engaged against this foe, and let me say to you, Go on! Go on! till the smoke will be seen no more to ascend from yonder distillery chimney. Go on! till the last tavern door shall be for ever bolted. Go on! till the last drunkard's wife will be seen weeping her life away because of the intemperance of her husband. Go on! till the last drunkard's child shall be heard to cry for bread. Go on! till the very last drunkard shall be reclaimed; until our now drink-cursed earth becomes freed from the greatest curse that can blight a nation.

For this purpose be united. "Union is strength." Take a long pull, and a strong pull, and a pull all together, and you shall succeed. "Stand as an iron pillar, strong and steadfast as a wall of. brass."

Let the past cast its shadows upon the future. We stand upon the vantage ground of David, who, when proud Goliath of Gath dismayed the hosts of Israel, resolved to face the boaster. For forty days, morning and evening, did the Philistine draw near and hurl his defiant challenge at the Israelites and said, "I defy the armies of Israel this day; give me a man that we may fight together." But David, with all that dignity which ever characterizes the man who has truth on his side, and God's glory for his aim, determined to meet him. Saul tried to dissuade him, remarking, "Thou art but a youth, and he a man of war from his youth." But David remembered the time when God delivered him out of the paw of the lion and the paw of the bear, and said, "This uncircumcised Philistine shall be as one of them." So David chose five smooth stones out of the brook, which he carefully deposited in his shepherd's bag and went to meet Goliath. "Am I a dog," cried Goliath as David approached, "that thou comest to me with staves?" and he "cursed David in the name of his gods." "Thou comest to me," answered David, "with a sword and with a spear and with a shield, but I come to thee in the name of the Lord of Hosts, the God of the armies of Israel, whom thou hast defied." "Come to me," tauntingly exclaimed the Philistine, "and I will give thy flesh to the fowls of the air and to the beasts of the field;" and David hasted and put his hand in his bag, selected a stone, placed it carefully in his sling, and breathing the prayer, "O thou God of Abraham, thou God of Isaac and of Jacob, let it be known that thou art God in Israel, and that I am thy servant." He winds the sling, the stone enters his forehead, his colossal figure falls upon the ground, while his gore stains the grass. He runs forward, leaps upon his body, and stooping down draws Goliath's sword from its sheath, severs his head from his body, and carries it in triumph to Jerusalem.

And, friends, a worse and more deadly enemy than Goliath is amongst us. King Alcohol, a hell-born giant, is not only threatening, but actually destroying thousands of our fellow-beings; and shall no youthful Davids come forward and try to kill and destroy this terrible enemy of God and man ?

In the midst of difficulty and opposition we are resolved to labour on, and leave the results to God. Work is ours, brethren, but results belong to God. Then, in the language of Barry Cornwall—

" Weave, brothers, weave! toil is ours ; but toil is the lot of man ;
One gathers the fruit ; one gathers the flowers ; one soweth the seed
    again.
There is not a creature, from England's King to the peasant that delves
    the soil,
That knows half the pleasures the seasons bring, if he have not his share
    of the toil."

Richard Cobden said : " Every day's experience tends
more and more to confirm me in my opinion that the
Temperance cause lies at the foundation of all social and
political reform ;" and that " out of six hundred and fifty-
eight members in the House of Commons, he believed
that the men who are the most temperate are the men
who bear the fatigue of the House the best. Water
drinkers will upset the moral world, and will turn it round
with a much better face to us when they have done with
it."

Experience confirms the soundness of Temperance principles. What is wrong in practice cannot be right in
theory. There is danger in drinking while it is safe to
abstain. Therefore, "on reason build resolve, that column
of true majesty in man."

I have had ample opportunities of observing the fruit
of this great enterprise, and have met with hundreds of
the trophies of our cause. I have knelt at the family altar of many who a few years ago were uttering the most
profane language that ever escaped the lips of mortal,
but now instead of blasphemy is heard the voice of
prayer and thanksgiving.

Mr. S—— was on a spree. Returning home " tight," he
observed the Sunday-school dismissing and was hurrying

home. The footpath was too narrow, even the road seemed too narrow, but he got home and lay down upon his bed. His daughter entered ere he fell asleep, and said " O, mother, is father drunk again ?" " Hush, child, why do you ask such a question ? " " Because the scholars said they saw him going home and he was drunk, and the road was not broad enough for him to walk upon." He heard this, and said he would never drink another drop. He keeps his pledge like a man, has considerable property, and is doing well.

If persons would calmly and thoroughly consider our principles, we think there is nothing in them but what would commend them to every Christian and philanthropic mind ; but some have taken up the defensive, and they seem unwilling to throw down the weapons of their warfare. Now it is a bad thing to take up and hold to the wrong side of any question merely for argument sake. There is such a thing as the possibility of getting a squint in one's intellect. There was a man in Cork who was remarkable for looking obliquely, and a young man there prided himself in trying to imitate this poor man, and he would twist and strain his eyes, which exhibited the perfection of infinite knowledge, until at last by his terrible efforts the muscles became unequally contracted or weakened, and he became the most terrible cross-eyed squinter in that entire neighbourhood. So, some persons may, by taking up a false position for the sake of argument or otherwise, beget a squint in their intellect; hence we would entreat all those who " see and approve of the better but follow the worse," to let nothing hinder them

from acting a wise and straightforward course, and doing
that which sound judgment and an enlightened conscience can approve. "To him that knoweth to do good
and doeth it not, to him it is sin." O, how much good
you might do if you would! One-half the world seems
satisfied with doing nothing but finding fault with what
the other half does, instead of trying by earnest individual
and united effort to make this old world better.

Sir H. Davy invented a lamp by which he could go
down into the coal mines and wander through their sub-
terranean passages amidst foul air and gases, and avoid
all danger of an explosion. This was a great invention ;
and, thank God, if we take the Temperance pledge, and
adhere strictly to its principles and be guided by its
safe light, we shall avoid all danger of an explosion, and
will be enabled to walk through this world without being
drawn into the vortex of intemperance.

Millions in time and millions in eternity have bitter
cause for regret that they indulged in the use of alcoholic
stimulants ; but I never knew a man to be sorry for being an abstainer. No, it will plant no thorns in your
dying pillow that you have practised and done all in
your power to promote the principles of Total Abstinence.

We want in this conflict men of iron. There are men
of clay and men of iron : men who are Temperance men
when in company with Temperance men, and tipplers or
nobodies when with drinkers ; men who take like the
clay the impress of whatsoever they come in contact with ;
but there are men of iron, who give their impression to
all they come in contact with—who are the same outside

the division that they are inside. O for more of these men of iron! such as the Hon. Malcolm Cameron, who, when he dined with the Prince at Sarnia—the Prince, who knew Mr. Cameron was a teetotaler, said, when the health of the Queen was proposed, "You will have to take wine now." Mr. Cameron replied, as he filled his glass with water, "The Queen has forty-five thousand as good subjects in Canada as she has in all her possessions, who will most cordially drink her health, not in wine, but water pure."

A. Lincoln, the late President of the United States, at a public dinner was asked to drink. "No, gentlemen," he replied, "I have drank none for fifty years, and I'll not begin now."

I remember hearing the late lamented Simeon Morrill, of London, Ont., state that at a great dinner party, the late Sir —— took advantage of his (Simeon Morrill) conversing with a friend, and poured some liquor into his glass. It was not unobserved, however, and when all rose to drink, he sat still. All waited until a waiter took away his glass, gave him a clean one with fresh water, which he filled, and then all drank. That day Sir —— was so drunk that Mr. M. had to assist him into his carriage, and Sir —— exclaimed, "Well, thank God the horses are sober." Truly, after all, the Temperance men have the best of it.

BE TRUE TO YOUR PRINCIPLES.

Some there are who take offence and leave the ranks for very trifling causes indeed. Now, what would you think of a soldier in Her Majesty's service who would go up to his officer and say, "I want to leave the army?" "Why?" asks the officer. "Because I don't like so-and-so." Would not that man deserve to be branded with the title coward and deserter? Then let no paltry thing ever lead us to betray that cause which we have espoused, and which should be dear to every Temperance man.

I remember well how I was sneered at when I embraced the principles of Total Abstinence. Some take particular pleasure in teasing those who become enlightened on this question; but generally they come off worst. There were three young men that resolved to do what no young man should, namely, to take a "rise" out of an old man, or to sport with old age. So they made it up that they would have fine fun. The first went out, and as he met the old man he said, "Good morning, father Abraham." "Good morning, young man," replied the old gentleman. The second said, "Good morning, father Isaac." "Good morning, young man." The third said, "Good morning, father Jacob." "I'm neither father Abraham, father Isaac, nor father Jacob," replied the old man; "but I'm Saul, the son of Kish, who went out in search of his father's asses, and lo! I have found them." Those who will not join us won't make anything by taunting us who have embraced the cause of humanity and the cause of God.

The *Westminster Review*, which was once one of the deadliest enemies of Total Abstinence, has now changed its opinion, and instead of winking at the evils of this traffic, is now bold in exposing the horrible results which flow from this abominable system. It declares that " it is impossible to exaggerate the evils of intemperance," and that " drunkenness is Britain's curse."

We have no hesitation in stating that the pledge is a great safeguard. Suppose that on your way home you were obliged to cross a broad, deep river ; here was a narrow plank dangerous to walk upon, and yonder was a broad, substantial bridge, with side railings and everything perfectly secure. Now, were the waves roaring beneath, the lightning playing around you, and the wind blowing a perfect hurricane, over which would you cross ? I know the ladies would choose the broad, substantial bridge, with side railing attached, that they could lay hold of. Well, this is the Temperance bridge, on which you may walk in perfect safety. But the other is the narrow plank of moderation ; every step you take it springs, and over it thousands have been precipitated and engulphed in the abyss of intemperance.

See that large mercantile establishment in flames. The merchant has one consolation : he has a patent fireproof safe ; his books, his notes, his cash are there ; he is not totally ruined ; he can start again. Oh, drunkard, enter our Lodge and adhere to our principles and you are safe.

Total Abstinence is our watchword ! Nothing less will do, poor inebriate. You may be sincere to amend your ways, but 'tis useless ; you must entirely abstain. See that poor shipwrecked mariner ; he grasps a straw ; he lays hold on a bubble ; but it vanishes—not that he was insincere, not that he was indifferent about saving his life, but the object at which he seized was incapable of

saving him. And so, poor inebriate, if you grasp at moderation it will prove a straw. Nothing less than total
abstinence can save you.

What a sermon, too, on the blessings of Temperance is
contained in the few lines in the third scene of the second act of "As you Like It," when Adam says to his
young master :

> " Let me be your servant !
> Though I look old, yet I am strong and lusty ;
> For in my youth I never did apply
> Hot and rebellious liquors in my blood ;
> Nor did not with unabashful forehead woo
> The means of weakness and debility ;
> Therefore my age is as a lusty winter,
> Frosty but kindly.   Let me go with you ;
> I'll do the service of a younger man
> In all your business and necessities."

There is a passage in classic history where a man was
brought up accused of being a traitor.   His friend, who
had rendered eminent services to his country, and in his
country's struggles had lost his arm in its defence, lifted
it up, and the Court felt the force of this silent appeal and
he was acquitted.   So the wounds and scars of those
who have been injured by drink appeal to you.

At a wedding party in the Eastern States the bride
was asked just to taste in honour of the company; she, however, refused.   Her husband and her father entreated her
just to put it to her lips.   They urged so strongly
that she took it in her hand, and holding it up between
her and the light she started back uttering a loud scream.
" Ah !" said she, " what a fearful sight."   " What did you

see?" "Away on yonder lone bank of a river in California lies a young man once beloved by his friends and all who knew him, with none but a lone comrade to wipe the damp sweat from his fevered brow, while the horrible 'delirium tremens' burnt up his very heart's blood. The demon Drink killed him. That loved one was my only brother; his lone comrade is now my husband. Father, shall I drink it?" "No!" uttered the father, as he wept. "Husband, shall I drink it?" "No! no!" uttered the husband. Then appealing to the company, she said, "Friends, shall I drink it?" "No!" responded every voice, and the entire company joined in the pledge.

There are two courses open for us: the one is to fold our arms and allow the demon Drink to go on doing its work of death; the other is to arise in all our might, majesty and power, and fight against the foe that threatens our homes.

"THE SHIP OF STATE."

Thou, too, sail on, O ship of state—
Sail on, O Temperance, strong and great;
  Humanity with all its fears,
  With all its hopes of future years,
Is breathless, longing on thy fate.

We know what master laid thy keel,
What workmen wrought thy ribs of steel,
  Who made each mast and sail and rope;
What anvils rang, what hammers beat,
In what a forge and what a heat
  Were shaped the anchors of our hope.

Heed not each sudden sound and shock,
'Tis but the wave and not the rock;

'Tis but the flapping of a sail,
And not a rent made by the gale.
In spite of rock and tempest's roar,
In spite of false lights on the shore,
  Sail on ; nor fear to breast the sea—
  Our hearts, our hopes are all with thee.
Our hearts, our hopes, our prayers, our tears,
Our faith triumphant o'er our fears,
  Are all with thee ! are all with thee !

LECTURE V.

OBJECTIONS CONSIDERED.

IT is well for humanity that public opinion has changed, so that now it is not so fashionable to treat as in years gone by. A man may now be a total abstainer even at the table of Her Most Gracious Majesty, without being called either a fanatic or an enthusiast. And yet how slow some men are to profit by observation and experience. When the centenary of Robert Burns was celebrated, the poem which took the prize read as follows:—

> "Yet while thy fate all Scotia mourns,
> We'll drink whene'er this day returns,
> The memory of Robert Burns,
> Here about and far awa'."

Here they acknowledge that drink was the failing of Scotia's noblest bard, and yet they quaff the deadly cup. I believe that much of the cause of Burns' folly was attributable to the drinking customs of the age in which he lived. No one could be more strongly impressed with the injurious effects of drink than the bard himself, for on one occasion he exclaimed, "Drink is the devil to me;" while on another occasion, writing to a lady, he remarks, "The people would not appreciate my company if I did not give them a slice of my constitution." Methinks if his spirit had been permitted to visit our earth on the night of that great celebration, he would have flown across the land, and, with his broad pinions, have swept from every table every decanter filled to his memory.

In the lines of the late lamented James Montgomery, on Burns, he says :—

> "Oh! had he never stoop'd to shame,
>   Nor lent a charm to vice,
> How had devotion lov'd to name
>   That bird of paradise."

It is the patronage and example of professors of religion, and persons holding important and influential positions in society, which keep up these customs. Suppose a young man would go to Toronto, and as he passes up Yonge Street he is accosted by a poor old degraded drunkard, with the elbows out of his coat and the crown out of his hat, and asked, "Hallo, young fellow, will you come and have a glass?" "No," he utters, if he deigns to reply at all; he is quite offended and insulted. But let him visit the house of a clergyman, and observe that minister partake moderately of the same, and quite another impression is made upon his mind; or let him go and visit his sweetheart. Now, in Ireland when young gentlemen go "sparking," they go on horseback; and in whatever else we may excel Irishmen, I think that in sitting a horse Irishmen, in general, can beat Canadians. One young Irishman, who was anxious to win the affections of a noble and beautiful heiress, and knowing that it was most important to be proficient in horsemanship, would go out by moonlight and practise. While reading the newspaper one day his eye caught an advertisement, "Chiffney's Receipt for Horse Riding; price ten shillings. Any person remitting the amount in postage stamps, or by post-office order, will receive copy by return." He mailed the money, and back came the receipt, as follows :—

> "Your head and your heart keep boldly up,
> Your hands and your feet keep down,
> Your legs keep close to your horse's side,
> And your elbows close to your own."

This was all he got for his ten shillings. But suppose you were going to see your sweetheart, not on horseback, but in your gay cutter, with the bells tingling, jingling. Bells, merry bells! And it is astonishing what excuses young gentlemen make when they want to be permitted an opportunity of seeing their sweethearts. One says he is sorry to hear the young lady's mamma has caught a severe cold, and he was driving past and just called to inquire after her health. This is kissing the child for the sake of the nurse, or courting the mother for the sake of the daughter. At last the wine and cakes are produced, and the young lady holds up the glass with the sparkling wine and says, "Will you have a little drop?" William looks not so much at the glass, nor even what it contains, as at the delicate hand that holds it, and as he gazes he becomes enamoured. "What a pity that I'm not an artist! what a model for an artist's pencil!" But the lady breaks the spell, and says softly, "William, won't you take a little?" "Thank you, Miss"—bows gracefully, and sips it up. Young man, that was the very same liquor that the old drunkard in Toronto wanted you to drink,

I

and which you spurned ; but when it was presented under
pleasanter circumstances you accept it.   When the drunkard offers it, you would not be seen in such company ; but
when the minister or the beautiful young lady offers it,
it appears desirable.

I know something of this so-called drinking for friendship.   I do not covet the friendship that is formed over
the bottle and glass—it is the most hollow under the sun,
and of it we may, with Goldsmith, inquire—

> " What is friendship but a name,
>   A charm that lulls to sleep ;
>   A shade that follows wealth and fame,
>   And leaves the wretch to weep ?''

The folly of drinking is illustrated in the following :

A German nobleman once visited Great Britain.
Wherever he went during a six months' tour, he was, by
custom, compelled to drink in honour of King, Queen,
Church, State, Army and Navy ; at last his visit drew to
a close, and, in a measure to requite the kindness he had
received, he provided a sumptuous banquet, and feasted his
friends to their hearts' content. The tables were cleared and
the servants entered with two immense hams ; slices were
cut and handed to each, and the host rose and with all
gravity said, " Gentlemen, I give you the King ; please eat
to his honour." His guests protested they had dined, but
the host was inflexible. " Gentlemen," said the nobleman,
" for six months you have compelled me to drink at your
bidding ; is it too much that you should now eat at mine ?
I have been submissive ; why should you not follow my
example ? You will please, gentlemen, do honour to your

King; you shall then be served with another slice in honour of the Queen, another to the health of the Royal Family, another to the Army, &c., &c., to the end of the chapter."

All who drink do not become drunkards! No, thank God, all who drink do not become drunkards; but because all who use alcoholic stimulants do not become intemperate, is that any reason why we should countenance the drinking customs of society, which have been the cause of all the drunkenness which abounds to such an alarming extent in our midst? And while all who have used strong drink have not been victimised by its fatal and seductive power, still, who can count the number of the unhappy victims which have been borne down the damnable stream, and engulphed in the horrid sea of intemperance?

The mighty problem cannot be solved by all on earth; it will require the day of judgment and eternity to reveal the number and doom of those unfortunate persons who have been ruined by this terrible source of misery, the drinking usages.

Suppose a mad dog was running at large through your neighbourhood, and just as you were about to pull the trigger, a friend stepped up and said, " Don't shoot that dog; it won't bite everybody." " I know that," say you, " but he may bite somebody;" and while it is not likely that every one will be bit, yet a strong probability that some one or more persons may, justifies you in destroying the life of the dog. And so in regard to drink, because it is morally certain that if the drinking customs of society are continued, as a consequence some will become drunkards.

One reason why some men don't become drunkards is, because they are too close-fisted; there are some such creatures in the world. A preacher once went to his steward and requested so many pounds to relieve the wants of his family : " Oh, I see it's for money you preach, and not for the good of souls," responded the steward. " I can't eat souls, sir," said the injured pastor, " and even if I could it would take a thousand such as yours to make a meal." I have heard of a man whose soul was so small that it could stand on the point of a needle, and leave room for a fiddler to dance round it ; but whether this be truth or fiction, we know most positively that there are some persons remarkably stingy. Why, when some men lift a five cent piece with their finger and thumb, if it were a living thing it would groan ; and if they press a Yankee quarter between their finger and thumb, you can almost hear the eagle scream.

These are not the men who are likely to become drunk-ards ; it is not your niggardly, miserly, stingy, selfish men, but rather those kind, generous, liberal, whole-souled men, who love not pelf but company, who are fond of so-ciety, who like a good laugh, a well-sung song, or a humo-rous joke ; it is men of intellect, men who are open, manly and generous ; it is the most promising, noble and glorious specimens of lordly creation that become the victims to this traffic ; it is the choicest, the kindest and the best who are ruined by drink.

Gaze upon the sea of life. See the innumerable number of skiffs which sail on said sea, every one of them with an immortal soul on board. Behold the rocks that rise threatening destruction to those frail skiffs. Here is the

rock of ambition, there the rock of self, yonder the rock
of the love of money ; but there is one rock against which
I perceive more shipwrecked than all the rest, and that is
Intemperance.

Judge Ray, Temperance lecturer, in one of his efforts
got off the following hard hit at "moderate drinkers :"

" All those who in youth acquire a habit of drinking
whisky, at forty years of age will be total abstainers or
drunkards.   No one can use whisky for forty years with
moderation.   If there is a person now in the audience before me whose experience disputes this, let him make it
known.   I will account for it, or acknowledge that I am
mistaken."

A tall, large man rose, and folding his arms across
his breast, said :—

"I offer myself as one whose experience contradicts
your statement."

" Are you a moderate drinker ?" asked the Judge.

" I am."

" How long have you drank in moderation, did you say?'

" Forty years."

" And never intoxicated ?"

" Never."

" Well," remarked the Judge, scanning his subject closely
from head to foot, " yours is a singular case ; yet I think
it is easily accounted for.   I am reminded by it of a little
story :—

" A coloured man, with a loaf of bread and a bottle of
whisky, sat down to dine on the bank of a clear stream.
In breaking the bread he dropped some crumbs into the

water. These were eagerly seized and eaten by the fish. That circumstance suggested to the darkey the idea of dipping the bread in the whisky and feeding it to them. He tried it. It worked well.

"Some of the fish ate of it, became drunk, and floated helpless on the surface. In this way he easily caught a large number.

"But in the stream was a large fish, very unlike the rest. It partook freely of the bread and whisky, with no perceptible effect whatever. It was shy of every effort of the darkey to take it. He resolved to have it at all hazards, that he might learn its nature if possible.

"He procured a net, and after much effort caught it, carried it to a coloured neighbour, and asked his opinion on the matter.

"The other surveyed the wonder a moment, and then said—

"'Sambo, I understands dis case. Dis fish is a mullet head; it ain't got any brains—dat's so.'"

"In other words," added the Judge, "you are all aware that alcohol affects only the brain, and of course those having none may drink without injury."

The storm of laughter which followed drove the "moderate drinker" suddenly from the house.

We admit that there are some instances where men who drink hard live to a ripe old age. But every old toper is a *Decoy Duck*, and no more proves that it is safe to drink and not become a drunkard, than the pensioner proves that it is safe to go to the field of battle and not be shot. While that veteran has returned, how many of his noble comrades have fallen on the field and been buried on a foreign shore! So while that man who for ten, twenty, or fifty years has practised drinking and has not become a drunkard (in the common acceptation of the term), how many, oh! how many of his moderate drinking companions have been ruined by drink.

DRINK STIMULATES.

Now, we teetotalers are in good spirits because we drink no spirits, and I would not give the snap of my fingers for the man who could not be in good spirits without the aid of a false spirit. What advantage would it be for me to get my watch to beat seventy ticks this minute, and fifty the next? So with alcoholic stimulants I grant that it puts a false spirit in a man for the time being, but afterwards comes the depression; for as a natural consequence, just in proportion to the elevation produced by spirituous liquors will be the languor that will necessarily ensue. Alcohol is a transient blaze, and the excitement produced by its use is like that of putting straw upon the fire: it gives a blaze for the moment, but soon expires and leaves the fire more languid than before.

When you spur your horse, or come down upon his back with a loaded whip, does that impart any more strength to the animal? No, it does not. No more does strong drink to man. While men under its influence may exert themselves beyond that which is prudent, let them remember that those who violate the laws of nature must pay the penalty. It is said that alcohol was first invented one thousand years ago, and used to stain the cheeks of the ladies of Arabia, and still it continues to redden portions of the human countenance.

It helps the imagination, say some of strong poetic genius. The truth is, some imagine good of drink, and evil of the Temperance movement. In some cases, however, we believe our objectors are correct, and admit that it does assist the imagination.

In the parish of Auchtermurchie, in Scotland, there lived two weavers (to those unacquainted with that truly magnificent country we would remark that it is not all covered with heather; nor do all the inhabitants wear kilts; nor is their chief diet composed of Scotch haggis, peas meal, brose and Campbelton whisky), who were remarkably intelligent—one of them was a great astronomer—but their fault was this, they were too fond of a spree. On this occasion they had "drowned the miller," and John the astronomer lay down on the bank of a stream and was quite unconscious; his companion was not quite so much intoxicated, and after a time lost sight of his friend. So he went about, crying, "John, whar are ye?" At last John, awaking from his slumber, looked down into the river, where he beheld the moon reflected beautifully on the placid waters, and exclaimed, "I dinna ken, but I ken yae thing. I'm far abin the moon onyway." So it does help the imagination.

> "For bring a Scotsman frae his hill,
>   Clap in his cheek a Highland gill,
> Say such is Royal Georgie's will,
>   And there's the foe ;
> He has nae thought but how he'll kill
>   Twa at a blow."

Men under the influence of strong drink often imagine themselves wonderfully clever, and think that they can do almost anything, while in reality they can do very little.

A woman in Glasgow was at the grocer's laying in her week's meal, but she had made too free with liquor. Returning home, she carried the child in one arm and the meal in the other ; at length, reaching home, she deposited the bag of meal in the cradle and placed the child in the press. Shortly after it began to scream, and the mother rocked the cradle with all her might. At last a neighbour woman entered. "What's the matter wi' the wean ?" she asked. " I dinna ken," responded the mother ; " I'm doing a' I can to quiet it, but it will no be guid a' I can dae." Then the woman pulled down the blanket to raise the child, but, lo ! it was a bag of meal. So the mother, under the influence of liquor, imagined that her baby had been converted into a bag of meal.

Dr. Cooke was once about to hire an Irish jaunting-car, when another driver accosted him with "Don't take that man's horse, your honour ; he'll never carry you ; take my horse, your honour." " Is your horse trustworthy ?" in-quired the doctor. " Yes, your honour," replied the car-driver ; " he's a illigant horse ; he's a poet of a horse, your honour." The doctor, struck with the element of poetry in a quadruped, got upon the car. They had not pro-ceeded far, however, till they reached an acclivity in the road, when suddenly the horse came to a dead stand. " You rascal, you," said the doctor ; " is that the value of your word ? Didn't you say he was a poet of a horse ?"

"And so he is, your honour," returned the car-driver, as he came down upon the poor animal with his loaded whip; "he's nothin' else than a poet; sure he's better in the imagination than the performance." So persons under the influence of alcohol are generally better in the imagination than in the performance.

IT STRENGTHENS.

Notwithstanding all the light that science has thrown upon the question, there are still some who seem to entertain the idea that intoxicating drink possesses strengthening qualities.

There is a great difference, I would remark here, between strong drink and strengthening drink. A few glasses of strong drink will knock the strongest man down; but strengthening drink, or pure cold water, will strengthen, refresh and invigorate all those who partake of this health-giving, heaven-sent beverage.

It has been demonstrated that in two glasses of sherry wine there is not more nourishment than is contained in one kernel of wheat, and that in a gallon of ale there is not more than is contained in a pennyworth of bread.

But to take an illustration from the Prize Ring. Let me ask what was it that Sayers and Heenan drank when they were being brought into condition for the great "National Prize Fight?" Was it liquor? Not one drop were they permitted to take. What, then, did they drink? Pure cold water. It was this that was to brace their nerves and bring them up into condition, and by it they were made perfect specimens of pugilistic training;

and when they stripped on the field and commenced that awful combat, as they struck at each other it resembled the beating upon a new drum.

As a proof of the superiority of cold water over strong drink, none but abstainers could endure the requisite fatigue at casting the shot for the Lancaster gun at Woolwich Arsenal.

I have had many years' experience myself of the cold water principle, and I am bold to assert that I believe we are better able to endure either heat or cold, work of the body or work of the brain, prosperity or adversity, upon cold water than upon alcoholic stimulants. During the first and second days of January, 1864, I had occasion to travel to fill my appointments, and while some of those with whom I travelled had constantly to resort to the aid of stimulants, I can say, without any boasting, that I endured the cold much better than those who drank liquor.

O the days are gone when claret bright inspired my strain,
When I sang on every festive night, Bright Champagne,
Prime thirty-four in floods may pour, and glasses gaily clatter,
But there's nothing half so safe to drink as plain cold water.

The bard may make a greater noise over his wine,
When with other Bacchanalian boys he chances to dine ;
But if he wake with a headache, and wonders what's the matter,
He'll find there's nought so safe to drink as plain cold water.

There's Dr. Hazel ; he proclaims that water's full
Of curious brutes in every pool.
If this be true, it seems to you a most important matter,
For there is meat as well as drink in plain cold water.

Professor Clark, of Aberdeen, says chalk is there,
And Monsieur Chattin iodine finds everywhere,

If that be true, it seems to you a most important matter,
For there's meat, and drink, and physic, too, in plain cold water.

Why, take but one drop of pure water and put it upon a flower, and it will bloom and send forth a heavenly fragrance; but put a drop of alcohol upon it and it will die.

Give one glass of spirituous liquor to the thirsty traveller upon the sandy desert of Arabia and he will turn away from it with loathing; but offer him a glass of cold water and he will drink it to the dregs, quench his thirst, and return the glass heaped with gold, if he has it in his possession.

> "Better than gold is the water cold,
>   From the crystal fountain flowing;
> A calm delight, both day and night,
>   To happy homes bestowing."

Dr. Livingstone, the great African explorer, states : " I have acted upon the principle of Total Abstinence from all intoxicating liquors for more than twenty years. My own opinion is that the most severe labours or privations may be undergone without alcoholic stimulants, because those of us who have endured the most had nothing else than water to drink."

Sir Charles Napier says : " When I was in India, I was tumbled over by the heat with apoplexy, and 43 others were struck, all Europeans, and all died within three hours except myself. The sun had no ally in the liquor amongst my brains. I do not drink."

I look upon the testimony of Captain Kennedy, who commanded the " Prince Albert," in Lady Franklin's pri-

vate expedition to the Arctic regions, as one of the strongest proofs on record in favour of Total Abstinence. The
"Prince Albert" was one of thirteen vessels that sailed in
search of Sir John Franklin in that year. It was the only
one equipped upon Total Abstinence principles, and it
accomplished more than any of the rest :

1st. By going out at a season when no other vessel
would venture out.

2nd. It travelled further in one extended track than
any other expedition.

3rd. It had less than other expeditions with which to
accomplish it.

The "Prince Albert," with 18 of a crew of Total
Abstainers, with stinted means, accomplished *four times*
the distance that Sir James Ross with 180 men and abundant means accomplished ; and although the men suffered
from snow blindness, Arctic lameness, hunger and thirst,
yet Captain Kennedy brought home every man he took
out with him, which none of the rest did ; and when the
"Prince Albert" arrived at Aberdeen it was remarked
that they never saw a crew return from an Arctic voyage
in such excellent health and spirits as the brave cold water
crew belonging to the "Prince Albert."

The Duke of Wellington, when being examined before
the House of Commons with relation to drink in the
army, on being asked the question, "Are spirituous liquors
injurious to the soldiers ?" answered, in his laconic style,
" Invariably injurious."

A student once, contrary to the rules of the institution
with which he stood connected, had brought into the

college a barrel of ale. One of the professors on hearing of it took the young gentleman to task, and asked how it was that he broke the rules of the college by causing a barrel of ale to be brought into it? To which he replied, by way of excusing himself, " I find that it strengthens me." " Prove it—prove it," cried the professor. " Well," said the student, "when that barrel was brought here, I could not move it, but now I can lift it and carry it any-where." The secret was, he had emptied its contents, and hence it became a very easy matter for him to lift it. So do some people try to prove that it strengthens them.

INSTEAD OF RELIGION.

You teetotalers place Temperance in place of Religion.

Now, in all my experience I never knew a man who did so. In all my intercourse with teetotalers I never met a man who rested his hopes of salvation upon his being an abstainer ; but while it is not religion, we rejoice to know that it subserves the interests of religion, and has in many cases proved to be a stepping-stone to that higher life.

If temperance, without being religion, will subserve the sublime interests of religion—if it will raise men from the gutter, and bring them " clothed and in their right mind " to the house of God, it is deserving of the appro-val and co-operation of every Christian man.

One of the most useful and consistent members of the W. M. Church in Portadown was once a poor miserable drunkard, so vile and low that the Church seemed to have no hope nor to take any interest in so worthless a wretch ; but the Temperance cause laid hold of him, and the labours of those men were owned of God in reclaiming him from his awful position. He became sober, obtained work, acquired means to purchase clothes, which enabled him to attend public worship, found religion, and became one of the brightest ornaments of Christianity in that entire neighbourhood.

The farmer, while he tills the soil and sows the seed, does not despise, ignore, or undervalue the gracious Providence which causes the dew to descend, the light and warmth of the sun to beam upon, and the refreshing showers of rain to fructify and mature the crop; no more do we lightly esteem the preaching of that ever-blessed Word which is "the power of God unto salvation to every one that believeth." But we believe that this movement is like the rolling away of the stone from the door of the sepulchre ; and as human power was acknowledged and exerted at the door of the sepulchre, we believe God owns and acknowledges the labour of his servants in this enterprise, as preparing the way in myriads of cases for the hearing and reception of divine truth and the further displays of the divine goodness. Would to God that we had more Hezekiahs (2 Chron., 30th chap., 14th verse), who were anxious that every idolatrous altar should be destroyed. And oh ! how many have, by using strong drink, been led to neglect the worship of the true God, and to bow down to the god Bacchus !

But there were no Temperance Societies in Apostolic days.

We read nothing about that, neither do we read about

hospitals, colleges and Sabbath-schools ; and would you think that a justifiable reason why we should not have such ? God has given us his word as the rule of our faith and practice, and we are bound to do good to all men. And if we can do men good by our labours in this department, we are doing that which, though not directly commanded, is acceptable and well-pleasing in the sight of God.

PAUL'S ADVICE TO TIMOTHY.

But did not Paul say to Timothy (1st Tim., 5th chap., 23rd verse), " Drink no longer water, but use a little wine for thy stomach's sake, and thine often infirmities ?"

Now, the quantity of wine prescribed was small, and the kind medicinal ; it was for his stomach's sake, not for his palate's sake ! Now, there was in use when this direction was given, the pure blood of the grape as well as fermented and intoxicating wines ; and we know that alcohol, when used frequently and in quantity, produces inflammation of this organ. And we believe the Apostle was a man of too good judgment to recommend anything that would be injurious to his patient ; but whatever may have been the description of wine recommended, up to the time of the prescription Timothy was a cold water man.

But how is it that so many doctors still recommend wine, &c. ?

There may be many answers given to this question. It may be because they really think it essential. Some well-meaning M.D.'s are much mistaken in reference to the value and quality of this article, or it may be that the doctor knows his patient is fond of it, or that the doctor is fond of it himself, and that in recommending it to others it may have a reacting influence; but whatever be the reasons some have for almost on all occasions recommending this article, we know that upwards of 2,000 physicians have certified :

1st. That a very large proportion of poverty, disease and crime is induced by the use of alcoholic stimulants as beverages.

2nd. That the most perfect health is compatible with total abstinence from all intoxicating beverages.

3rd. That persons accustomed to such drinks may with perfect safety give them up, either at once, or gradually after a short time.

4th. That total and universal abstinence from these beverages would greatly contribute to the health, prosperity, morality and happiness of the human race.

THE MARRIAGE IN CANA.

" But did not our blessed Lord make wine at the marriage in Cana?" He did; but if I cannot prove that it was unintoxicating wine, no more can you prove that it was intoxicating: besides, there is a strong probability that it was not intoxicating. Let us suppose, first, that this wine was unintoxicating, (and we think this reasonable), because we cannot imagine that the blessed Saviour, who said, "If ye being evil know how to give good gifts unto your children," would give that wine which Solomon declares to be a mocker, that which "biteth like a serpent and stingeth like an adder." Or let us suppose, secondly,

J

that it was intoxicating wine; then the language of the
Governor would indicate that they had drank enough,
for he remarked, " After they had well drank." Can you
believe it possible that the adorable Redeemer would,
" after they had well drank," provide them with eighty to
one hundred and twenty gallons more, while Solomon declares that " no drunkard shall inherit the kingdom of
heaven ?" 'Tis monstrous to think that he who " tempt-
eth no man " would act thus while he declares " Woe
unto him that putteth the bottle to his neighbour's
mouth." Again : it was customary to produce inferior
wine at the last, when they would not be able to detect
it; but here they observed at once that the last was the
best, which is strong evidence in favour of the view that
it was unintoxicating. People have difficulty in under-
derstanding how anything unintoxicating in its nature
can be called wine; but it is simply prejudice. Pliny
states that there were three hundred and ninety-five
kinds of wine, only one of which would burn. Captain
Freatt states that when he was travelling in the south
coast of Italy in eighteen hundred and forty-five, that
the wines most esteemed were sweet and unintoxicating.

I am no linguist, but this I can see, that there is a wine
mentioned in Scripture which has the approval of God,
and there is also wine which has his disapprobation, and
I cannot think that that which is pronounced a blessing can
possibly be the same as that which is pronounced a
curse.

" But is it not a good creature of God ? " I answer, no
alcohol exists in the natural condition of anything in

this world ; it is only a circumstance in the process of decay. Alcohol is only obtained by arresting the natural process of decay in its first stages. Alcohol can only be produced after life has departed, and is the product of death, and death only. Alcohol is the intoxicating principle in all intoxicating drinks, and it is the antagonism of alcohol to life that produces those manifestations called drunkenness.

Gold is a good creature of God ; but was it right for Aaron to make a molten calf, to cause the people to fall down and commit idolatry ? An ox is a good creature of God, very valuable in the logging field ; but if you turn it into a china shop on King Street, Toronto, it may do much damage in a short time. Now, alcohol may be, and often is, very useful when skilfully applied ; but often it has been made a curse rather than a blessing, by being too freely administered.

Capt. Stewart, when stationed in India, proceeded with a party of coolies (or native soldiers). In course of their march, as they approached a village they heard a loud and terrible scream, and met the entire inhabitants, old and young, halt and lame, making their escape as best they could, beating upon their breasts in awful trouble. "What's the matter?" inquired the Captain. A royal tiger got into the village and was gorging himself with the blood of the infirm, the sick, the dying, and the helpless babe. What's to be done? They approach to where the tiger lay; the Captain orders his men to fire, but they were afraid they could not kill him, and would not shoot. The Captain creeps forward alone, raises his gun to his shoulder, takes aim for the tiger's heart, fires. The tiger springs upon him, throws him into a ditch, and walks away and crouches down upon the top of a hill which overlooked the village. The Captain recovers from the shock, goes to his men again, examines their guns, and directs them all to fire together. Every trigger is cocked, and just as they are about to fire, "Stop! stop! stop!" cried an old grey-headed Brahmin, "don't shoot that tiger; he's a valuable creature and a creature of God, and was created for some useful purpose." The soldiers again drop their guns, and were too conscientious to fire. The Captain pointed to the blood and victims that were strewed around, and told his men he'd shoot a Brahmin if he acted as that tiger had done. A part obeyed; the huge animal was killed, and thus many valuable lives were saved. What think you of the religion and arguments of the Brahmin? There is danger in the tiger Drink.

It is not too much to say that those who patronize the drinking customs of society are a party to the horrid effects of intemperance. If I were to ask you for a donation, "What is it for?" you ask. "To murder Jim Brown," I reply. "I won't give you a cent," say you; "if I was to give you anything I would thereby become a party to the murder, and amenable to the laws of the land." So with drink. The drinking customs of society are murdering their thousands, and your moderate drinking is perpetuating those customs, and leading to the perpetration of murder and death by wholesale; and I ask you, are you not a party to the sad results?

I DISLIKE THE PLEDGE.

If an enemy were to land upon our shores, would it be unmanly in us to enrol as volunteers and go forth and fight in the defence of our Government, our nationality, our homes, our wives and our children ? If slaves were to band themselves together and say, another manacle shall never be placed upon our hands, and strike for freedom, would there be anything unmanly in all this ? No ; and alcohol is the worst enemy that ever visited our beloved country, and shall we not endeavour to crush the foe ? The appetite that is formed by the use of these drinks is the worst slavery that ever cursed a freeborn. subject. Man is a bundle of habits, and shall we not pledge ourselves to stand by each other and avoid being caught in this fatal snare ? Some of those persons who object to take our pledge do not object to other pledges ; for instance, a young gentleman who wishes to get joined in the bands of " holy matrimony," does not object to the pledge which is administered at the Hymeneal altar, and perhaps some young ladies would not object to take this latter pledge who hitherto have not taken the former. Paul, the great Apostle of the Gentiles, took a pledge—a longer one than we ask you to subscribe to, when he said, " If meat make my brother to offend, I will eat no flesh while the world standeth." He shows here that he was prepared to give up even wholesome meat, which was useful and nutrit'ous, for the sake of his weak brother, and that not for a month, nor a year, nor for life, but " while the world standeth." Now, Paul was no dwarf either in piety or intellect ; he was a full-grown man, and could

boast before the Chief Captain that he was free-born, and
no doubt valued his freedom as much as any man, yet for
the sake of others he would pledge himself and deny himself; and shall not we deny ourselves the use of that
which is unnecessary and injurious for the sake of our
brothers ?   Besides, which, I ask, is the free man ?   Place
a glass of spirits there before a man who has acquired an
appetite for the same, and his language is, I hate you, yet
I love you ; and while he knows it to be his enemy, he
takes and drains its contents, and becomes its servant.
" His servant ye are whom ye obey."   But place a glass
before a total abstainer, and he turns away from it ; he
hates it with a deadly hatred.   It possesses no charm for
him ; he sees the blood of murdered victims staining the
glass, and cries—

> " Begone, strong drink, I pray thee begone from me—
> Begone, strong drink, thee and I shall never agree.
> Long time thou hast been tampering here, and fain thou wouldst
> · me kill,
> But I'm resolved, but I'm resolved, thou never shalt have thy
> will.
> A pledge we'll sign, a song we'll sing, and merrily pass the day ;
> I hold it one of the wisest things to drive strong drink away.
>   Away, away, &c."

Some think to sign a temperance pledge is to sign away
their freedom ; whereas it is to preclude the possibility of
their becoming slaves.   " Indeed, now, Robert, I'll not let
you sign the pledge," said a newly-married wife to her
husband, who was desirous of joining our ranks at one of
our meetings.   " Indeed, I won't make a boy of my husband by signing a pledge."   A few years rolled past, and

that same woman, with tears and entreaties, implored some of the leading men connected with that same society to do what they could to rescue her husband, who a few years before wanted to act the wise and cautious part.

That dandy young man won't sign the pledge, but sticks up his collar like a tall stalk of wheat. He won't sign away his freedom. Just take the trouble to go up and examine his head, and you will find there is nothing in it.

SELFISHNESS.

We are too prone to think and act as if the whole business of life was to spout in our own circle, enjoying all the rich blessings of a benign Providence, and to anticipate, when done with those enjoyments here, a glorious exit to the Eden above. But we must not forget that this life is the great theatre upon whose stage we must play the all-important drama of life ; and if we would act our part well and merit the applause of myriads of spectators, we must not limit our operations to the home circle, but, with large-hearted benevolence, we must labour for the welfare of our race, and live out the injunction, " Work while it is called to-day, for the night cometh when no man can work." O, for the burning zeal of Paul !

There is a picture which represents a professor in one of our Glasgow Universities running with all his might, and the aspiring students following after, hard holding on by his skirts, with the proverb, " The deil tak the hindmost," engraven under the picture. So it is in the world ; every man for himself. Selfishness, which is the very first thing at which religion aims a blow, still rules supreme in many hearts, and unless they see how they themselves are likely to become advantaged by giving up drinking, they are not willing to do much for the sake of their weak brother. They are very much like the Scotch baillie who lived in a rising village, the inhabitants of which thought it essential, before all the available ground would be taken up, to erect a commodious market-house. All the baillies save one were in favour of the scheme. This selfish baillie would not consent; he said " it would involve considerable outlay, and that we should not be benefited in proportion to said outlay." "But," said one of his brother baillies, "while we shall not be benefited, posterity shall." "Well," said the baillie, "if you can show me where posterity has benefited us, then I have no objections." So with some persons; they are not willing to make any sacrifices for the sake of others. They are so thoroughly selfish that they resemble the man who carried the mail between Kirkintulloch and Glasgow. When he arrived at the latter place the post-office was in flames, and stepping up to one of the firemen who was playing upon the building, and clapping him upon the shoulder, he shouted, "Play upon the Kirkintulloch mail bag; play upon the Kirkintulloch mail bag." So he did not care if all the mail bags in the post-office were destroyed if only the Kirkintulloch mail bag, the one he went for, was safe. So "let me be safe if the world should perish," is the cry of many.

Cain is now a long time dead, but it would seem that there are many in the world who have imbibed his spirit, and by their conduct still cry, "Am I my brother's keeper?"

They seem to think that they are at perfect liberty to drink away, so be that there is not much danger of themselves personally becoming addicted to drink. If their neighbour chooses to drink to excess, that's his own business; give them enough to feed and clothe their own family, a home education and position in society for their own children, and they care nothing about their neighbours. They may drink, die, and perish. If I myself can sip my glass of wine in moderation, and if from my peculiar temperament I am not likely to become a drunkard, why should I give it up for the excess of my brother? Exactly: " Am I my brother's keeper?" Many there are who look upon this enterprise with a prejudiced eye; they condemn it without ever examining its principles and objects, and hence, being unacquainted with its operations and aims, they cannot appreciate the noble efforts that are being put forth to rescue mankind from the curse of intemperance.

An Irishman once landed upon Glasgow Quay early in the morning, while the inhabitants of that populous city were sound asleep, and as he wandered forth he saw a dead monkey lying on the street, and fancying it to be one of the inhabitants of the land of the mountain and heather, he exclaimed, "Poor Scotland! they cannot bury their own dead!" So it is with many in reference to the Temperance enterprise; they do not go to the trouble of investigating carefully our principles and objects, hence they form a partial judgment not favourable to our cause. No man can look at our movement, contemplate our object, observe our self-denying efforts and mark the glorious success which has crowned our labours, without beholding much that is worthy of his highest admiration; and the more we know of this great cause, the more will it commend itself to our judgment.

It is reported that once an Irishman was driving a horse and cart over Derry walls. When under Walker's Monument, his sword fell down and broke the shaft of Patrick's cart. Pat, looking up, said, "Arrah, but you hould your spite a long time." So it may be said of some in reference to Temperance, they retain their prejudices notwithstanding the good that has been accomplished through the efforts put forth by temperance societies.

They condemn it without ever examining its principles and objects, and hence being unacquainted with its operations and aims, they cannot appreciate the noble efforts that are being put forth to rescue mankind from the curse of intemperance.

A clergyman once said to one of his flock: "John, will you not give up this whisky drinking? it is ruining you; do quit it, I pray you." "Sure, your reverence, I'm just doing what the Scriptures teach me," said John. "How is that?" exclaimed the minister. "Sure, it teaches me that I'm to love my enemies;" and holding up a glass of spirits said, "That's the worst enemy I've got, and I love it in my heart." Now, I think it is evident that the reason why some will not join our movement is, they like a little drop. Nothing, I know, will give such offence as telling the naked truth. For instance, a man returned home one evening, and commenced to kick the chairs, table and furniture through the house, and otherwise exhibit his naughty temper. "What's the matter, my dear?" whispered his meek, loving wife. "Neighbour B. has said I told a lie." "Oh," replied the wife, "never mind that; he can't prove it, my dear." "But he has proved it," cried the husband angrily. This was what pained him, that it had been proved. So if the truth were revealed, we believe that the reason why many do not join our ranks is because they like it, and even all the sufferings our common humanity has endured through this custom seems insufficient to lead them to deny themselves the gratification which this drink affords them. And then if you accuse them of liking it they get vexed and angry. Sometimes those very persons who are so offended when accused of being fond of liquor, by their own confession prove that it really is so. And yet some persons, however much they are addicted to this vice, would feel quite insulted if you said they were drunkards. At a temperance meeting once a man rose up and said, "You don't call me a drunkard, do you? I drank eight or ten glasses to-day. I take nearly that much every day, and no one ever saw me the worse of liquor. You don't call me a drunkard, do you?" "Well," replied the lecturer, "if I owed the Devil one hundred drunkards, and had only ninety-nine to pay him with, and if I offered him you for the one hundredth, and he would not take you, I would remain in his debt for ever."

It is useless to reason with such persons. They will not be convinced, and though beaten at every point they will have the last word, like a tailor in Paisley whose wife was very unbearable. She would have the last word, and the tailor resolved to conquer her if possible; so he took her to the canal and put her into the water to bring her into submission. But no, she was not to be so easily conquered as all that; so he put her down under the water and held her there until he thought her life was in danger, and, to his mortification, when she was under the water she raised her hand above it and snapped her fingers at him. So some oppose this cause as determinedly as she did her husband.

Temperance men have the same old song at their temperance meetings. True; but the wolf and the bear in our northern country may as well object to their being killed in the old way by steel and musket, as our enemies refuse to hearken to our old arguments.

> " This night we vow before the world's great bar,
> Never to pause, or quit this holy war,
> Till Drink's vile temples fall."

LECTURE VI.

INTEMPERANCE.

DR. GUTHRIE once said, "Drunkenness is our national curse, our sin, our shame and weakness."

Go with me, if you please, to the drunkard's home, and see that desolate habitation. Empty cupboard, broken-hearted wife, ragged children. Think of the tears of fathers who have lost their sons, and of mothers who have been robbed of their daughters; of wives who have lost their husbands, and children who have lost their parents, and listen to the wail of the lost. O! methinks if you could hear the groans of the countless multitudes who have fallen victims to this horrid traffic you would haste to the rescue.

Behold the drunkard's wife; gaze upon that pale, wan face, that wrinkled brow. The hue of health has left the cheek, the countenance is sad, the hair is prematurely grey; the step is feeble; the keenest anguish fills her soul, and wrings the very life-blood from her heart. Where, oh where is there human suffering to surpass that of the poor drunkard's wife? And yet there are countless thousands of such who are suffering through the intemperance of their husbands.

It is one of the saddest things upon which I reflect. I look upon an aged man who hàs toiled hard for years, and, after accumulating a little of this world's goods, sends his boys to the Normal School or some other institution to have them educated. As they leave home the father puts his hands upon their heads as he says, with broken accents, "May God bless you, my sons !" They leave home with a father's blessing and a mother's prayers ; but they are attracted by music, and begin to follow the example of their seniors. At length the appetite for drink is formed, and with a shattered constitution and blasted life they return, not to bless but to curse their parents. Thus instead of their being a support and comfort to them in the decline of life, they drag down their grey hairs with sorrow to the grave.

How many are weeping over the intemperance of their sons ! I have found a father pacing his office in an agony as he pulled the grey hairs from his head, and exclaimed, " My son is breaking my heart."

Once I was addressing a meeting in the parish of Glenavy ; the Rev. Rector occupied the chair. At the close of my lecture an aged man with white locks asked permission to say a few words. "Certainly," replied the worthy rector. " I was present," said the old man, " at the trial of Moore for the murder of his son. His daughter, a fine young woman aged about twenty years, gave evidence against her father. The judge asked the daughter, "Did your father love his child ?" "Love him!" said she ; " no father could love a child dearer than he did; he called him his Benjamin ; but, your worship, he came home intoxicated, and lifted a hatchet, and with one blow he severed the head from the body." The old man added, "I saw him hanged at Carrickfergus jail; and you all know that I lost myself as fine a lad as ever stood in Glenavy parish church by drink. The lecturer has said some hard things against drink, but the half cannot be told." Drink

> " Plucks from our breast
> The friends that loved, the friends that blest,
> And leaves us weeping on the shore
> To which they can return no more."

Intemperance brings shame, not honour; misery, not happiness; weakness, not strength; sickness, not health; poverty, not wealth; death, not life.

INTEMPERANCE RETARDS.

I hold that intemperance retards our progress; that it throws barriers in the way of national as well as personal prosperity; that it stints our mental, moral and religious growth; it hushes the aspirations of the student in his scholastic pursuits; it stops the enterprise of our merchants, and counteracts the preaching of the ever blessed gospel, for

> " Wherever God erects a house of prayer,
> The devil's sure to build a tavern there."

Well might a foreigner remark as he did when he visited Great Britain. He said, " It is well those Anglo-Saxons are such a drunken race, for, were it not for this, with their energy, talent and power they would become

the masters of the world." We do hold the keys of the
physical world, such as Gibraltar, the Cape of Good Hope
and Malta, but we shall never wield that mighty influence for good which the Almighty designed we should
use until we put away this evil from us. It acts like a
mighty millstone around the national neck, and if we
would become truly

> "Great, glorious and free,
> First flower of the earth and first gem of the sea,"

we must give up this custom, which is degrading us at
home and spoiling our influence abroad.

What was it that discouraged the noble heroine, Florence
Nightingale ? It was not with toil or watching ; it was
not the breath of sickness nor the fierce blaze of an orien-
tal sun, as she nursed, God bless her! our sick soldiers at
Scutari, but it was the sad, sad effects of intemperance.
" Banish," cried this noble lady, " this deadliest of all foes
from your ranks." And it does pain the mind of the philanthropist to see the havoc and misery which Drink is
causing.

Some years ago, James Silk Buckingham, member for
Sheffield, obtained, to his own surprise and the astonishment of the House of Commons, a select committee to
inquire into the causes and consequences of the prevalent
vice of intoxication amongst the labouring classes, and
that committee gave a report which showed that the consequences of the drinking habits of the people were:—destruction of life, disease in every form and shape, premature decrepitude in the old, stunted growth, debility and

decay in the young, loss of life by drowning, burning, madness, &c. He was quite sure any society that had for its object the amelioration of those great evils, ought to be listened to with attention.

The evils of intemperance are far more numerous and widespread than any are aware of. I can take you to towns in Canada where almost every yard of ground is stained with the blood of the victims of intemperance. I remember speaking on this subject to Mr. J. J. E. Linton, of Stratford, and he offered to take me through that town, and give me a history of the deaths that had occurred there, in proof of this painful fact.

Have you read *Othello*, the most finished and perfect of all Shakspeare's tragedies ? What is it but a solemn temperance lecture ? Whence come all the horrors which close around the scene of that awful and magnificent drama ? Is it not from the wine with which Iago plied Cassio ? What is Iago himself but a human embodiment of the great master of evil ? and as that master goes abroad over the earth seeking whom he may devour, where does he find a more potent instrument than in the treacherous wine-cup ? This dark tragedy, with its crimes and sorrows, is but an epitome, a faint transcript of ten thousand tragedies which are all the time enacting on the theatre of daily life. How many are there, to-night, who can use the words of Othello's sobered but almost frenzied Lieutenant, and say :

" O, thou invisible spirit of wine ! if thou hast no other name to be known by, let us call thee, devil."

K

"That men should put an enemy into their mouths to steal away their brains."

" O, I have lost my reputation! I have lost the immortal part of myself, and what remains is bestial. My reputation, Iago, my reputation ! "

" To be now a sensible man, and by-and-by a fool, and presently a beast, O, strange ! Every inordinate cup is unblessed, and the ingredient is a devil."

We have known men, through habits of intemperance, to become reduced from positions of wealth and affluence to the most miserable want and poverty.

In the year ending at Michaelmas last, ninety-four thousand nine hundred and eight persons, or two hundred and sixty a day, were proceeded against before justices in England for drunkenness, or for being drunk and disorderly; and sixty-three thousand two hundred and fifty-five of them were convicted. The great majority were only fined, but above seven thousand were committed to prison. The returns show a great increase over the previous year, for only eighty-two thousand one hundred and ninety-six were then charged with drunkenness, and only fifty-four thousand one hundred and twenty-three convicted. Of the persons thus charged in the last year, twenty-two thousand five hundred and sixty were females, and more than ten thousand women were convicted for being drunk. Coroners' inquests, in the year eighteen hundred and sixty-two, found two hundred and twenty-one verdicts of death from excessive drinking. One hundred and fifty-five men and sixty-six women thus ended their days.

What is drunkenness? or, what do we mean when we say a man is drunk?—that a man has taken into his physical system a certain amount of a physical thing called alcohol, which has produced a certain physical result which we call drunkenness? But is not gluttony as bad as drunkenness? There is nothing in the nature of bread to create an artificial appetite for an immoderate use of the same, nor is bread pronounced in Scripture a curse. It is written, "Woe unto him that putteth the bottle to his neighbour's mouth;" but nowhere is it stated, Woe unto him that putteth a loaf of bread to his neighbour's mouth.

There were slain in Liverpool, in 1864, through drink, no less than three hundred and fifteen souls.

In Kingston, Ont., thirty-one out of thirty-six deaths, in one year, were directly caused by intemperance.

Dr. Howe, in his report on *Idiocy*, to the Legislature of Massachusetts, states: "The habits of the parents of 300 of the idiots were learned; and 145, or nearly one-half, are reported as 'known to be habitual drunkards.'"

Dr. Hill, Superintendent of the Asylum at Columbus, O., says :

"A citizen of this State married an intelligent lady, who bore him ten children. After the birth of the first three, the father became intemperate, and during his career as an inebriate four children were borne to him. The first three were smart and intelligent, and became useful men and women, and so of the last three. Of the four borne to him during his inebriety, two have died in the lunatic asylum, another is there, and the fourth is an idiot. The demonstration is complete and certain, and there is no room left for doubt as to the cause of idiocy and insanity in these cases. Thus an intemperate man or woman transmits a depraved constitution and an impaired intellect to children and even grand-children.

"The statistics in regard to the idiots of Massachusetts, published a few years since, furnished a volume of statement. The more this subject is investigated, the more it will be shown that the use of liquors is impairing the health and reason and shortening the lives not only of those who drink, but of their descendants. In self-defence, the State will, sooner or later, be compelled to interpose its strong arm, or the race will become deteriorated physically, intellectually, morally and socially. If a man has a constitutional right to degrade himself below the level of a decent brute, he has no right to people the land with imbeciles and lunatics."

What a fearful amount of pauperism is occasioned by intemperance. If you visit the workhouses which stud the Old World, and listen to the reports of those in charge of such institutions, you will be convinced that the drinking usages of society are the mighty feeders of this sad state of things.

It is customary for the inmates to go out one day in the week to visit, and their friends treat them on such occasions, so that they often return drunk ; but when they die, no friends are seen, and as the hearse driver performs the last ceremony, you cannot but think of the verse—

"Rattle his bones
Over the stones;
'Tis only a pauper,
Whom nobody owns."

Wonderful are the changes and reverses in some men's lives, but how many have been brought down from positions of respectability and affluence through indulgence in strong drink! It was startling to see Napoleon Bonaparte, as it were but yesterday, carrying the world before him on his victorious march, and causing kings and nations to tremble at his nod; but behold him a few days after, powerless! and chained like a felon to an isolated rock in the midst of the ocean. If you would avoid the degrading, debasing and demoralizing course of the drunkard, never take, we implore you, the first step on this damnable ladder. It is the first step, young man, on it that leads down to all the rest.

"Don't speak to me about the evils of intemperance," said a poor unfortunate victim; "I know, alas! too much of its sad consequences. I well remember the time when I sang praises and made melody in my heart to God, and O how I did pity those who frequented the tavern, and I grieved as I heard their profane talk and listened to their immoral songs; but I have been overcome. I tampered with the enemy, and step by step I was led to ruin, until now I'm a poor degraded drunkard. I have forfeited the friendship of all my true friends; I have turned my own flesh against me; I have wasted my means; I have sacrificed my health; and worse than all, I'm a slave, a self-made slave, and bound with chains more difficult to be broken than those of iron. Good God, I'm a lost man!—lost soul and body—lost for time, lost for eternity!"

There is a poor woman in ———, named Sally, whose husband is a terrible victim to the bottle. How does she get her husband (Irish Jemmy, as he is called) home? She carries a jug of whisky and goes a few yards before him, and coaxes him along step by step. Only for drink they might be well off. I met them at one of my meetings, and his son, a fine young man, joined the lodge.

A friend of mine was passing a tavern door in Toronto, when he saw the tavern-keeper take a man by the collar and push him out upon the footpath as he lifted him with the toe of his boot. "How dare you use that man so?" said my friend; "I know that man." "I don't care whether you know him or not," responded the tavern-keeper, "he's the most contemptibly mean man in the city." "How is that?" "Because he comes into my bar and calls for liquor, and takes it, and walks away without paying for it." Who was that mean man? A short time ago he held a situation as book-keeper in the city of Toronto at a salary of a thousand dollars per annum; that mean man has a brother who is an esteemed minister in this Province; and that mean man's wife and five children were, the last time I heard of them, dependent upon the charity of a few friends for a subsistence. What is it that has cast that book-keeper out of employment? Drink! What is it that has plunged that man's wife and family into such misery? Drink! What is it that has made that man so mean? Drink! Only for this seductive, damning drink, that man would be a useful member of society—a loving husband and an affectionate parent.

"We don't see such misery as you temperance folk represent." No, because you don't look for it. Suppose you were to stand upon the island opposite Toronto, and fire off a cannon, and a messenger was to go to you and say, "You are by your firing destroying property, wives and children." "But I don't see it," say you. "No; but come over in the boat with me and I will show you the effects produced by your firing." So with this traffic; if you will but follow the inebriate home, and mark well the results of your business, you will see degradation, poverty, misery, disease, lunacy and death are the sad consequences.

To those persons who have unfortunately acquired an appetite for strong drink, I would say, give up the habit at once and for ever. I have no faith in becoming sober by degrees.

A man addicted to drink was asked by his wife to give it up; he promised to quit by degrees, but still came home drunk. One night he fell in the well; the wife heard the splash, and ran out. He cried "Nancy, Nancy." She turned the windlass, and up he rose. Then she would undo it, and down he would go again. This was repeated several times, when he cried, "Nancy, what are you doing?" to which she replied, "O, I am bringing you up by degrees, the way you were going to quit the drinking." "Let me up," he exclaimed, "and I'll never taste it again."

Some may be ready to exclaim that there is "no use trying." Alas! alas! this is the rock on which is wrecked every life that ever yet was a failure—the mournful epitaph which might be written over the grave of every buried resolution for good which was ever born in the soul of man.

"No use trying!" Did ever a fouler lie enter through the doors of a living heart? Don't believe it, dear reader! don't for an hour—no, not for a moment. No matter how many times you've fallen, get up again; this very fact of your "trying" proves that you have "life" in you. You are only dead when you cease trying. Have you evil tempers or indolence, selfishness or pride, wrong imaginations or foolish thoughts to conquer, and have you been vanquished again and again?—don't give up! You have gained something, whether you know it or not. Sit right up, and "buckle to" again, for only in despair is defeat. Look all your losses and failures bravely in the face and say, "I know that you've gotten the victory over me many and many a time, but I'm undaunted yet, and if I fall a thousand times I shall get on my feet and go right at the struggle again. I shall keep trying, with God's help, so long as there's a breath of life within me!" And, amid all the blessed eternal records to be unsealed by the hand of God, there shall not be found written the name of one soul who has boldly, earnestly, and reverently said this, and persistently lived it; and every other life has been a mock and a failure.

Some years since I gave up the use of tobacco; however, I found it a much harder task than I at first anticipated. It really afforded me unspeakable pleasure to sit down and, with a long pipe, enjoy a smoke, and I did admire much the fantastic shape that the smoke assumed as it went curling up beautifully to the ceiling. At length I parted with the pipe, but I retained a little bit of tobacco in my vest pocket, and how I longed for a taste! What a mighty power it exerted over me! I was almost like a kitten in the grasp of a lion. I would lift it and almost touch my lips, and then return it to my pocket, and for minutes would be tempted and tried as no human language can describe. At last I thought, "Well, is it not passing strange that this small piece of a weed should have such a power over me? It's but a weed; I'm a man—or ought to be one; now, either it will master me, or I will master it." So I flung it over the garden hedge, and from that day to this I have never chewed a bit nor smoked a whiff of tobacco. "How am I to give up drink?" says one. Go and do likewise—put away the enemy far from thee; resolve like a man that you will no more touch it, and look to God for strength to enable you to keep your solemn vow. For intemperance is a national sin, carrying desolation and death from the centre to the extremity of the land. In view of such results, surely "strong drink shall be bitter to them that drink it." Others suffer from this vice. Not only does the poor drunkard suffer himself, but those with whom he stands related in life also suffer. Every day we see illustrations of the assertion that the "innocent suffer with the guilty." We had a man in Armagh who was in the habit of attending Portadown market almost every Saturday. It made little matter whether he had business or no; to market he would go, and pretty freely he would drink too, and then it was time for his old hat to look out. Already it had many dinges, but every market day it was a sufferer, for he would give it a tap and swing his shillelagh, and cry, " Do you all know who I am ? Do you know who I am? "Why, I'm Mr. ———, of the Foy. I've got three chimneys on my house ; I've land for ever and moss for eternity. Hurrah ! St. Patrick's Day in the morning ! "   When Mr. ———'s boy would be going to school, some witty customer would' give his hat a tap and say, "I'm Mr. ———, of the Foy ;" and when his daughter would be going to the post-office, some young man, who should have known better, would cry round a corner, "I've three chimneys on my house."   So that this man's family suffered considerably through the intemperance of the father.

Not only do children suffer, but, ah! how severely in particular do wives suffer !   One night I was awoke from my slumber, while guest at a friend's house in Toronto, by a loud noise and a cry, "Open and let me in."   My friend opened, and his own sister-in-law entered with her two children, one under each arm. "What's wrong ?" " O, my husband came home with a bottle of brandy, and lifted an axe and would have killed us, and I had to fly for my life."   Who is that woman ?   She is the daughter of pious parents, tenderly reared and much loved by all who know her ; but, through the intemperate habits of her husband, she was obliged to leave him, and although only fifteen months have elapsed since she left old Ireland, with ample means to start business in Toronto and do well, so miserable had her life been through drink, that she was obliged to steal away with her two children to seek an asylum in her father's house, while her husband, a smart and clean fellow only for drink, was wandering about through Toronto, when I last heard of him, looking for employment.

I have heard the drunkard's wife exclaim, "I would work for him, I would nurse him; but, oh, to see him coming home drunk, it breaks my heart!"

A husband in Liverpool returned home one evening under the influence of drink, and said to his wife, "Mary, you did not kiss me." And as she approached him he plunged a knife into her heart's blood, and she fell a lifeless corpse at his feet. It was drink that caused it.

> "O 'tis monstrous, 'tis monstrous;
> Methought the billows spoke and told me of it,
> And the thunder, with its deep and dreadful organ pipe,
> Pronounced the name of murder."

Not ten years ago, Mrs. Mary Campbell, of the County of Perth (see *Stratford Beacon*, 15th April, 1864), hanged herself through despair, on account of the drunkenness of her husband. Well might the coroner of that section exclaim as he did, "Drink, Drink, when wilt thou be satisfied?" A family of six or seven children left without a mother, one only seven months old!

And mothers suffer also by this vice. And oh! how much they suffer! A young man was returning home one evening to his widowed mother in Glasgow, and he observed two men quarrelling and stepped forward to separate them, when one of them drew a knife and stabbed him to the heart. Here was a kind son, the only support of his widowed mother, killed by a person in liquor.

A father returns home, and looking at his wife inquires
"Is Tom home ? "   " No," she replied.   " Well, if he aint
home by the time I get my supper, I'll bolt the door and
he won't get in to-night."   O, young man, ofttimes the
door might have been bolted against you if your mother
had not interceded for you.   The father ate his supper
and went to bed.   The mother also retired, but not to
sleep.   As soon as the husband fell over in a sound doze
she arose, unlocked the door, listened, but heard no
sound of Tom returning.   Putting her shawl about her
head, she wandered off to a tavern that Tom unfortunately
frequented.   " Is Tom here ? " inquired the poor mother.
" No."   A recruiting sergeant had been there; Tom had
taken the shilling and was off to the war.   The mother
returned home with a sorrowful heart.   Time rolled past;
five years had now elapsed, and a letter came informing
the mother that her son was returning.   Her heart leaped
for very joy.   She could not wait, and walked many weary
miles to meet her boy.   When she arrived at the barrack
gate she looked at the sentinel.   " You're not Tom," said
she ; " Tom was not so stout nor broad as you.   Where's
Tom ? "   " Walk inside, and some of his comrades will inform you all about Tom."

Tom, under the excitement produced by liquor, stabbed
his sergeant, was tried by court-martial, found guilty and
sentenced to be shot.   He was brought out, placed beside his coffin, and five minutes were given him to address
his comrades, which he did thus : " Comrades, don't drink.
'Twas drink that drove me from my mother's roof; 'twas
drink that caused me to commit that bloody act for which

I am about to suffer. Comrades, if you love peace of mind, don't drink. If you would value heaven and escape hell, don't drink. O! comrades, don't drink. I implore you, don't drink." The word was given : Shoulder arms ! present ! fire ! Six bullets penetrated Tom at once ; he fell back upon his coffin a lifeless corpse. His mother listened while her heart was breaking, but as the comrade who had informed her all about Tom stood beside his grave and said, " There's the last of poor Tom," it was more than a mother's heart could bear, and she threw herself down upon his grave, and in a paroxysm of grief clasped the cold grave in her arms, and in mortal agony expired, uttering " My poor Tom ! "

If from intemperance a father dies at thirty instead of fifty, humanly speaking twenty years of a father's affection, care and industry are lost to the family; but there is also the loss of his income. Suppose he could save only ten shillings stg. per week, in twenty years, with interest, it would raise a fund that would provide fifty pounds a year to his poor family.

Besides, the sober portion of the community have to bear a vast deal of the expense of supporting the destitute as well as for the punishment of offenders brought on by intemperance. There was a certain Quaker barber in England who received a note for church-rates for five shillings and sixpence. When he got it he called upon the clergyman and said, " Pray, friend, what dost thou mean by this note ?" " Mean ! why it's for church-rate don't you see." " Yes, friend, but what is that for ? " " Why, for the repair of the church and the maintenance of public worship." "Well, friend, what have I to do with that? I don't attend thy church." "O! that don't signify; the church is always open, and it's your own fault if you do not attend; besides, it's the law, and you must pay." "Well, friend, I think that a very unjust law that obliges me to pay a ministry and a religion which I don't attend. Fare thee well." A few days after the minister received a note: "Dr. to Timothy Saulters, for shaving and hair-cutting, five shillings and sixpence." On receipt of it the minister ran to the barber and said, " What do you mean by sending me this bill? You never cut my hair nor shaved me in your life." " Nay, friend, but thou knowest my shop is always open, and it's thine own fault if thou dost not come to be shaved." And we think it a very unfair thing that total abstainers should be taxed for the support of those made destitute, and the punishment of those made criminals, by a traffic which they hate. By right, those who make money by this business should be accountable for the evils arising out of it.

I remember the Rev. Mr. Macpherson telling me of a mule his brother had bought. The man from whom he purchased it was a great drinker, and had accustomed the mule to stop at almost every tavern, and he would treat it as well as himself; so that Mr. Macpherson's brother was greatly annoyed with stopping at every tavern, and it positively refused to go till it would get its treat. So sometimes you see persons suffer from even buying an animal from one who drinks.

We suffer great loss by intemperance. A man was

brought up before the Mayor some time ago in one of our cities for being drunk. The fine was $2 and costs, or 30 days in jail. The man told the Mayor that it was his own money that he drank and got drunk on. The Mayor said he must pay the fine or go to jail. He had no funds, and was sent down. Observe, he thought he had a right to drink and get drunk on his own money, but the rate-payers had to foot the bill.

The sober portion of the community have to stand considerable risk on account of intemperance.

Some of the saddest accidents which have occurred both by land and sea have originated through drink.

The late Quebec fire is a painful illustration of this. The *Globe* stated that—

" The fire originated from drunken debauchery in a tavern, near daylight. The men were disputing over their ill-gotten gains at cards. From words they came to blows, and the table being upset, on which was a coal-oil lamp, in a moment the oil became ignited, then the furniture, and then the building in a few minutes more. Alarm became general in the vicinity, and in half an hour the Fire Centre had word. In one hour the hose was laid and water let on. In ten minutes after, the first line was cut by some miscreant, and soon after a similar thing happened to the second run. The fire now became unmanageable, and the populace panic-stricken.

" It should be understood that only about one-third of the buildings destroyed are in the city proper. In this portion is comprised the best class of buildings of stone and brick, the greater part of which were insured. It is

here the Quebec, British America, London and Liverpool
suffer so heavily. The two-thirds of the burnt districts
without the city were built of wood; the owners were
generally the occupants, who preferred to build of wood,
live in narrow streets, and have no water, than pay one
cent of tax or be insured. The total loss to the city and
St. Sauveur cannot be less than $3,000,000 by fire."

By this sad accident no less than 2,500 houses were
destroyed, 18,000 persons left houseless, and three million
dollars worth of property destroyed, while four persons
lost their lives.

One of the survivors of the ill-fated "Anglo-Saxon," in
which 263 persons were drowned, told me that the Captain was intoxicated; and when the mate warned him of
a passing schooner, and asked him to sound, his stern reply was, "I'll sound when I please."

If tavern-keepers pocket the gain, the sober portion of
the community are obliged to bear much annoyance.
Travelling up Yonge Street one evening in a public stage,
I had an encounter with a drunken man that will illustrate this point. After I got nicely seated, the door was
opened, and the stage driver assisted the poor drunkard
inside. After we started, the man began to swing his
arms about, much to the dread of the inmates; he became
very quarrelsome, but we were not disposed to quarrel
with a poor man so much the worse for drink. Then he
began to sing—

> "Rule Britannia, Britannia rules the waves,
> Britons never, never, never shall be slaves."

And then he tumbled down into the bottom of the stage,

Oh ! angels, seraphs in the spheres !
Behold our eyes suffused in tears ;
Must drink-made sorrow ceaseless flow,
And breaking hearts no respite know ?
Must we resign to such a foe
All that we cherish here below ?
Forbid it, mighty God of love !
Forbid it, angel hosts above !
Oh, joy ! our souls with rapture glow—
We hear the angels chanting, No !

Young ladies, never walk with your arm in a whisky jug. There are some young men positively much more offensive than a jug with whisky in it. We have sometimes been shut up in a close carriage with one or two of this sort, and know whereof we affirm. The poet has said—

"Full many a gem of purest ray serene,
The dark unfathomed caves of ocean bear ;
Full many a flower is born to blush unseen,
And waste its sweetness on the desert air."

There is no mistake ; the fragrance, if such it may be called, which emanates from the victim of intemperance is felt by many ; it does not " blush unseen."

How foolishly some persons act while in liquor. Men who are smart and clever when sober, under the influence of liquor are guilty of the most foolish things imaginable. There was a schoolmaster who, under its influence, was fond of soliloquising. When asked by a friend how he, spake to himself so much, he replied that " he had two reasons—first, he liked to talk to a sensible man ; and secondly, he liked to hear a sensible man talk." ·

L

It makes one man so quiet that he will sit down upon
the floor and not speak a word, while it makes a perfect
madman of another.   One man under its influence becomes so playful, that he will bulk marbles with the children ; while another goes home and breaks the delph and
kicks and destroys everything in the house.   It causes
another to go home and hug and kiss his wife almost to
death, while it makes another act in the most cruel manner.

There is a very good man now living in the State of
New Jersey, who was at one period of his life very much
addicted to intemperance.   On one occasion he stumbled
into a graveyard and fell into a new-dug grave, and remained there till morning.   When the grave-digger entered
the charnel-house, he heard some awful unearthly moaning, and tremblingly approached, and looking saw Mr.
So-and-so, and wondering what he would say, he stepped
back and made a noise.   When he rose to his feet and
looked round at the grave-stones and monuments by
which he was surrounded, he said, " Laws-a-me.   Resur-
rection morn, and I am first up."   My friends, " on reason
build resolve, that column of true majesty in man," and
dash aside that cup which makes the wisest of men act
while under its influence so foolishly.

A butcher who killed meat for my father in Paisley
was greatly addicted to drink.   His wife was obliged to
make black puddings in order to procure a living.   One
night the husband arose to take a drink of sour milk ; he
had been drinking heavily the evening before, but instead
of taking milk, he went to a can of blood which the wife

had for to make puddings of. He did not observe his mistake; became very sick, and vomited considerably. The doctor was sent for; the poor man was very penitent. O, he was done; he had burst a blood-vessel at last, there could be no disputing it; there was the blood. But the wife knew better. She saw that he had been at the blood can, and told the doctor so, but cautioned him to not let the husband know, and to warn him to quit the drink He obeyed, and this was a salutary warning to him, and he kept sober through fear for some time.

How wickedly men act while under the influence of liquor; if they merely acted foolishly it would be bad enough, but when we consider that, under the excitement produced by these stimulants, men otherwise quiet and gentle are made mad and dangerous, we think this another reason for endeavouring to discontinue their use. Mr. Trethewey, a friend of mine, was staying with a minister, who pointed to a picture and said, " That illustrates the following incident : A man named Stufford, in a village in the State of Pennsylvania, stood at a tavern bar as a funeral passed by, and as he lifted his glass, he said to the landlord and those who were standing by ' When I die, I want to be buried in a hemlock coffin, pitched over with tar. I want to go to hell cracking.' ' Next day,' said the minister, ' as I sat in my study, I heard a noise, and going to the window I saw a crowd of persons running down to the low part of the village, where there was a saw mill. Fearing that some accident had occurred, I quickly followed, and when I arrived at the spot I found that Stufford, while under the influence of

drink, had come into contact with the saw, and was liter-
ally cut in two.   After his death his companion declared
that he appeared to him in his room in living fire, while
balls of fire were falling from his toes and fingers.' "

We think we are warranted in saying that men under
the influence of liquor say desperately wicked things, and
do desperately wicked things also. See that father; he returns home, maddened by drink. Instead of lifting his
darling child, and imprinting a sweet kiss upon its rosy
lips, what does he do ? He puts its little soft hands into a
steel trap; and as the child shrieks and cries in awful
agony, does it touch his heart ? No! but he laughs like a
very fiend, and mocks its sufferings.

LECTURE VII.

THE LIQUOR TRAFFIC.

IN a History of the Waldenses there is the following
passage: "Taverns are fountains of iniquity and schools
of the devil," and we may add that publicans are the
schoolmasters.

If there are any who think of starting this business, we
would urge you to abandon the thought. A man in Belfast, who tried almost every business and invariably
failed, as a last resource commenced tavern-keeping at
Peter's Hill, and put up on his sign-board "The Last
Shift;" and surely it is the last shift to deal out that
which is injurious in its nature and results. But some
say, "I keep a respectable house." Talk not to us of rec-
titude within a moral pest-house—we care not how re-
spectably you sin.

"On best, on worst, this sentence we record,
Your trade's abomination to the Lord."

It is the nature of your business to make drunkards.
A little boy was passing a tavern one day, and he observed
a drunken man lying at the bar-room door, and he went
in and said, "Landlord, your sign-board has fallen." The

landlord went out, and nearly stumbled over the inebriate, and looking up saw the sign-board up as usual, but realised the meaning of the witty boy's remark, that the drunkard was his sign-board.   Yes, the drunkard is the fruit of tavern-keeping.

A tavern-keeper said the other day, " I only sell to sober people." So much the worse ; if you only sold to drunkards they would die off, but the mischief of your business is that it finds men sober, and never leaves them till many of them are poor drunkards.

The Reverend John Wesley says that " the men who traffic in ardent spirits, and sell to all who will buy, are poisoners general ; that they murder their fellow-men by wholesale; neither does their eye pity or spare.   And what is their gain ? Is it not the blood of these men? Who would envy their large estates and sumptuous palaces ? A curse is in the midst of them.—The curse of ￲God is on their gardens, their walks, their groves ; a fire that burns to the nethermost hell; blood, blood is there ; the foundation, the floor, the walls, the roofs are stained with blood. And canst thou hope, O man of blood, though thou art clothed in scarlet and fine linen, and fared sumptuously every day, canst thou hope to deliver down the fields of blood to the third generation ?   Not so ; there is a God in heaven.   Therefore thy name shall be rooted out, like as those whom thou hast destroyed, both body and soul ; thy memorial shall perish with thee."

There was an advertisement, a short time ago, going the rounds of the English press to this effect : " £500 Reward.—Five hundred pounds reward will be given to any person or persons who will prove before competent judges that the third generation has been benefited by the traffic in intoxicating drinks." Now, there are plenty of money-loving Englishmen, anxious Scotchmen, and ambitious Irishmen, who would be glad to snap at five hundred pounds, but, although this advertisement has been going the rounds of the press, none have come forward to demand the money. And why? Because they could not do it. The curse of a holy and just God rests upon this cruel traffic.

How long, tavern-keeper, will you live upon the wreck, ruin, and misery of thy fellow-beings. Thy business is debasing, degrading and demoralising. The Scriptures declare that "Love worketh no ill to his neighbour," and can you doubt that your business works ill? O, if thou wilt but come with me to the haunts of intemperance; if thou wilt follow the inebriate home and see the effects produced by this destructive traffic, thou wilt tremble at the havoc thou art accomplishing. Bear in mind that so long as you continue in the business you are living on the diffusion of rags and wretchedness, and thrive, like toad-stools, on social disorganization and decay.

Some of those engaged in the liquor traffic speak as if we were influenced by evil and vindictive motives in advocating Temperance principles. While, however, no such feelings actuate the author of this volume, still he will endeavour to show that there are no men in the land who would be more largely benefited by the total suppression of the liquor traffic than those men themselves who are engaged in it; and more, I think there are no families in the community that would derive more advantage by putting a veto on the traffic than the families of those men engaged in the business.

This traffic is not only an injury to the poor purchasers, but it is bad to the tavern-keepers themselves. I have known men to keep taverns for years and not become drunkards; but while they themselves have escaped, I have known their sons to become victims to intemperance. I have also known men to come fresh from the plough with strong, healthy constitutions, and before eighteen months to expire in a fit of "delirium tremens."

One morning I was passing a tavern at Elma Centre, County Perth, and the gentleman who was driving me said, "Do you see that tavern there?" "Yes." "Well, during the last two years, two tavern-keepers have been buried out of that place. Did you observe two widows sitting opposite you last night in the front seat?" "I did." "Well, those were the wives of those two men, who died from the effects of drink, and there is a third man there now, and the other evening they were waiting upon him; he's now on his last legs, and cannot long survive unless he quits drinking."

I have made it my business to keep a record of all that I have known who have died through drink during the past twelve years; the black list is now before me, and not only is it long, but it is startling. Without lifting the curtain, I may state that judges, ministers, statesmen, orators, physicians, lawyers and others have fallen victims to the drinking customs of the age. Some of the most generous, gifted, and noble have been drawn within the whirlpool of custom, and engulphed in the vortex of intemperance.

The following is taken from " Extracts by Rowland Burr, from the Report of the Select Committee of the Legislative Assembly of Canada on the Prohibitory Liquor Law," and printed by order of the Legislative Assembly : "I have the record now before me, kept by myself, of the liquor dealers of Yonge Street for fifty-four years past, one hundred in number, and I will mention the abstract of the record, viz. :—

Number of ruined drunkards in the one hundred families.. 214

Loss of property once owned in real estate......... £58,700

Number of widows left 46

Number of orphans..................................... 235

Sudden deaths.. 44

Suicides publicly known............................... 13

Number of premature deaths by drunkenness..... 203

Murders.. 4

Executions.. 3

Number of years of human life lost by drunkenness 1,915

I have been acquainted with these 100 families, and I have kept written records of them, for the purpose of printing them, leaving out the names."

If an apothecary gives poison by mistake he is tried and punished, but the tavern-keeper sells poison knowing it to be such, and yet nothing is done to him. He has a license to sell as much as he pleases, and the more he sells the more money he makes, and the more mischief he accomplishes.

Rather than I should have anything to do with this traffic, I would suffer the amputation, one by one, of every finger and toe upon this poor body; allow every tooth in my poor head to be extracted, my eyes to be plucked out of their sockets, and bear all the tortures that earth and hell could invent and execute. I might have accumulated this world's pelf by engaging in this business. My grandfather was a distiller, and I have had tempting inducements made to embark in this business; but I have seen so much of the fearful fruits of the bottle that I dare not countenance it. I live to avenge the wrongs that this traffic has wrought upon some of those I love, and some whose memory still to me is dear. And yet how custom has blinded the eyes of the people in reference to this business. A man in Glenarm, Ireland, was returning home one night and called at a tavern and got liquor, and was sent on his way incapable of taking care of himself, and he fell into a canal and was drowned. At the coroner's inquest, and all throughout Ulster, there was the greatest fuss raised about the canal not being properly fenced; but there was scarcely a word about the man who sold the liquor and made him incapable. There was not a word about fencing up the door of that tavern lest another poor victim should get drunk and meet his death thereby. No, my friends, the people are greatly at fault in this particular in permitting this traffic which is so dangerous.

The following illustration is deserving of careful perusal :—

A gentleman stepped into a tavern, and saw a filthy drunkard, once a respectable man, waiting for his liquor. He thus accosted him :

"G——, why do you make yourself the vilest of men ?"

"I aint the vilest," said the drunkard.

"Yes you are," said the gentleman ; "see how you look. Drink that glass and you will be in the gutter."

"I deny your po-iz-zi-tion," said the drunkard. "Who —who is the vi-vilest, the tem-tempted, or the tempter ? Who—who was wor-worst, Sa-Satan or—(hiccup)—Eve ?"

"Why, Satan," said the gentleman.

"Well—hiccup—well, be-behold the tempt-tempter," said he, pointing to the bar. The bar-keeper flew into a passion and turned the poor fellow out of his house without his dram.

Have you observed a spider as it entangled a silly fly into its cobweb and drained the last drop of blood from its victim? Just so is this drink traffic draining the life-blood from the nation. It is the moral sepulchre where have been buried some of the most promising beginners in life's battles.

It has been remarked that the tavern-keeper is worse than the highwayman. The latter asks "your money or your life," but the tavern-keeper takes both "your money and your life." Give up, we pray you, this business, or depend upon it conscience will thunder and remorse will goad you. I care not how wealthy you become by the traffic ; its accumulation will afford you no joy, either in death, judgment, or eternity. There was a man in Limerick, Ireland, who committed murder, and was

seized with remorse for the horrid crime he had committed, and in two hours his hair, which had been as
black as jet, became as white as snow; and when you
see the ghosts of those whom you have been instrumental
in destroying following you, and hear the shrieks, the
groans and the wailings of those whom you have ruined,
you will curse the day that you embarked in so hellish
a traffic. I know that many have an interest in this
traffic; they have houses to rent and ground to sell, and
friends in the business, and livings to gain from those
connected with it; but it must come down. The truth
shall prevail. "Every valley shall be exalted."

Surely it is time something was done to stop this
frightful system of iniquity. There are no less than
twenty taverns to one baker's shop in the City of Toronto.
Now, we think, instead of increasing the number of these
taverns, that they should be dried up; and how are we to
dry up taverns? How do you farmers dry up your cows?
Don't you take the calves from them? So, could we take
the whisky calves, the whisky suckers away, then the
taverns, as the result, would go dry. They would lose
their means of support, and give up the business for some
more honourable one.

I remember a remark that the Mayor of Stratford made
one evening that he presided at a grand Temperance
demonstration that was given to me at my farewell lecture in the County of Perth. He stated that sometimes
he felt deeply sorry when he was compelled to pronounce
judgment against some poor unfortunate creatures who
were taken up upon a charge of drunk and disorderly, and

he wished he had got it in his power to punish the parties who gave them the liquor which led them to commit the offence with which they were charged.

Now I believe that if you can convince the judgment of some men engaged in this business they will give it up. Such was the case of a Mr. Mathers, who kept a country store. A man called one evening and got a quart of liquor out of his cellar, and on his way home, after drinking freely, he became intoxicated, and lay down on the railroad track. Next morning, very early, his wife, accompanied by a few friends, went out in search of the missing husband, and found him stretched across the railroad track; and if he had remained there but a few minutes longer the cars which were passing would have killed him. When Mr. Mathers heard of this, he thought, "Well, had that man been killed I would have been at fault; he got the liquor at my store; I'll sell no more liquor;" and so he gave it up. But while some will act thus, there are others who will not quit unless the strong arm of the law compels them to desist, and hence kind words and entreaties prove abortive to such. They put me in mind of a dialogue between an Irishman and a farmer. The farmer had a very savage dog, which followed Pat to his great annoyance; but Pat armed himself with a pitchfork one evening, and resolved, if the farmer would set his dog upon him that night, he would see how he liked steel. As usual, the dog ran out ferociously at Pat, and Pat up with the pitchfork and stuck it into the dog's head. The farmer ran out and asked him why he didn't run at his dog with the other end of the pitchfork. "Blood an' ouns," answered Pat, "why didn't he run at me with his other end?" So with some tavern-keepers. They will not give up the traffic, howsoever injurious it is, so long as the law sanctions it; and in order to meet such cases we must seek a prohibitory law to prevent such men from engaging in a business which is positively injurious to the community.

"I'm going to give up selling spirituous liquors," said a tavern-keeper in New York to a Temperance friend. "How is that?" "Because there came into my store this morning at a very early hour, a young man who, looking up to the brandy bottle which stood upon the shelf, exclaimed, with a fearful oath, ' Come down! come down! You killed my grandfather and you killed my father; come down now and kill me.' What that young man said," continued the grocer, "was but too true. His grandfather died a drunkard, and with liquor obtained at my store. His father died a drunkard, and with liquor obtained at my store—both drank from the same bottle, and both were dead—both the grandfather and father; and now the son had come to claim the sad privilege of drinking from the same bottle, and dying as his grandfather and father had died. I looked at that young man. I thought of the past, and it seemed as if the way to hell from my store was very short—that I could look from behind the counter where I stood quite into it. I felt that the business of selling liquor was a bad business, and I made up my mind to quit it." And he did so.

"You Temperance men want to rob us." Nay, we are

even willing to tax ourselves to pay the capital invested, in order that the evil may cease.

We will be the greatest robbers in the world, nevertheless; we will rob the jail of eight-tenths of its drink-made criminals; rob the workhouse of seven-tenths of its drink-made paupers; rob the lunatic asylum of one-half of its crazy inmates; rob the doctors of one-half their fees; and rob the last enemy, Death, of thousands of its drunken victims annually.

There is another thing worthy of remark in reference to drink, and that is, that it is the effect that is punished and not the cause. To illustrate this point: Suppose a farmer goes early in the morning with a grist, and he starts without his breakfast, and he meets some companions who treat him, and in his turn he does the same; but the two glasses prove too much for him on an empty stomach, and he is overcome and found in a state of intoxication. Some members of his church prefer a charge against him. He is tried before a number of deacons, found guilty and expelled; but there may have been some men trying that unfortunate who can take their glass in the morning, another after breakfast, and several glasses between that and dinner-time, and yet be sober as judges and say that they never were drunk in their lives. Mark you, the man who got drunk on two glasses is expelled; but the men who could drink ten glasses and not get drunk are respectable members of the church, and kick out the poor fellow who took the two glasses, because he could not stand as much as themselves. I verily believe that many a man is brought up and fined before a magistrate for

being drunk anfl disorderly, who has considerably less
liquor in him than the magistrate who convicts him.

Joseph ——, of——, told me that he had been a moderate drinker for forty years, and that he never was
drunk in his life ; and yet he was stoving with drink
while he uttered those words.   He was saturated with
alcohol, and was in danger, if he came in contact with the
light, of adding to the list of those who died of sponta-
neous combustion.   This man drank almost as much each
day as would make several drunk, but he timed it nicely
and just managed to keep on his feet, but was stupid
with drink all the time, and had difficulty in walking
straight.   O, how drinkers are deceiving themselves!—
they cannot see themselves.

You will also find that the rules which regulate every
legitimate department of business are inverted as regards
the drink traffic.   It is the demand that regulates the
supply in every lawful trade.   If you increase the number of bakers' shops, butchers' shops or grocery stores in
any village, you do not thereby increase the consumption
for said articles, but if you increase the number of taverns you will find the demand augmented.   The publicans of Birmingham, England, admit this, for in a petition
which they presented to the British House of Commons,
they state, " We find that vice and crime are just in proportion to the number of public-houses, and the facilities
afforded for obtaining spirituous liquors."

It is also a *first* principle in every proper business to
develope it to its utmost extent, but the advocates of the
drinking usages would not consent to this.   They want

certain restrictions and limitations to be placed upon the Drink traffic. We, however, are convinced that ." it is impossible satisfactorily to limit or regulate a system so essentially mischievous in its tendencies."

In further proof that the rules which regulate every proper business are inverted as regards the liquor traffic, I would add: H. A. Massey, of Newcastle, is not ashamed to send his mower and reaper to the World's Fair, and label them with his name and address; but did you ever know a tavern-keeper to send a few drunkards to the Exhibition, and label them with his name and address? I never did; and yet the mower and reaper are not more certainly the result of the employment of Mr. H. A. Massey than are the inebriates the result of the traffic in which the tavern-keepers are engaged.

Again, when men go to the bar, as a general rule they drink anything that may be emptied out of a decanter; but when they go to the dry goods merchant to purchase cloth, they will ask " Is it all wool, sir ? " and they will beat him down to the lowest possible price; but at the bar it is "Come along, boys; have something to drink." And they will take anything, no matter how it is adulterated, and *pay* for it without a grumble; but when they are getting an equivalent for their money, they will beat the merchant and the mechanic down to the lowest possible price.

M

LECTURE VIII.

THE PHYSICAL, SOCIAL AND MENTAL EFFECTS OF THE DRINK TRAFFIC.

IN proof that the Liquor Traffic is injurious to man as a physical being, I refer to the aborigines of this country. Since the "fire-water" has been introduced, the Red race has degenerated sadly. A century ago they numbered about sixteen million souls, and now they do not number over two millions. All the Indian chiefs which I have conversed with on the subject declare that the "fire-water" has disgraced and killed many of their brethren, and they are unanimous in wishing it banished from the land.

But our observation is not confined to the Indians. We have only to look round on the circle of our friends and acquaintances, to see the injurious effects of alcohol upon the physical system: there is the bloodshot eye, the painted nose, the fevered lip, the trembling hand, the tottering gait, and everything indicative of the wreck and ruin that "strong drink" is effecting upon the physical constitutions of thousands of our fellow-beings ; and, as Dr. Justin Edwards remarked, "were the body transparent, you would see the foot-prints of the enemy *on*

the inside, long before you discover them on the outside."
Now, there is a religion of the body as well as a religion
of the mind.   We are ·exhorted in Scripture to " Glorify
God in our *bodies* and in our spirits, which are His;" and
" Do thyself no harm " is as much an injunction of the
Great Moral Governor of the Universe, as " Thou shalt
not kill."   Yet, Cleopatra did not more certainly take
away her life when she applied the asp to her breast, than
are some men, who look upon the commands of the Most
High as obligatory, striking the suicidal blow to their
own existence by indulging in spirituous liquors.   Nor
does the evil rest here.   Dr. Darwin and other distinguished physicians assert that all the diseases arising
from drinking spirituous or fermented liquors are liable
to become hereditary, even to the third generation ;
gradually increasing, if the cause be continued, till the
family becomes extinct."

Much light of late has been thrown upon the injurious
nature of alcoholic drinks now in use.   It is a fearful
fact that the most noxious and poisonous substances are
being resorted to in the manufacture of said liquors.
" Can a man take fire into his bosom and his clothes not
be burned ?"   The use of said drinks, even in small quantities, is most destructive to health.   Would that all who
drink were as honest as a certain J.P. that I met with a
few months ago.   At the close of one of my lectures, this
gentleman got up and said : " Friends, you all know me ;
I have been born and brought up in your neighbourhood ; I have been a strict moderate drinker for over
thirty years.   Not one of you can accuse me for having

been once drunk; and, yet, friends, although I have been
a strict moderate drinker in the common acceptation of
the term, I must acknowledge that I have seriously
injured my health and undermined my constitution by
my so-called moderate drinking." Dr. Cheyne, of Dublin, has given it as his opinion, after 30 years of medical
practice, observation and experience : " Let ten young
men begin, at 21 years of age, to use but one glass of
spirits of only two ounces a day, and never increase the
quantity : nine out of ten of those young men will shorten
life upon an average more than ten years." Besides, we
have the testimony of over 2,000 of the most distinguished
physicians in Europe and America to the fact, that " the
most perfect health is compatible with total abstinence
from all such intoxicating beverages, whether in the form
of ardent spirits, or as wine, beer, ale, porter, cider, etc."
And, notwithstanding all this, I have conversed with men
who use considerable spirituous liquors, who would consider themselves insulted if you were to accuse them of
being intoxicated, or affirm that they were injured by indulging in said drinks ; and some of them will even get
up in our Temperance meetings and state, " For 40 or 50
years I have been a moderate drinker, and before I came
to this meeting I drank three glasses, and feel nothing the
worse for it. Do you call me a drunkard, sir, or say I'm
injured by what I drink—eh ? " Now, some men of this
class might be compared to a sponge. Take a sponge
saturated with water and compress it, and the water will
ooze out; so if you were to compress some such characters as I have just named, the alcohol might ooze out of

every pore of their body; and yet if you were to state that they were drunkards, or that they were injured by these liquors, they would be mightily offended. While a man may stand up and declare that for so many years he has used alcoholic stimulants moderately and has not become a drunkard, let him only deal honestly and look back upon the past, and while he may have escaped as with the skin of a tooth, how many of his school-mates and companions, by following his example, may have fallen into drunkards' graves. The man, therefore, who lives to a good old age, notwithstanding his intemperate habits, lives in spite of his drinking, not on account of it. Some of the best constitutions are reduced to mere wrecks, and that in a very short period, by drink; and I believe that much of the physical debility of the present age is attributable to this cause.

Dr. Caldwell says : "*By habits of intemperance, they not only degrade and ruin themselves, but transmit the elements of like degradation and ruin to their posterity. This is no visionary conjecture, the fruit of a favourite and long-cherished theory. It is a settled belief resulting from observation—an inference derived from innumerable facts.*" These are weighty statements; and all are ready to admit that soundness of body and mind has much to do with the true prosperity of a nation. Why, then, not at once admit the right of a legal power in the hands of an enlightened people to interfere with any business that produces such effects ?

There are thousands of living witnesses to prove what two thousand medical men have testified, that the most perfect health is compatible with total abstinence from all intoxicating liquors ; and the truth is, a man in health no more requires alcoholic liquors than a duck requires an umbrella.

"Here, then," cried Seneca, describing the fatal effects of drunkenness, "the hero unconquered by the toils of prodigious marches, exposed to the dangers of sieges and combats, to the most violent extremes of heat and cold ; here he lies subdued by his intemperance, struck to the earth by the fatal cup of Hercules."

It is alarming the social evils and miseries that are inflicted upon society by this traffic.   A world of woe is in that one word drunkenness ; its very utterance fills our minds with trouble, and there are few who can look round upon the circle of their friends and say, " That foul monster never injured any one belonging to me!"   It has made inroads into many a once happy family circle ; it has converted the Bethel into a Brothel ; it has transformed the once affectionate father into a fiend, and made the once devoted mother treacherous, cruel and unkind.

Many a fond mother to-night is sitting in her almost empty dwelling, while the chill winds are whistling their night dirge through her once comfortable but now desolate home. There with sorrowful heart she rocks and sings " Hush, my dear, lie still and slumber," while her husband is away at the tavern, spending his money " for that which is not bread ; " there he sits, furnishing the tavern-keeper's dwelling, while his own is almost empty ; supplying the tavern-keeper's children with bread, while his own are starving, and " the wee mice micht be seen running through his ain cupboard with tears in their een, because they canna get any crumbs tae eat."

It is worthy of remark that, just in proportion as a man begins to love strong drink, the love of house, love of home, love of wife, love of children, love of everything that should be dear and sacred to a man, diminishes in the same proportion.

There was a man in Scotland named John ——, one of nature's noblemen; he got married to Sarah ——, one of the most gentle, loving and affectionate of her sex. For the first few years of their married life, all was joy and sunshine; but, unfortunately, by following the drinking customs, John acquired an appetite for liquor. He would squander his earnings at the public-house, and prefer his pot companions to the wife he once so fondly loved· A few years wrought a wonderful change in John and his circumstances; and yet Sarah, womanlike, clung to him as the ivy to the ruined building, nor did she cease to plead with God in private for him; she loved with a love stronger than death, and her "Father which seeth in secret himself" rewarded her "openly." One Sabbath evening John returned home after a long carousal; he spent a miserable night, and in the morning he said to his wife, "Sarah, I want you tae gang awa to the publican, and ask him for the len o' seven shillings till Saturday nicht." "Weel, John, I dinna like tae gang, but if I maun gang I wul gang, but I dinna like tae gang, John." "Come, noo, get ready fast, and gang awa tae the publican, and ask him for the len o' seven shillings till Saturday nicht." And did ever you observe a poor drunkard's wife going

off to a publican to ask an obligement ? She put an old
threadbare shawl about her head, and only leaving room
for her eyes, that she might not stumble, off she wandered.
At length she reached the public-house, and was met by
a fine, rosy-cheeked landlady, who accosted her thus :—
" What brought you here this morning, Sarah ?" " Oh,
what brought me here ? John sent me tae see if you would
be sae good as tae len' him seven shillings till Saturday
nicht." " Umph ! I'm no 'sic a fule as.a' that. You should
rather pray for his death, Sarah. Has he no been the big-
gest curse ye hae met wi', the drunken vagabond ? I would
rather gie something tae bury him, and get him oot o' the
road, woman." " Is that what ye say noo, after John has
spent a' his hard earnings wi' you for the last six or seven
years ? Ye say I should pray for his death. No, no ! I'll
no pray for his death, but I'll tell you what I'll pray for ;
I'll pray that God may gie him strength as long as he
lives that he may never darken your door, nor anither
publican's door," and, suiting the action to the word, she
whirled round and walked home. " Pray for his death !"
thought she; " no, no; he wasna aye a drunkard until he
gaed tae the drunkard-maker and was converted into ane ;
besides, he's my ain husband, and ' wi' a' his faults I lo'e
him still.'"

     With this she entered. John was anxiously waiting
her return, and as she approached he scanned her every
feature as he inquired, " Did ye get it ? did ye get it ?"
" No, no, I didna get it." " What did she say ?" " Oh,
what did she say ? Dinna ask me, John." " Tell me this
minute what she said." " Weel, John, she said I should

pray for your ——" (with this she burst into a flood of
tears.) " Tell me," cried the husband, " tell me this minute
what she said, or I'll knock you doon as flat as a flounder."
" Weel, John, keep quate and I'll tell you.   She said that
I should pray for your ——"   " Oot wi' it," cried John.
" ' Pray for your death,' she said ; but I said ' No, no, I'll
no pray for his death, but I'll tell you what I'll pray for ;
I'll pray that God may gie him strength as long as he
lives that he may never darken your door nor anither
publican's door :' and come noo, John, gang down on
your knees, John, and we'll pray God tae give you that
strength."   John was submissive ; he knelt beside his
wife, while she sent up her earnest prayer to the throne
of grace, that God would enable her husband to make and
to keep that resolution.   Afterwards they went to the
secretary of the Temperance Society and enrolled their
names.   John returned to his employer, told him what he
had done, and asked for work.   His employer kindly replied, " John, you shall have work while there is a job of
work in the shop."   John was a good workman (and it is
those men who are in most danger of being led astray).
He applied himself diligently throughout the week ; at
length Saturday night came, and with it hopes and fears
alternately occupied Sarah's mind.   At length she heard
his footstep, and, thank God, he was sober.   When he entered, he looked into his wife's face with a smile, and said :
" Sarah, sit down ; hold your lap, woman " (you all know
how a woman holds her apron when she expects to get
anything), and he emptied his earnings into her lap, as
the little ones cried, " Come and see this ; my faither has

emptied thousands of shillings into mither's apron." Presently the baker's boy entered with some bread, and the grocer's lad with some groceries, and the little ones thought their father was going to open a grocery shop. Such is the blessed effects of temperance.

Dr. Franklin, in summing up the domestic evils of drunkenness, said : " Houses without windows, gardens without fences, children without clothing, principles, morals or manners."

Dirt, disorder and discord are its effects; scolding, swearing and fighting its results ; lying, stealing and imprisonment its fruits ; disease, wretchedness and starvation its natural consequences. In fact, it is the monster social evil—the plague spot—the grand impediment in the way of all genuine reform.

A poor drunkard was once pursued by the police, and for safety he ran into the publican's parlour ; and as he looked at the beautiful furniture and costly paintings, he inquired " Where did you get all them nice things ? " " From you fools," replied the landlady. " Well," thought the poor inebriate, " I've been a fool too long ; I'll fool no more ;" and he became a sober man, and furnished his own parlour and bought silk dresses for his own wife.

Ye working men, I would warn you against drinking. A poor man once lay intoxicated opposite a tavern bar. " What is this fellow doing here?" inquired a customer. " O, never mind him," replied the landlord, " he is taking shingles off his own house to put them on mine." The man was not insensible, though intoxicated ; he heard what passed and profited by it as well, and he resolved he would no longer shingle other people's houses, so he left off drinking. Some time after the tavern-keeper met him : " Well, Jemmy, what are you doing these times? it's a long while since I saw you. Where did you get them nice clothes, Jemmy?"   " Well, landlord, as to what I have been doing, I have been shingling my own house, not yours ; and as to these new clothes, I bought and paid for them with the money I would have spent at your bar, only the last time I was there I overheard you say I was taking shingles off my own house and putting them on yours ; and indeed it was very true, for my house was beginning to leak pretty bad."

Dr. David Livingstone, the celebrated African traveller, says the only thing he is proud of is, that one of his forefathers was renowned for wisdom and prudence. On his death-bed he gathered his children around him and said : " None of your forefathers could ever be charged with dishonesty, so if you are dishonest it does not run in the blood. So my last charge to you is, 'be honest.' "

Certainly there is no grander sight in the world than to behold the honest poor man as he struggles hard to earn an honest living. Working men are the golden pillars of society ; it is to the working men the rich are indebted for the many comforts and luxuries they enjoy. They brave the stormy ocean to fetch from foreign climes rich fruits and precious delicacies with which the rich may gratify their tastes ; they build that noble mansion, from which you look upon the surrounding country; they till the soil; they build that carriage in which you ride; that yacht in which you sail for pleasure; that sofa on which you recline in ease. Then why should not the working men give their hair an aristocratic sweep, and enjoy the fruit of their toil ? Drink is the worst master that the poor man ever served.

What social debasement hast thou wrought, O foul Intemperance—how hast thou injured the most promising members of society ! Some of our noblest and most gifted sons have been ruined, and by thy treacherous power some of our fairest daughters have been sacrificed.

THE MENTAL EFFECTS OF INTEMPERANCE.

It is all moonshine to say that total abstinence is good enough for the vulgar, the unlettered and the working classes ; both high and low, rich and poor, noble and mean, have been ruined by drink. We could almost weep for those of immortal memory, gifted with extraordinary talents, and possessed of rare natural genius, who by these deluding customs have been drawn into the vortex of intemperance.

Witness the cases of Byron, Burns and Edgar Allan Poe, three illustrious poets who fell victims to the killing influences and tendencies of this fearful indulgence.

Ye men of letters, who work with head and brain, take warning. Some of the most clever men who ever played their part upon the theatre of life have been overcome. Intemperance has brought ministers down from the sacred desk ; orators, statesmen and philosophers have been ruined by drink ; men of ten talents, giants in intellect and brilliant in genius ; kings, warriors and earthly potentates have been slain by King Alcohol. There is to be seen wandering through the streets of London an old grey-headed man accompanied by his miserable-looking wife; he carries a tin in one hand and a staff in the other, while he looks for charity from the passers-by. Who is that old man? But a few years since he was a respected and influential minister of the church, but drink, love of drink, caused him to be deposed from his sacred office, and now he wanders a poor object begging his bread. Who are those miserable-looking objects we see dragging their steps into yonder splendid gin palace? They look like persons who had risen from the grave to get a last glass, and had forgotten their way back again. Fashionable young gentlemen gather up the skirts of their coats as they pass them, lest they should get them soiled. Those young gentlemen call for wine, beer, ale, brandy, or whatever they fancy, but these miserable creatures ask for a pennyworth of "all sorts." Now, "all sorts" is well named: the counters are covered with zinc, with holes perforated in it, and a vessel is kept to contain the dregs that are spilled, and this is called "all sorts." But did those poor creatures begin with drinking "all sorts?" No! Many of them are men of education; many of them were once leading and influential members of society; but they have descended by drink, and many of those who now despise them will ere long, we fear, be as low as they are.

O, young man, if thou would'st ascend the scale of intellectual eminence, avoid drinking. Remember, while "there is no royal road to intellectual eminence," that the tavern, instead of giving an impetus to your aspirations after knowledge, will contrariwise keep you back; you must not

loiter about the bar-room, but you must study hard and
work hard to attain your object, remembering that—

> " Those heights by great men reached and kept,
>   Were not attained by sudden flight ;
>   But they, while their companions slept,
>   Were toiling upward in the night."

Sir Wm. Hamilton had the following aphorism above
his study door : " In the world there is nothing great but
man, and in man there is nothing great but mind." And
is it not very humiliating that man so endowed, with a
mind open to the infinite and destined to the eternal,
should by drink become debased and degraded ?

Mind elevates man above the brute creation, and makes
him but " a little lower than the angels." It is the greatest work of God. All else is dust; but the mind is immortal, immaterial, incorruptible as the everlasting Jeho-
vah. If you ascend those everlasting mountains, the tops
of which have been covered with snow ever since creation dawned, howsoever broad their base, majestic their
height, or ponderous their weight, they are but matter ;
they cannot think, feel, nor reflect, and these, together
with

> " The cloud-capped towers, the gorgeous palaces,
>   The great globe itself, shall melt away,
>   And, like the baseless fabric of a vision,
>   Leave not a wreck behind."

But when the stars shall fall like fig leaves from heaven,
and the earth pass away as a scroll, man shall outlive
them all, and survive the " wreck of nature and the crash
of worlds."

By mind man can look abroad upon the vast universe of God, and view the variety, beauty, and usefulness of those gifts which the Almighty has spread with such bountiful hand. It digs down into the bowels of the earth and throws light upon the past; it studies the animal and vegetable kingdoms, with its three hundred thousand varieties of the former, and its hundreds of thousands of the latter; it examines the minute and comprehends the great, from the mite to the elephant, from the shrimp to the whale; it throws its tape line around the globe, and fathoms the depths of angry ocean.

It wings its flight to the starry heavens; it contemplates the size of those heavenly bodies, their distances from the sun, and the amazing celerity of their movements.

It looks from nature up to nature's God, and contemplates the Deity, who summons into being with like ease the whole creation or a single grain, and exclaims:

> "These are thy wondrous works, parent of good,
> Almighty! thine this universal frame.
> Thus wondrous fair, thyself how wondrous then!"

Yea, it raises him to the very heavens; he muses upon the august throne of the eternal; he beholds the spheres rolling beneath his feet, obeying the impulses of Him at whose behest they sprang into being, and by whose Almighty arm they have been kept in motion till this hour, and it enables him to commingle his songs with the blood-royal of heaven. And oh! to think that a mind capable of such expansion here, and such advancement in heaven, that instead of it enjoying God, and basking in his smile for ever—" a perpetuity of bliss is bliss,"—it should be ruined and made eternally miserable by drink. The very thought is awful, and rouses every manly feeling in my soul, so that I hate drink with a perfect hatred.

Philanthropists, ye that love the race, " haste to the rescue." The drinking usages are retarding our progress and development, stunting mental and moral growth, and withering much that once was full of promise.

Drink has hurled reason from its lofty seat, and left nothing but the wildest fancy playing like the forked lightning through the shattered walls of a ruined castle ; it has sundered the fondest ties that ever pure affection bound together ; it has bloated the fairest features that ever smiled around the family hearth ; it has made the happiest homes wretched ; it has made the strongest men powerless ; it has fevered the most marvellous brain ; it has silenced the most eloquent tongue ; it has closed the brightest eye that ever flashed in human countenance ; it has laid cold in death the warmest hand that ever shook in human friendship ; and has made for ever silent the pulsations of as warm a heart as ever beat in human bosom.

Many of the brightest luminaries in the world of science, and some stars of the very first magnitude in the great galaxy of human intellect, have had their resplendent light for ever dimmed by the black presence of the demon Drink.

Ah ! when we take into consideration the fact that many, very many, of the most gifted men that have ever

lived have become victims to this vice, we are admonished
to beware.   One day Mr. ——, a writer ·for the press,
called to borrow fourpence from the writer; the week
before he had received thirty-seven pounds ten shillings
stg. from the London *Times* for an article which he had
written.

Who can estimate the injury inflicted by drink?

What if Newton's judgment had been impaired by
drink when he saw the apple fall which suggested the
law of gravitation.

What if Watt had been intoxicated when the boiling
tea-kettle suggested the power of steam.

What if Lawrence Koster had been under the influence
of liquor when he cut the letters on the smooth bark of a
tree, which suggested the art of printing. And yet these
and other important discoveries have originated in ·con-
ceptions faint enough to be extinguished in a glass of
wine ; and who can tell the loss the world has sustained
by the stupefying influences of strong drink ?

The noblest product of a nation is its men.   Whatever
improves or elevates men increases the power of the nation ; while, on the other hand, whatever weakens or debases men diminishes the power of the commonwealth.

Now, shall we have a sober or a drunken Dominion ?

Would you see Canada thrive in material prosperity,
rise in moral grandeur, and advance in true piety, then
discountenance the drinking customs of society. The
root and origin of all true property is the mind and intellect, and the most real property is the minds of the individuals who compose the nation,

N

The brain is the great central organ of the nervous system, where the mind has its seat. The nervous system might be compared to a telegraph—the nerves are the wires, and the brain the central office. Professor Miller states that "The brain suffers most injury (from the effects of alcohol), both in structure and function; but there is no vital organ in the body in which there is not induced, sooner or later, more or less disorder and disease."

Hugh Miller says: "Two whole glasses of whisky came to my share. A full-grown man would not have deemed a gill of usquebagh an over-dose, but it was considerably too much for me; and when the party broke up and I got home to my books, I found, as I opened the pages of a favourite author, the letters dancing before my eyes, and that I could no longer master the sense. I have the volume at present before me—a small edition of the 'Essays' of Bacon. The condition into which I had brought myself was, I felt, one of degradation. I had sunk, by my own act, for the time, to a lower level of intelligence than that on which it was my privilege to be placed; and though the state could have been no very favourable one for forming a resolution, I in that hour determined that I should never again sacrifice my capacity of intellectual enjoyment to a drinking usage, and with God's help I was enabled to hold by the determination."

Sir Fowell Buxton has remarked that "a man of genius without perseverance may run the career of a rocket, but can never be a star; and he that has perseverance without genius will be a bright and steady star, but can never be a sun; but the man who has genius and perseverance combined will be the sun of his own system." We ask you then to persevere in your attainments, to avoid the tavern and the drinking usages, and to take for your motto:

> " Higher, higher let me climb,
> Up to the mount of glory,
> That my name may ever shine
> In my country's story."

Earl Russell said, " I am convinced there is no cause more likely to elevate the people in every respect, whether as regards religion or political opinions, or as regards literary or moral culture, than this great question of temperance."

LECTURE IX.

THE MORAL AND RELIGIOUS ASPECTS OF THE QUESTION.

THE drinking usage is injurious to man as a moral being, the publicans themselves being judges. In the Birmingham publicans' report to the House of Commons, there is the following startling paragraph (startling as coming from the publicans themselves): " That it is clearly shown by Parliamentary Returns, that vice and drunkenness are in proportion to the number of public-houses and the facilities for obtaining intoxicating drinks." Besides, often have publicans rented a house in the country to prevent their children from coming in contact with those who frequent their place of business; and I have known a grocer and publican who would not allow his daughters to cross over or serve on the whisky side.

Some time ago a minister related the following at the close of a temperance meeting : " Travelling in the County of Victoria with some other ministers, we put up at a tavern. While warming ourselves by the fire until the dinner would be prepared, I heard a strange sound in the back part of the house, and I asked the landlady what caused that noise. She replied, " It is a parrot, sir."

" Why don't you keep it in the bar?" I asked. "It would be a source of entertainment to travellers," I added. She answered that she did formerly keep it in the bar, but it was beginning to learn to swear, and she "had to put it in the back part of the house to keep it from swearing." Now, there stood beside her a dear little girl, and yet, while the landlady was fearful that the morals of the parrot might become corrupted if it remained in the bar, she seemed to forget that her own dear children were growing up under the blighting influence of the bar-room.

John Cassell, in his able paper upon Education, states that, in order to test what became of Sabbath scholars after they had left the school, a circular was addressed to the chaplains of the principal prisons in England, Scotland and Wales, when by their report it appeared that out of ten thousand three hundred and sixty-one inmates, six thousand five hundred and seventy-two had been Sabbath scholars. Hence arose the question, "What is the cause of this?" Answer, "Almost uniformly, strong drink is the cause." Sunday-school teachers, teach Total Abstinence in your schools, or drink will undo your efforts.

The popular historian, Sir A. Alison, says of the records of the Glasgow House of Refuge :—

" These highly curious annals of crime show, in the clearest manner, the fatal influences of the drinking of whisky upon the lowest classes of the people, for out of 234 boys who are at present in the institution, it appears from their own account that the drunkenness of their parents stood thus :—

Had drunken fathers........................ 72
Had drunken mothers..................... 62
Had both father and mothers drunken. 69

So that upwards of two-thirds of the boys in the institution have been precipitated into crime through the use of liquor by one or both of their parents.

CRIME IN LIVERPOOL.

The report of Major Greig, head constable of Liverpool, on the state of crime in the borough. Census taken 29th September, 1868.
Total number of licensed houses........ 2,598

RESULTS.

Apprehended for drunk and disorderly, drunk and
incapable, and drunk and assaults............. 16,770
Number brought to the Detective Office and Bride-
well, but not locked up............................ 3,010

It has been estimated that every public-house in Liverpool makes ten paupers annually.

Every two public-houses keep a policeman. Every public-house sends eight persons to the police court.

Every public-house imposes a tax of one hundred and sixty pounds per annum upon the ratepayers.

At the great Permissive Bill banquet in Manchester, 19th April, 1865, Sir Walter C. Trevelyan, Bart., said, in speaking of the drink traffic: " Too well it does the nefarious work, as is shown by the ghastly annals of our gaols and gallows, our poor-houses and mad-houses, our hospitals and cemeteries, our penitentiaries and reformatories, our brothels and other dens of vice; not to mention the countless victims whose sad career, though not exposed to public view, bring unutterable lamentation and woe and sorrow to the domestic hearth. Few are able to escape its destroying power; for, worse than the dire hosts of war, pestilence and famine, which cease from their cruel work after they have run their appointed course, the work of this army never ceases, its commanders are never satisfied, but go 'on, dealing death and destruction around, night and day, from year end to year end."

In the British Parliament, Sir Morton Peto called the attention of the House to the fearful state of immorality around our camps and dockyards, and stated that in Plymouth alone there were nine hundred prostitutes under the age of fifteen years; and could you go to them and inquire how they became seduced, you would find that drink had much to do in effecting their ruin and shame. Not only does drink nerve the assassin's arm, but it also gives the deceiver a mighty advantage in accomplishing his deeds of wickedness.

Wendell Phillips, in a speech delivered in the City of Boston some time since, stated: " In ten years, forty-five men out of every hundred in this peninsula of Boston are arrested for crime; forty-five out of every hundred, nearly one-half of the population, in ten years pass through the station-house or the gaol. Now, go with me to Berkshire County, in this State (Mass.), where the law against the liquor traffic is enforced; less than

two men out of one hundred are subjected to imprisonment in that county."

Owing to the democratic foreign population of Boston,
the law was not enforced in the city.

On the 28th of April, 1865, a very large meeting was
held in Dublin, for the total suppression of the liquor
traffic.   After dwelling upon the statement that the traffic is immoral in its tendency and criminal in its results,
the mover of the first resolution stated among other things
the following startling facts : " When they consumed in
Ireland, in four years, two million gallons less of spirits,
they had 22,000 less paupers, and £214,000 less poor
rates ; when 2s. a gallon was added to the duty, they had
19,300 less committals to prison than when the duty was
low.   In Scotland the Sunday closing reduced the committals in Edinburgh by three-fourths, and a new gaol
projected was never erected because it ceased to be necessary.   In Glasgow, with all its drunkenness, while its
population increased by 67,000, its criminals decreased by
18,500 under the operation of Sunday closing of public-
houses.   Oliver Goldsmith, their own countryman, who was
no teetotaler, said, " In all the towns and counties I have
ever seen, I never saw a city or village where miseries
were not in proportion to the number of public-houses."

*Extract from a Report of a Committee appointed by the
Canadian Parliament, February 24th, 1859.*

1. That indulgence in the use of intoxicating liquors is
the cause of most of the suffering and sorrow, the poverty
and crime which afflict Upper Canada ; and,

2. That it is the duty of Parliament to mitigate, diminish, and if possible to extirpate the cause of these evils.

Extract from reply of G. L. Allan, Esq., Governor of Toronto Gaol, to queries addressed to same Committee.

From my experience in such matters, having been now going on 14 years dealing with them, I unhesitatingly assert, that were the criminals not actually committed for drunkenness analyzed, it would be found that three-fourths of them committed the offences with which they were charged through the agency, directly or indirectly, of intoxicating drinks.

Through the drinking customs of society the once white garments have become sullied; those who stood high on their moral elevation have been hurled down into deepest degradation, and there they have writhed and groaned, and at last expired.

The effect of indulgence in strong drink is set forth by Professor Miller, in his admirable work on "Alcohol: its Place and Power." He says: "What is specially human is lessened; what is merely animal is intensified; the passions rise rebelliously, and defy all moral control; and the man becomes, under his own act, what the law has quaintly termed him, 'Voluntarius demon.' He is temporarily *insane*, and fitted for any act of violence to himself or others."

Drink is the great cause of most of the crime that is perpetrated in the land.

Between Ross and Waterford there is a heap of stones placed, to commemorate the murder of Mr. Leonard by

Thomas Malone.   Malone's mother sent him out to commit the bloody act, but when he saw Mr. Leonard he had not the hardihood to perpetrate so foul a deed, and returned and told his mother that when he looked in the gentleman's face he smiled so pleasantly that he could not kill him.   The mother, however, was not to be thwarted in this way, and taking from the press a bottle of poteen (home-made whisky, very strong), and handing it to her son, she said, " Here, drink that." He drank it, and while under its influence he committed the murder that he refused to do when sober.   Yes, my friends, drink nerves the assassin's arm !   Malone was tried, found guilty, and sentenced to be hanged.   After sentence had been pronounced, Malone turned round in court to an aged woman, with grey hair, and addressed her thus : " Mother, twice you made me do it.   When I returned home and told you I could not find in my heart to kill so innocent a looking man, you handed me a bottle of poteen, and said ' Drink that,' and when I drank it, and was robbed of my senses, I killed the gentleman.   Mother, 'twas you made me do it, and I'll curse you with my last breath."   O, parents, do not encourage your children to drink ; they may begin to drink soon enough, to your shame and to your sorrow, but O, if they will drink, do not you teach them.

THE RELIGIOUS ASPECT.

Who, I ask, is to suppress this mighty Hydra ? I believe that Temperance Reform is legitimately the work of the Church, and I would despair of success in this glorious enterprise if I did not believe that the day is fast approaching when the Church shall enter earnestly and heartily into this movement. I do sincerely believe that outside the Church there is not moral power enough to suppress this evil; hence, we solicit the co-operation of all Christian men and women, and ask you, both by pre-cept and example, to frown down those customs. Let the ministers and members of Christian Churches withdraw their support from the drinking customs of society, and there is no power on earth, nor in hell, that can withstand our progress.

Which of the ten commandments has not been, and hourly is not being broken by drink? I hesitate not in affirming, that the Church (with some noble exceptions) is asleep in reference to this evil. O! in view of the terrible havoc which drink is making, the alarm note should be sounded from every pulpit, and the people warned of the danger of tampering with strong drink. O, ye watchmen in Zion, hear the pleadings of one who was all but ruined by the alluring customs, and remember Ezekiel xxxiii., 6th verse—" But if the watchman see the sword come, and blow not the trumpet, and the people be not warned; if the sword come and take any person from among them, he is taken away in his iniquity; but his blood will I require at the watchman's hand." A worse destroyer than the sword is in our midst, not only killing the body but ruining the souls of thousands around us. O, it is a responsible and important as well as a sacred office, that of the minister of God. And few can form any estimate of the power which he exerts over those committed to his care. How very requisite then

that the ambassador should be faithful in discharging his
solemn duties, and use that vast influence which he has
to frown down vice and to promote virtue. "If the
preacher appeal to the intellect, the philosopher will rival
him; if to the passions, the mob orator will surpass him;
if to the imagination, the poet is his master; but his
power over the conscience no man shares. As the Czar
of many lands, he wields his sceptre over the master
faculty of man."

Drink has robbed the Church of some of her most
worthy members. In Belfast, a friend of mine went to
visit a gentleman on his death-bed. The whisky was in
a glass on a table at his bedside, and my friend said to
him, "Samuel, do give up this liquor; it is killing you;
do, my friend, put it away." "Do you see that, Charles?"
said Samuel, lifting the glass with whisky in it. " I
do," said Charles. " Well," said Samuel, "if I were to be
in hell the next minute after drinking it, I would drink
it, Charles." He drank it; soon died, leaving sixty thousand pounds sterling behind him, bequeathing so much to
the church with which he was identified, so much to the
hospital, the Royal Infirmary and other charitable institutions, and was buried with all the honour and respect
that the Church and the community could confer upon
him.

What influences are you using to suppress the evils of
intemperance? Alas! that so many still stand aloof from
this good cause, and refrain from trying to counteract
the evils under which humanity groans; and it is cause of
sorrow that so many, by their example, are doing much to

continue those evils. It must be patent to every thoughtful mind, that proportionate effort is not being put forth by the Church and professing Christians to stem the torrent of intemperance ; this vice is the parent of all vices ; and we have got so accustomed to the evils of intemperance that the frightful results which daily occur make but little impression on some minds.

The Church is at fault in this particular. She has not lifted her voice as a trumpet, and cried against our national vice. Nay, she hath too frequently lent herself to the promotion of intemperance ; she has kept silence while the monster serpent has been coiling itself around her members, and they have been unexpectedly destroyed in his foul embrace.

When ministers visit their flock it is no rare thing for the wine, &c., to be handed round, and those who patronise this custom lend themselves to the formation of those habits which have slain their millions.

Christians, in their mistaken kindness, have done everlasting injury to the ministers of the Gospel ; they have injured their constitution, and taken up much precious time needlessly ; besides, many young men on their first pastoral mission, who never were accustomed to much liquor, knowing it was offered in kindness, and afraid to refuse lest it should give offence, have allowed themselves to be persuaded to take more than they were able to bear, and have been almost unconsciously overcome and rendered unfit to perform aright the duties of their sacred office. Some again imagine that a little wine is requisite after preaching, but this has been tested, and is found to be both unnecessary and injurious.

Hearers watch with a keen eye the acts of their spiritual teacher, and think they may safely tread in the same path until they form an artificial appetite which is insatiable. If there is one habit more than another which the Church ought to cry and war against, it is drinking; drink has undone her noblest ministers, ruined her most useful members, slain her brightest sons and loveliest daughters.

Religion has suffered by this awful traffic, and the success of the ever blessed Gospel has been much retarded both at home and abroad. Its injurious influence in this respect is beyond all human calculation. In a letter from the Archdeacon of Bombay there is the following statement, that " for every convert to Christianity in India, the drinking practices of the English have made a thousand drunkards." O, my friends, if this be true—and I believe it to be so—what, I ask you, must these natives think of Christianity? To take the Bible in one hand, teaching them to abstain from all appearance of evil, and in the other hand to take that soul and body destroying drink, which has been fitly termed "liquid fire."

It is worth a thought, to which denominations, or how many, is this traffic confined? It is confined almost entirely to three, namely, the Presbyterian, Church of England, and Roman Catholic. When will these churches discountenance the manufacture and sale of these drinks?

"God of the silver bow, thy shafts employ,
   Avenge thy servants and (not the Greeks) the drink destroy."

Let the united prayer of every friend of the human race be—

> " Quench, mighty God, with thine own power,
> By law or love, or spring or well,
> By flood or storm, or hail or shower ;
> But quench, O quench this fire of Hell."

The drinking customs not only retard the spread of the ever blessed Gospel at home, but it is producing the very same results in foreign lands. Listen to what Archdeacon Jeffrys states: "If the English were driven out of India to-morrow, the chief traces of their ever having been there would be the number of drunkards they have left behind.'

Mr. Thompson, missionary in Africa, remarks : " I blush and hang my head for shame, my soul is agonized when I think of it; the other day I counted fifty barrels of spirits just landed from the very State that sent me here to preach. Since then I counted seventy-five more. How awful, when the very ship that takes me out to preach ' temperance, righteousness and judgment to come,' has its hold filled with a flood of damnation and death."

Bishop Burgess has said : " We might as well expect to be freed from any fearful pestilence, solely by prayer, where it arises from the exhalations of a noxious pool, which we are either too indolent or unwilling to remove, as to imagine that the world will be ever relieved from the crying sin of intemperance, whilst the social custom of drinking and the traffic is so universally upheld."

That eminent Scotch divine, Dr. Guthrie, says in his work, " The City : its Sins and Sorrows" : " So long as re-ligion stands by, silent and unprotesting against the temp-

tation with which men greedy of gain, and Government
greedy of revenue, surround the wretched victims of this
basest vice, it appears to me an utter mockery for her
(religion) to go with the Word of God in her hand teaching them to say, 'Lead us not into temptation.'"

Rev. Theo. L. Cuyler, of Brooklyn, N. Y., says: "Every
true and timely moral reform should be born, and nursed,
and reared, and supported in the Church of Jesus Christ.
There is not a single moral precept which sinful humanity
needs, but the Church should teach it; there is not a wholesome example to be set, but the Church should practise
it. That Christian Church will be the most *Christ-like*
which does the most to ' seek and to save the lost.'

"Among all the great moral reforms, none has a stronger
claim on Christian men and Christian ministers than the
enterprise for saving society from the crime and curse of
drunkenness. And intemperance never will be checked,
the liquor traffic never will be prohibited, the drinking
usages of social life will never be overthrown until the
members of Christ's Church all feel that they are also
members of Christ's great Temperance Society. If the
Church does not save the world, then the world will sink
the Church. And what a burlesque it is to style that
Church organization a 'salt of the earth' which has a trim-
mer in its pulpit, and tipplers in its pews !

"Our final recommendation is, that every church member
should make Temperance a part of his daily religion. The
bottle is the deadliest foe to Christ in our churches and
our communities. A friend of Christ *must* be the enemy
of the bottle. More souls are ruined by the intoxicating

cup than by any single vice or error on the globe. Every professed Christian who gives his example to the drinking usages, is a partner in the tremendous havoc which those evil customs produce."

Mr. Smith, of Edinburgh, states: "You may erect a church and a reformatory in every street in the city, but if you leave taverns every few doors as at present, they will, with the seductive nature of drink, and the inherent depravity of man, do more to promote evil and crime than all the ministers and philanthropists in the city can remedy."

The following is worthy of careful perusal:—

Ministerial Declaration, adopted at the Ministerial Conference held in Manchester, June 9th, 10th, and 11th, 1857.

"We, the undersigned Ministers of the Gospel, are convinced by personal observation within our sphere, and authentic testimony from beyond it, that the traffic in intoxicating liquors as drink for man is the immediate cause of most of the crime and pauperism, and much of the disease and insanity, that afflict the land; that everywhere, and in proportion to its prevalence, it deteriorates the moral character of the people, and is the chief outward obstruction to the progress of the Gospel; and these are not its accidental attendants, but its natural fruits; that the benefit, if any, is very small in comparison with the bane; that all schemes of regulation and restriction, however good so far as they go, fall short of the nation's need and the nation's duty; and that, therefore, on the obvious

principle of destroying the evil which cannot be control-
led, the wisest course for those who fear God and regard
man is to encourage every legitimate effort for the entire
suppression of the trade by the power of the national will,
and through the form of a legislative enactment."

And yet, although drink has ruined its thousands and
its tens of thousands, many professing Christians continue
to encourage those drinking customs, and not unfrequently
are they found at bar-rooms, giving their sanction and
countenance to this awful custom.   I do not think that is
what is meant in the admonition of the Saviour, when He
said : " Let your light so shine before men," &c., &c.   We
should be zealous for the glory of God, and for the unsullied beauty of the Christian character.   A young man
was asked to engage in prayer during the Ulster revival
in eighteen hundred and fifty-nine, after the sermon,
which was from the text above quoted, and he earnestly
implored that if any of his companions would attempt to
hide their candle under a bushel, that it might burn the
bottom out of it, so that it might shine.

O, my friends, be not a party to the licensing of those
houses which are devastating our land, clothing countless
widows in sackcloth, and multiplying orphans.

Professing Christians should be very careful of their
example.   A young man in Belfast, who had once been
very much addicted to drink, became an abstainer.   On
one occasion he was invited to a party ; when there he was
asked to take a little wine ; he refused.   At last he saw
an eminent minister of the gospel, a man of undoubted
piety, take a half glass of wine. " Well," thought he, " there

can be no harm in my taking a little when the minister takes it." His resolution gave way; he partook of the wine; it awoke his old appetite for alcoholic stimulants, and on his way home he went to a public-house, got more drink, and was taken home to his parents dead drunk.

Moderate-drinking Christians, you are responsible to a very great extent for the sad consequences of intemperance. The intemperate man finds a good excuse for his immoderate use of alcoholic stimulants in your moderate use of the same. I believe that it is the patronage of professors of religion and of leading minds in our communities which perpetuates these customs.

I am further of opinion, that you have not done all that it is your duty to do in reference to this question unless you abstain. In view of the dangerous nature and injurious tendency of the drinking customs of society, and from the sad havoc which drink has made in the past, we think you ought to discountenance those customs.

If all the money now wasted upon drink was appropriated to Christian objects, and if all the time now squandered through the drinking usages was applied to improve the mind, and acts of charity, what a change would this world present. But some good people will say, " Let your moderation be known unto all men." Now, what is scriptural moderation? I think it is the right and proper use of things good and lawful, and total abstinence from what is injurious. Now, Dr. Parkes, Dr. Carpenter, and others who stand at the top of the profession, declare that " spirituous liquors are invariably hurtful to the healthy body." Hence, total abstinence from what is injurious is, in the strict sense of the term, scriptural moderation.

Some say that total abstainers " disparage the grace of God." Before it be proved that we are guilty of the crime alleged, it must be proved that we attempt what grace alone can accomplish. May not the idle become industrious ; may not the thief become honest, without the special interference of Divine grace ? Why then condemn us when we urge the drunkard to become sober ? Because we man the life-boat to save the shipwrecked crew, do we thereby employ a substitute for the Gospel ?

The teaching of grace is " Lead us not into temptation ; " but if we, in spite of its teachings, enter into the same, the act and consequences are our own.

We have many noble examples in Scripture of the Temperance principle, including Samson's mother, John the Baptist, Daniel and his three companions, who preferred pulse and water to the king's wine, and who were " fairer and fatter than all the children who did eat the portion of the king's meat."

Religion, some say, does not prevent us from drinking in moderation. Nor does it compel us to drink. This is all we claim. It leaves us free to abstain from that which is injurious. Others speak of the possession of religious principles as the only safeguard.

Did it protect Noah ?

Did it protect Lot ?

The truth is, Alcohol is a physical agent, and produces in the mind and body its natural results, apart altogether from our religious opinions and principles. If a man partake of arsenic, it matters not the extent of his piety, it will produce its ordinary results ; and if a man partake of alcoholic liquors, whether Christian or infidel, its tendency is to create the drunkard's appetite."

Our opponents will do well to consider that grace deals with a man's reason and affections, but grace does not deal with a diseased stomach or a fevered brain.

Let those persons who have any doubts upon the propriety of using intoxicating liquors listen to Paul : " And he that doubteth is damned if he eat, because he eateth not of faith : for whatever is not of faith is sin."—Romans xiv., 23rd verse.

There is no doubt but the Bible, rightly interpreted, is the best temperance book in the world—that total abstinence has the Divine aproval, and is consistent with piety and wisdom.

Surely it never was designed that man should degrade himself by indulging in the use of intoxicating liquors· Man was created in the image of God. " In the image of God created he him, male and female created he them." Man was made to walk erect, and with face uplifted to the blue vault of heaven, to gaze upon the wondrous works of God, and view—

> " The spacious firmament on high,
> With all the blue ethereal sky ;
> The spangled heavens, a shining flame,
> Their great Original proclaim."

Man was constituted capable of looking from nature up to nature's God ; and contemplating the divine character, capable of knowing, loving and serving the Most High, and to accomplish this in its highest sense, let Christians of every name discountenance the drinking customs.

I think I am justified in asserting that persons generally do not treat drink as they do anything else. In illustration of this I may here state that on one occasion a party visited Niagara Falls. A young gentleman of rather a rash disposition lifted a young girl, the joy of the party, with lovely blue eyes, and golden ringlets hanging down her snow-white neck, and standing upon a jutting crag, he caught her by the waist and held her over the mighty abyss. "O, don't do that," screamed one. "It's dangerous," cried another. "O, stop, stop," shouted a third. But no! he would show how regardless he was, and again held her over. She got timid and nervous, and gave a sudden spring, and fell into the surging waters below. "My God, what shall I do?" cried the young man, and he leaped in after the child, and both met a watery grave. Not a shred of their clothes was ever seen. Have any from that day until now repeated the dangerous trial? Not one! And yet, although one after another, father after father, mother after mother, brother after brother, sister after sister, son after son, friend after friend, companion after companion, has been borne down the deceptive stream of moderation into the rapids of intemperance, and finally engulphed in the horrid sea of drunkenness, men, Christian men, continue to patronize the cause of all the mischief, the drinking customs.

Drink is "no respecter of persons." It has brought ministers from the sacred pulpit, it has laid orators, philosophers and statesmen low. Kings, warriors and earthly potentates have been ruined by King Alcohol.

One of the most promising young ministers that ever ascended the pulpit in the City of Dublin became a victim to the drinking usages of society. It was thought that no soirée or party was complete without his presence. He was a young man of great promise and of fine parts. Friends invited him to dine. Drink was offered. He was too good-natured to refuse. By-and-by he began to like it; was eventually overcome; was seen going home at midnight from one of these parties, linked between two members of his church, and, to prevent being expelled, he sent in his resignation, went to London, and became a penny-a-liner to the "Wesleyan Times," and when last heard of was dismissed from that situation for intemperance, and was wandering through the metropolis without a coat. O, friends, he was somebody's boy; he was tenderly reared; his father sweat many a drop to give him a finished education, and his poor mother wept many tears and prayed many prayers for her boy, but he became another victim to the long list of drunkards.

> "I knew him this, I knew him all
> That fondest heart could crave;
> And yet, O God! his blacken'd pall
> Covers a drunkard's grave!"

The great folly of the drink traffic consists in this, that it aims at upsetting the ordinance of God.

The fourth commandment reads thus, "Remember the Sabbath day to keep it holy." But the brewer, during the malting season, keeps men at work in open violation of Heaven's decree; so that what God wrote with his finger on the table of stone on Mount Sinai is trampled on by the brewer, and he keeps men at work during the hours of the sacred Sabbath.

We shall never occupy that position amongst the nations of the earth which the Almighty designed us to occupy, nor will we wield that influence for good which the Almighty designed us to wield, so long as we foster this dire drink traffic, which is injuring us at home and ruining us abroad.　Would you see the Dominion of Canada advance in material prosperity?　Would you see her rise in moral grandeur?　Would you have her exert a mighty influence for good in a religious point of view?　Then sweep away the traffic in drink, which is counteracting almost every effort which is being put forth to elevate the race.

We shudder at the thought of Pagans offering up human sacrifices, but in Great Britain alone sixty thousand lives are offered up annually to the god Bacchus; fifty thousand in the United States; three hundred thousand in France; and Sweden has one hundred and seventy thousand distilleries to three millions of a population; besides the havoc drink is causing in other parts of the world, where no estimate has been made of its extent.

Wherever you go, let your empty wine-glass proclaim your silent protest against the drinking customs of Society; and fashion, which now commands us to drink, will with all-potential voice command us to abstain. There is no denying the fact that the abstainer is the only real friend of this movement, and he that is not with us is surely against us. "But I don't like that word teetotalism," says one; "it's a poor thing if a man can't keep himself sober without having to pledge himself." Now, let me ask what is teetotalism? It is a compound, chemical compound, of two things—science and common sense. Science says: Alcohol will do you no good (if in health); and common sense says: Better leave it alone then; and teetotalism says: "Done," and the bargain is struck.

Of all the sins that teetotalers are guilty of—and they are neither few nor small—they are clear of this one sin, the sin of drunkenness, and they are not found encouraging and perpetuating this evil. I know there are some who would join us if we would substitute moderation for total abstinence, and many remedies would they resort to but the one which has been tried and never has failed.

In view of all that God has done for you, what are you doing for him and for humanity? Are you striving to leave the world better than you found it?

The recent pastoral address of the Bishops of the Methodist Episcopal Church contains the following timely utterance on the Sabbath and Temperance questions:

"The leading reform of the hour is the abolition of the sale and drinking of intoxicating beverages. These stimulants are sending multitudes annually to a drunkard's grave and a drunkard's doom. They are undermining our national life. They are the cause of almost all the crimes that infest society. They are the chief foe to the progress of the Church. The record of our Church in two successive General Conferences is in favour of prohibition. This is the ultimate goal of her efforts. She will not rest from these labours until the use and sale of intoxicating drinks follow to their grave other iniquities, once as powerful as these, and as deeply rooted in the appetites and interests of society. Let Prohibition receive your support, in your personal abstinence, and in all other Christian efforts for the overthrow of intemperance."

LECTURE X.

THE MEDICINAL USE OF ALCOHOLIC STIMU-LANTS.

I APPREHEND great danger from the medicinal use of alcoholic stimulants, from the fact that some persons of my own acquaintance, by using alcoholic stimulants by advice of their medical attendants, have been led to acquire habits whereby they have been ruined. I have no doubt but in some instances alcohol may be very useful; but I believe that the free use of alcohol to patients in a weak state of health has assisted wonderfully in spreading drunkenness through the land.

If alcohol is to be administered medicinally, it should only be prescribed by wise and skilful physicians, and that with very great caution and care.

Science designates alcohol as a poison, to be convinced of which you have only to try a few simple experiments. Sir Astley Cooper said, " We have all been mistaken in these things ; we'have considered them as restorative and nutritious, we now find that they are merely stimulants."

Hold some whisky in your mouth for five minutes, and you will find it to burn severely. Inspect the mouth, and you will observe that it is inflamed. Hold it for ten or fifteen minutes and you will find that various parts of

the interior of the mouth have become blistered. Then
tie a handkerchief over the eyes, and taste, for instance,
water, vinegar, milk, or senna, and you will find that you
are incapable of distinguishing the one from the other·
This simple and easy experiment proves to a certainty
that alcohol is not only a violent irritant, but also a nar-
cotic ; for in this experiment you have objective evidence
that it has inflamed and blistered the mouth, and subjec-
tive evidence that it has also for the time being paralyzed
the nerves of taste, and, to a certain extent, those also of
common sensation. Now, this is not an experiment or
fact upon which any doubt has ever been or ever can be
thrown ; and I ask you, can you believe that the still
more tender and more important internal organs , of the
body can be less injuriously affected than the mouth ?

It is in the nature of strong drink to create an appetite
for more. Stopping with a physician some time ago, his
lady related the following :—" My husband recommended
me to use beer (medicinally, of course), and I got to be
very fond of it; so much so, that after we had retired to
rest I would get up and sit by the fire waiting till my
husband would fall asleep. Sometimes he would say,
' Why don't you come to bed, dear ? ' ' Go to sleep, love,'
I would reply ; ' I don't feel very well; I'll retire by-and-
by.' Thus I would sit by the stove while moments of
eternal duration passed, until my husband fell asleep ;
then I would go to the press and take, as they say in
Scotland, ' a right guid willie-waught' o' the beer, and
then I would go to sleep. But when I found the habit
gaining on me, I resolved I would give up my beer. I

joined the Temperance Society, and my husband, through my example, has done the same." And I may add that her husband's personal appearance has very much improved since he joined the cold water army, and his patients have now a vast deal more confidence in their sober doctor than they had aforetime in their drunken doctor, and his practice has more than doubled itself. So in every way you look at it you will find that he has been benefited by connecting himself with the Temperance cause.

Professor Miller, in his work on "Alcohol, its Place and Power," relates the case of a lady who became a frightful dipsomaniac, and whose malady originated, or had been, as it were, suggested by the habit of carrying strong spirits occasionally in the mouth for the cure of toothache. "Against her own better judgment and the voice of conscience she is forced on," says my correspondent; "for days on end she has been out of one stupor into another. On two succeeding days of this week she has consumed a quart bottle of strong whisky; the next day, or rather night, when people were asleep, she got hold of some key which was supposed to secure from her a bottle of spirits and another of wine, and within twenty-four hours this was also consumed, no one being able to snatch it from her."

Not only should doctors guard against administering stimulants, but it is important that they should be practical teetotalers. There are at least two classes of professional drunkards, namely, doctors and lawyers, and it is sad that medical men, who know more of the evil effects

of intemperance than any others in the land, should be set
down as one of the two drunken classes.

If it is necessary that any man should be strictly sober,
I think the doctor is that man ; valuable lives are committed to his care, and surely the intellect should be
clear and unclouded by men occupying such a responsible
position.   Sad have been the consequences of medical men
prescribing while under the influence of the demon
drink ! Last year a M.D., while intoxicated, administered
to one of his patients morphine instead of quinine, thereby
causing immediate death.

I know that it is hard to get out of the old beaten path ;
the French *habitans* cling to their one-horse winter vehi-
cles with the shafts straight before them, thereby causing
their winter locomotion to be almost twice as laborious
as it might be if they would only take a common sense
view of things and make the double track ; so with some
of our medical men, they as tenaciously and persistently
cling to the old system.   However, as in the political
world we have some leaders, men who are prepared to
keep pace with the age ; so in the medical profession we
have noble heroes, who come out boldly and act from a
high sense of duty.   Out of the long list of worthies I
might name Dr. Bailey, Dr. Mudge, and Dr. Monroe, who
for years have practised on the non-alcoholic principle.
Even the *Lancet* has lately declared : " Whereas the question used to be between much alcohol and little ; the question now is, between a very little and none at all."   And
Professor Gairdner, M.D., of Glasgow, at a meeting of the
British Medical Association (see that Journal, 22nd June,

1868), advocated the administration of stimulants on a much lower scale than Dr. Todd and others.

One of our most eminent medical men told me some weeks since, that he was convinced that during the past he had been administering alcoholic stimulants too freely, and while he would not promise to discard alcohol entirely from his practice in future, yet he would promise in future to be very careful in administering the same ; for he was satisfied that for one case where they had proved beneficial, he knew of two where they had been injurious, and several where the results were doubtful.

Dr. Nicholls, of the Longworth Union (Ireland), has not admitted one drop of wine or spirits inside the institution for over eighteen years, and the statistics of the Longworth Union have been compared with other institutions where drink has been administered, and the balance is in favour of the non-alcoholic treatment.

It is gratifying to know that a great change for the better has taken place, during the past few years, in reference to alcoholic medication. Numbers of most eminent medical practitioners, both in Europe and America, do not resort to alcoholic stimulants ; they have found other remedies less dangerous and equally efficacious, and . wisely shun a practice which has proved so fatal.

Science has demonstrated that alcohol is not serviceable either as a nourisher, a repairer of waste, or a sustainer of animal heat. Liebig's theory, that alcohol is oxydized in the human system, has been shown to be baseless. Alcohol, when taken into the body, is eliminated by the various excreting organs—the skin, liver, lungs and kidneys—passing out unchanged as it went in, and can be extracted from the brain, liver, blood, &c. This is true, whether these drinks are taken "moderately" or " in excess."

Dr. Lees, at the great Permissive Bill meeting held in the Rotunda, Dublin, on the 28th April, 1865, the Right Hon. the Lord Mayor in the chair, challenged all the doctors in Dublin " to prove that a single drop of alcohol was ever yet assimilated with the human system. Alcohol was eliminated from the system, not assimilated with it. It came away by the breath, by the pores of the skin, and by the other excretions of the body, just as it entered the system. Bread did not do this, nor a mutton chop, nor a beefsteak. As well might they say that the cinders which fell through from the engine carried them from Dublin to Killarney, as to say that alcohol helped them to work or gave strength to the body."

Professors Todd and Bowman, in their great and standard work, " The Physiological Anatomy of Man," remark, " Were these drinks not rapidly absorbed from the stomach, it would be utterly impossible that digestion could go on in those who use them."

Whisky is not good for the body, unless it be a dead body. It is admirable for preserving enlarged livers and rotten bones. If you want to keep a dead man, do as the sailors did with their admiral, when they placed his body in the puncheon of rum—give him plenty of spirits. If you want to kill a living man, give him spirits too.

Professor Miller says :—" Suppose a medical man to order opium, to relieve pain or procure sleep, in needful and urgent circumstances, and that he neglects either to regulate the dose or to order its discontinuance when the necessity for its use has ceased. The convalescent, improperly left to himself, finds, first, that he must increase the dose to attain the ordinary effect; and secondly, that after a time he can ill do without it. Ere ever he is aware, he becomes an opium-eater—the victim of an infirmity most difficult of cure. And so with alcohol. Left without due control, the dose is increased, and the habit becomes confirmed ; the system refuses to part willingly with its use, and the man, besides being brought into a morbid state of bodily frame, is in extreme moral danger of intemperance."

The most recent teachings of science upon the subject are thus summed up by Professor Miller, of Edinburgh :— " Chemistry and physiology have demonstrated undeniably, that alcohol can be of no manner of use to man in the way of nutrition or food. It is quite indigestible. The stomach, bowels, and other organs can make nothing of it. For the gastric juice, even in its most concentrated and active state, it does not care one straw. As it went into the man, so, at its leisure, it goes out; unchanged and unchangeable. Why, then, will he spend his money for that which is not bread ? Why, instead of food, will he swallow a stone ? Poultry, no doubt, gobble up pebbles, under the guidance of a wise instinct; for they have a muscular organ in their crop, which makes good use of such things, in grinding the corn and seeds. But to every animal that happens to have no gizzard, surely the internal presence of such millstones must prove a burthen

P

rather than a benefit. Alcohol, like a stone, indigestible, is, like a stone, too, a grinder ; not of the man's food—for it in no way helps, but rather impedes digestion—but of the man himself. Another science—pathology—tells us that by reason of its tarrying for a time in certain organs, —preferentially the brain, the liver, the kidneys—it produces disease there ; while, acting not so intensely, though no less surely, on the general frame, it hastens the progress of tear and wear in that, and 'does the work of time.' The alcoholic man lives ' fast,' in all the senses of the term.   *   *   In fact, no intelligent person can fully' investigate the present aspect of the Total Abstinence controversy .without perceiving that drink and not drunkenness is the giant evil with which temperance reformers are called upon to contend.   Drunkenness is only one of the evils floating on the surface of this dead sea of drinking, the kindred ills that roll beside it, in the shape of poverty, disease, immorality, and crime, being almost infinite in number and extent."

Combe, in his work, "The Constitution of Man," states: "It will be remembered that in 1847 fever prevailed to an alarming extent in Ireland ; the consequence of des-·titution.   And.through the immigration of the Irish people, the fever was brought across the water, and it spread in.Liverpool, Glasgow, and other seaport towns.   In Glasgow, as a precaution for the poor, a number of rules, upon diet and cleanliness, were drawn up, printed and circulated.   The last rule runs as follows :—'Take a very serious thought on the subject of whisky—the grand source of poverty, want and disease—the grand destroyer of health, of morals, of character, of home, of comfort, and peace. Ask yourself this question :—Is the enjoyment of the dram or the tumbler a good bargain for the loss of all these ? ' Sensible men are taking this thought. Many a young man is resolving to have done with drinking, and enjoy life *really*, which no man does who drinks. He lives a wretched life; and mark this, he must ever continue poor. No drinker ever *rises* above the lowest poverty. Mark this, too—typhus fever finds out the drunkard and fastens on him."

How long shall we have to wait before politicians and men of God will see the policy of locking the stable-door before the horse is stolen, and not after ?

Dr. —— informed me that, during the emigrant fever in Toronto in 1847, liquors were furnished by the city in great abundance and were freely used, and he believed that nineteen-twentieths of the deaths that took place were caused by drink.

Some, I fear, forget that alcohol is a chemical, not a vital substance.

I know a lady who resides at Burford, who during the past twenty years has visited thirty-four death-bed scenes, and dressed two hundred and thirty-three persons in their grave-clothes, and some of them went "drunk into eternity."

Surely Bacchus has drowned more than Neptune, and the most voluptuous of all assassins is the bottle.

The doctor recommended A. to drink for his health's sake. He became addicted to it, neglected his business, impaired his constitution, lost religion, and at length ran away.   His poor wife suffered ·much.   The church of which he was a leading member has been disgraced, and all (I believe) the result of the doctor ordering him to drink medicinally.   For years they continue to take this prescription; not so with castor oil and other offensive medicines.

But all the blame must not be placed upon the doctors. Some patients are fond of stimulants—how much the faculty are at fault in creating that desire I cannot say—but it is to be feared that many in the present day affect to take a little wine "for their stomach's sake," when, if the truth was told, they take it more for their palate's sake than for the sake of their stomach.

I have a strong suspicion that the shrewd but eccentric Abernethy was not far wrong in his judgment. A patient presented himself before the gruff doctor on one occasion, and was met in the usual style in which the doctor met his patients, " Well, sir, what's the matter with you?" "Indigestion, sir."   " Put out your tongue, sir; do you take ale or porter?"   "Yes, sir; a glass with my dinner and a glass with my supper." " H'm! Do you take wine?" " Very little, sir, very little indeed; a glass now and then." " Why do you take it?"   " Oh, doctor, I take it because it does me good." "You lie, sir, you lie—*you take it because you like it!*"

MEDICAL DECLARATION ON THE USE OF INTOXICATING LIQUORS.

The following has been signed by upwards of 2,000

medical men, including many of the leading members of
the profession :—

"WE ARE OF OPINION :—1st. That a very large portion of human misery, including poverty, disease and
crime, is induced by the use of alcoholic or fermented
liquors as beverages.

" 2nd. That the most perfect health is compatible with
total abstinence from all such intoxicating beverages,
whether in the form of ardent spirits or as wine, beer, ale,
porter, cider, etc., etc.

" 3rd. That persons accustomed to such drinks may with
perfect safety discontinue them entirely, either at once, or
gradually after a short time.

" 4th. That total and universal abstinence from alcoholic
liquors, and intoxicating beverages of all sorts, would
greatly contribute to the health, the prosperity, the morality, and the happiness of the human race."

AN APPEAL.

I cannot close this lecture without making an appeal to
the Christian public. As I have before stated, I do not
consider that there is sufficient moral power outside the
Church to grapple with Intemperance ; while at the same
time I am fully satisfied that if Christian men of every
name would unite against this giant evil, it would speedily
be overcome.

Think of the injury that drink is causing. It maddens
the brain, poisons the body, debases the mind and ruins
the soul.

The truth is, the world is groaning and hearts are breaking on account of this traffic. O, could we hear the wailings of the departed drunkards, and see the eternal misery which this vice has entailed upon them, or could we listen to the lamentations which are now ascending, and count the tears which are now being shed, by intemperance, we would be glad to wash our hands clean of this awful traffic.

Two little boys returning from school stopped at a monument which had been raised to the memory of a mighty warrior. On the summit of it was placed a statue of the hero. One of the little fellows put his hand into his pocket and took his pencil and wrote upon the monument, "Could I concentrate around this spot all the blood that thou hast spilt in the gratification of thy ambition, thou couldst drink of the same without bowing thy head." And could we erect a monument to the god Bacchus, the top of which would reach to yonder cloud, and could we gather around it all the misery, wretchedness, crime, disease, tears, groans, ruin and death that have been caused by this parent evil, we could also say, "Thou couldst drink of the same without bowing thy head."

Dr. Lyman Beecher has remarked: "It is an immortal being who sins and suffers, and as his earthly house dissolves, he is approaching the judgment seat in anticipation of a miserable eternity. He feels his captivity, and in anguish of spirit clanks his chains and cries for help. Conscience thunders, remorse goads, and as the gulf opens before him he recoils and trembles, and weeps, and prays, and resolves, and promises, and reforms, and seeks it yet again. Wretched man!

he has placed himself in the hands of a giant who never pities and never releases his iron grasp. He may struggle, but he is in chains; he may cry for release, but it comes not, and lost, lost, may be inscribed upon the door-posts of his dwelling. And now the vortex roars, and the struggling victim buffets the fiery wave with feebler stroke and warning supplication, until despair flashes upon his soul, and with an outcry that pierces the heavens, he ceases to strive and disappears."

Lord Byron said, "Oh! God, it is a fearful thing to see the human soul take wing in any shape, in any mood." But, oh! my friends, think of the death of the poor inebriate.

Philip, Emperor of Macedon, had a servant to knock at his bed-chamber every morning and repeat those words: "Philip, remember that thou art mortal." Let this thought animate us to work while it is day, and, seeing death, judgment and eternity are before us, let us put forth all the effort in our power to reclaim the inebriate and bring up the young in paths of sobriety.

ADDENDA.

PROHIBITION.

LEGISLATIVE ACTION.

Report of the Select Committee of the Senate respecting a Prohibitory Liquor Law, presented on the 14th May, 1873.

COMMITTEE ROOM,
14th MAY, 1873.

The Select Committee to whom were referred the Petitions presented to the Senate, praying for the enactment of a Law to prohibit the manufacture and sale of Intoxicating Liquors in the Dominion, have the honour to submit the following as their Report.

The number of Petitions referred to your Committee to this date is 447: of which one is from the Legislative Assembly of the Province of Ontario ; 68 are from Municipal Councils, 3 from Church Courts, and 375 from an aggregate of 36,224 individuals; 25,945 of whom are of the Province of Ontario, and 10,279 of the Province of Quebec.

The individual petitioners are men of all ranks and classes of society, of all professions and trades, and of all shades of Religious and Political opinion ; and many of them occupy high positions in Churches and in Municipalities, in the Medical and Legal Professions, and in the Provincial and Dominion Legislatures: constituting in the aggregate such a large and influential representation of the intelligence and public sentiment of the country as to entitle their testimony and their prayer to the fullest and most favourable consideration of the Senate,—while the fact of so many Municipal Councils and the House of Assembly of Ontario joining in the same prayer, clearly indicates the deep-felt and urgent need of the Legislation petitioned for.

Your Committee do not regard the absence of Petitions from the other Provinces as evidencing any lack of sympathy with—much less any opposition to—the Petitions from Ontario and Quebec; they know from unofficial but thoroughly reliable sources that a Prohibitory Law is desired by large numbers in those Provinces, who will doubtless send in their Petitions at the next session of Parliament.

The united unvarying testimony of all the Petitioners is, that the vice of intemperance is spreading—mainly in consequence of the facilities afforded for the sale of intoxicating liquors. That the traffic in these liquors is the prolific cause of three-fourths of the crime and pauperism in the country. That so long as the traffic is licensed and protected by law, the evils resulting from intemperance cannot be repressed—all the various attempts by stringent License laws having signally failed—and they therefore pray for absolute prohibition of the manufacture and sale of intoxicating liquors as beverages.

Their testimony is fully sustained by the evidence already collected, and presented to the House of Commons now in Session, by a Committee of that Honourable House in their second report, where they state that, they find four-fifths of the crime in Ontario, and the same proportion of commitments to gaol in Ontario and Quebec, are directly or indirectly traceable to the traffic in and use of these liquors.

Your Committee are fully convinced that the traffic in intoxicating liquors, in addition to the evils already mentioned, is detrimental to all the true interests of the Dominion, mercilessly slaying every year hundreds of her most promising citizens; plunging thousands into misery and want; converting her intelligent and industrious sons, who should be her glory and her strength, into feeble inebriates, her burden and her shame; wasting millions of her wealth in the consumption of an article whose use not only imparts no strength, but induces disease and insanity, suicide and murder, thus diverting into a hurtful channel the capital that should be employed in developing her resources, establishing her manufactures, and expanding her commerce; in short, it is a cancer in the body politic, which, if not speedily eradicated, will mar the bright prospects and blight the patriotic hope of this noble Dominion.

Your Committee are not unmindful of the serious *apparent* diminution of revenue which would temporarily result from the suppression of the manufacture and sale of these destructive liquors. That it would be much less in reality than appearance is perfectly clear, for a very large amount of the expenditure for criminal jurisdiction, and maintenance of gaols, penitentiaries, and asylums would be saved immediately, and should be deducted from the apparent loss ; but even were it otherwise, your Committee would regard it as directly contrary to the spirit and fundamental principles of our truly British code of laws to allow any consideration of loss of revenue to hinder the removal of this great national evil, or to accept any amount of revenue as an equivalent for legalizing a traffic so pernicious in its inevitable effects . upon the community. They are, moreover, firmly of opinion that, instead of impoverishing the revenue, the effect of a Prohibitory Liquor Law, faithfully enforced, would be largely and permanently to increase it, saving the fifty millions of dollars now expended annually in the Dominion for these liquors, and converting that immense sum, now lost, into a capital yielding large returns from its being employed in trade and manufactures.

Your Committee regard it as the first and highest duty of Parliament to legislate for the peace, happiness, and material prosperity of the people, and consequently for the removal and prevention of evils such as are proved to be now injuring and threatening the country through the common use of intoxicating liquors ; and concurring in the opinion of the Legislative Assembly of Ontario, as expressed in their Petition, "that a Prohibitory Liquor "Law, such as prayed for by the petitioners, would be "most beneficial in its results" to the Dominion, would respectfully recommend that the prayer of the petitioners be favourably entertained ; and inasmuch as at this late period of the session it would be impracticable to carry through a well-considered, comprehensive Prohibitory Law, that the Senate, at the commencement of the next session of Parliament, do appoint, with the concurrent action of the House of Commons, a joint committee of both Houses upon the subject, to consider what steps should then be recommended to Parliament in connection therewith.

All which is respectfully submitted.

> ALEXANDER VIDAL, *Chairman.*
> D. CHRISTIE.
> BILLA FLINT.
> J. O. BUREAU.
> J. FERRIER.
> L. LACOSTE.
> M. A. GIRARD.
> JAMES R. BENSON.
> A. R. McCLELAN.

Ottawa, 14th May, 1873.

Report of the Select Committee of the House of Commons, presented 9th May, 1873.

The following is the report of Mr. Bodwell's Prohibitory Liquor Law Committee, presented to the House to-day :—

" Your Committee, to whom were referred the petitions presented in favour of a Prohibitory Liquor Law, beg leave in presenting their second report to call the attention of your honourable House to the following considerations, the result of their most careful deliberations, and based upon the facts to which they have had access so far :—

" 1. That the traffic in intoxicating liquors is an unmitigated evil, widespread in its effects, reaching with more or less virulence every class of the community, destroying and blighting with its baneful influence the existence of many of the most useful and promising members of society, producing untold domestic misery and destitution, and leading to the formation of habits alike opposed to the moral and intellectual advancement and prosperity of the country.

" 2. That the petitions presented, 384 in number, to your honourable House, and signed by 39,223 individuals, as well as the petitions from 82 municipalities and the Legislature of the Province of Ontario, praying for a Prohibitory Liquor Law, show that the people of the Dominion are very strongly impressed with the enormity of the evils alluded to, and that, in view of this strong and unequivocal demand, your Committee feel bound to urge the necessity of some action on the part of your honourable House to meet the wishes of the petitioners, and if possible remove the evils complained of.

" 3. That in examining the answers received from the Sheriffs, Prison Inspectors, Coroners, and Police Magistrates, one hundred and fourteen of whom have voluntarily given evidence, your Committee find that four-fifths of the crime committed in the Province of Ontario (answers have not yet been received from the other Provinces) is directly or indirectly connected with the manufacture, sale and consumption of intoxicating liquors.

"4. Your Committee further find, on examining the reports of the Prison Inspectors for the Provinces of Ontario and Quebec, that out of 28,289 commitments to the gaols for the three previous years, 21,236 were committed either for drunkenness or for crimes perpetrated under the influence of drink, thus corroborating the statements of the magistrates and others above alluded to.

"5. Your Committee find also, from the reports of one hundred and fifty-three medical men, as well as from statements made by medical practitioners in the United States and Great Britain, that the use of intoxicating liquors as beverage is not essential to the health or wellbeing of the community, but, on the contrary, it often leads to disease and premature death.

"6. Your Committee have also to report that they have made, as far as time would permit, enquiry into the operation and effect of the Prohibitory Liquor Law in the State of Maine, accepting its operations there as the fairest test of its success, and find that although there are violations of the law, in many cases flagrant and glaring, yet from the evidence received your Committee is convinced that a Prohibitory Liquor Law would mitigate, if not entirely remove, the evils complained of.

"7. In considering the immediate effect which the passage of a Prohibitory Liquor Law would have upon the revenue of the country, your Committee are bound to admit that for some time at least there might be a falling off; yet in the face of the evils arising from the liquor traffic alluded to in the first paragraph of this report, they cannot recommend any other course to your honourable

House than a ready compliance with the prayers of the petitioners. The reasons on which your Committee base this recommendation are the following :—Although the revenue arising from the traffic is now very large, amounting last year to $5,034,543.58, yet the expense of the administration of justice, the maintenance of asylums, hospitals and penitentiaries, consequent upon the habitual use of intoxicating liquors, would be largely diminished, thus furnishing a very considerable offset to the amount lost to the revenue ; that the capital now invested in the traffic, large as your Committee believe it to be, would, if diverted to other purposes of trade, add largely in a very short time to the general wealth of the country, and open up new and even more profitable sources of industry, which, in their turn, would contribute to the revenue without those baneful associations which vitiate the returns accrued from the liquor traffic ; that the effect upon the industrial prosperity of thousands who are now impoverished by their dissipated habits, would be such as to enable them to consume other dutiable goods, the law of supply and demand being such that wherever there is a surplus for capital it will find for itself some field of investment; that it is clearly the duty of the Government, when the social, moral and civil standing of the subjects are imperilled by the existence of any traffic or trade, that, apart from all considerations of the gain or profit, the interests of the subject should not be sacrificed even to the expansion or maintenance of the revenue; that the principle of protection to the subject against evils which may be and which are sources of revenue is already

conceded in Acts passed on former occasions in the Legislature of Canada, such as the Dunkin Act, sanitary laws,
and other laws of a similar nature.

"8. In view of these facts, your Committee would most
respectfully submit to your honourable House the importance of speedily removing the evil complained of, by the
enactment of a Prohibitory Liquor Law; that is, a law
prohibiting the importation, manufacture, and sale of all
intoxicating liquors, except for medicinal and mechanical
purposes, regulated by proper safeguards and checks."

E. V. BODWELL,
Chairman.

Ottawa, 9th May, 1873.

SUCCESS OF PROHIBITION IN MAINE.

Testimonies as to the workings and results of the Maine
Law, procured by Hon. Neal Dow from the Governor of
the State, Senators and Representatives in Congress,
Mayors, ex-Mayors, Judges, Ministers, Sheriffs, Internal
Revenue Officers and others :—

(From His Excellency Sidney Perham, Governor of
Maine.)

EXECUTIVE DEPARTMENT, AUGUSTA,
MAINE, June 3, 1872.

DEAR SIR,—In answer to your enquiry in regard to the
effect of the Maine Law upon the liquor trade in this
State,—probably one-tenth, in some places, is sold secretly
in violation of the law, as many other offences; but in
large districts of the State, the traffic is nearly or quite

unknown, where formerly it was carried on like any other trade.

Very respectfully yours,

SIDNEY PERHAM,
Governor of Maine.

To General Neal Dow.

(From the Senators and Representatives of Maine.)

FORTY-SECOND CONGRESS, U. S. HOUSE OF REPRESENTATIVES, Washington, D.C., May 29th, 1872.

MY DEAR SIR,—Your favour of the 26th instant, containing an enquiry, is before me; and in reply, while I am unable to state any exact percentage of decrease in the business, I can and do, from my own personal observation, unhesitatingly affirm that the consumption of intoxicating liquors in Maine is not to-day one-fourth as great as it was twenty years ago; that, in the country portions of the State, the sale and use have almost entirely ceased; that the law under a vigorous enforcement has created a temperance sentiment which is marvellous.

WM. P. FRYE, M.C. of Maine,
and ex-Attorney-General of same State.

The Hon. Neal Dow.

[Concurred in by Senators Lot M. Morrill and H. Hamlin; also by Members of Congress J. G. Blaine, John Lynch, John A. Peters, and Eugene Hale.]

Q

(From a Mayor, ex-Mayors, &c., Portland, Maine.)
PORTLAND, May 28, 1872.

As to the diminution of the liquor traffic in the State of Maine, and particularly in this city, as the result of the adoption of the policy of prohibition, many persons with the best means of judging believe that the liquor trade is not now one-tenth as large as it was formerly. We do not know but such an opinion is correct, but content ourselves with saying that the diminution of the trade is very great, and the favourable effects of the policy of prohibition are manifest to the most casual observer.

BENJ. KINGSBURY, Jr.,
Mayor.

[Concurred in by four ex-Mayors.]

(From County and City Officers and a Judge.)
PORTLAND, May 28, 1872.

We are of the decided opinion that the liquor trade is not one-tenth of what it was prior to the adoption of the Maine Law.

EBEN LEACH,
Registrar, Cumberland County, and others.

(Pastors of various Churches in Portland.)
PORTLAND, May 31, 1872.

As to the effect of the Maine Law upon the traffic in strong drinks in this city, the quantity sold now is but a small fraction of what we remember the sales to have been. If the trade exists at all here, it is carried on with secrecy and caution, as other unlawful practices are. All our people must agree that the benefits of this state of things are obvious and very great.

[Signed by 12 Pastors of Churches in Portland.]

(*From a Democratic Mayor.*)

PORTLAND, MAINE, May 29, 1872.

MY DEAR SIR,—I have had good opportunities of observing the condition of the State compared with other States where there are no prohibitory laws, and I am certain that the rural portions of Maine are, and have been, in an infinitely better condition with reference to the sale and use of such liquors than similar portions of other States referred to ; and are, and have been, comparatively free from both the sale and use, and this must fairly be considered the result of prohibitory legislation. At the present time the law is probably enforced in large towns and cities as thoroughly, at least, as any other penal statute.

WM. S. PUTNAM.

[Mr. Putnam was Democratic Mayor four years ago. His party has always opposed prohibition. Hence the special value of his testimony.]

(*From the Mayor of Bangor.*)

MAYOR'S OFFICE, CITY OF BANGOR, ME., May 30, 1872.

The law is being enforced throughout the State as never before, and with wonderful success. It is safe to say that in our city not one-tenth part as much is sold now as in years past, when the law was not enforced.

J. S. WHEELWRIGHT,

Mayor.

[Concurred in by Aldermen, City Officers and others.]

(The Supervisor of Internal Revenue District, Maine.)

DOVER, N.H., May 31, 1872.

In the course of my duty I have become thoroughly acquainted with the state and extent of the liquor traffic in Maine, and I have no hesitation in saying that the beer trade is not more than one per cent. of what I remember it to have been, and the trade in distilled liquors is not more than 10 per cent. of what it was formerly. Where liquor is sold at all it is done secretly, through fear of the law.

Yours truly,

WOLCOTT HAMLIN,

Supervisor of In. Rev. Dist. of Maine, N. H. and Vt.

To Gen. Neal Dow.

(From Col. Elliott.)

BRUNSWICK, MAINE, June 3, 1872.

The Maine Law is not a failure, but, on the contrary, almost a complete success. We are doing finely here. Scarce the least evidence of strong drink in town.

DANIEL ELLIOTT.

[Brunswick is a manufacturing town with a great water

power—the seat of Bowdoin College—a railway centre— a most flourishing and beautiful place. N. D.]

(From Gen. Chamberlaine, ex-Governor of Maine.)

BRUNSWICK, MAINE, May 30, 1872.

The declaration made by many persons that the Maine Law is inoperative, and that liquor is sold freely and in large quantities in this State, is not true. The liquor traffic has been greatly repressed and diminished here and throughout the State, and in many places has been entirely swept away. The law is as well executed generally in the State as other criminal laws. We say without reserve that if liquors are sold at all, it is in very small quantities compared with the old times, and in a secret way, as other unlawful things are done.

JOSHUA L. CHAMBERLAINE.

GEO. C. CRAWFORD, *Postmaster.*

[General Chamberlaine was Governor of the State for four years preceding the term of the present Governor. He is now President of Bowdoin College.]

(Convention of Pastors of Free Baptist Churches in Maine.)

PORTLAND, May 31st, 1872.

To whom it may concern.—It is often said by persons —unfriendly to the temperance cause, and to the policy of prohibition of the liquor traffic—that the Maine Law has failed to accomplish its purpose. Now we, the undersigned, pastors of Free Baptist Churches in various parts of Maine, assembled at a denominational convention in Portland, state that the liquor traffic is very greatly diminished under- the repressive power of the Maine Law. It cannot be one tithe of what it was formerly, and if it is carried on it is with secrecy and caution, as other unlawful practices are. The grog-shops are put by the law in the same category with gambling-houses and brothels, and prohibited as at war with the interests of the State and people.

Approved by vote of Conference. (Signed also unanimously.)

(Convention of Good Templars, Maine.)

CAPE ELIZABETH, May 29, 1872.

It was unanimously resolved,—That the Chairman certify, in the name of the Convention: That by the operation of the Maine Law in this State, the happy effects of this change are everywhere apparent. That in this town, where formerly the people were great sufferers from strong drinks, and generally throughout the State where the traffic yet lingers, it is covertly, as other offences against the law are, and that the quantity of liquors now sold in this State cannot be one-tenth as much as it was formerly.

Signed on behalf of the Convention,

DANIEL R. DRESSER,

Chairman.

[This convention was held in the Wesleyan Church, which was packed full, and many were standing for want of seats.]

(From the Rector St. Stephen's Protestant Episcopal Church.)

PORTLAND, MAINE, June 4, 1872.

MY DEAR GENERAL,—To make this law a still greater blessing, all that is needed is to enforce it as faithfully in the future as at the present time.

Truly yours,

A. DALTON.

Hon. Neal Dow.

(Hon. E. G. Harlow, Maine.)

DIXFIELD, OXFORD COUNTY, MAINE,
June 4th, 1872.

I have been travelling over the State considerably this spring. I am now thoroughly acquainted with my own county (Oxford), and do not hesitate to say there is not now a gallon of liquor sold where there was a barrel before the Maine Law of 1851. At our last term of Supreme Judicial Court, in March, not a single indictment for any crime was found. Our (county) jail is empty; our workhouse greatly reduced ; and the improvement wonderful.

Truly your friend,

E. G. HARLOW,
Member of Executive Council in Maine.

(From the Secretary of State, Maine.)

AUGUSTA, June, 1872.

As to the present extent of the liquor traffic in Maine, as compared with its condition in former times, there can-

not be any difference of opinion among intelligent citizens
of the State to the fact that the traffic is greatly less than
we remember it to have been.   If we were to say that the
quantity of liquors sold here is not one-tenth so large as
it was, it would not be above the truth, and the favourable effects of the change upon all the interests of the
State are plainly seen everywhere.

O. G. STACY,

Secretary of State, and other State Officers.

(*City Marshal, ex-Mayors, &c.*)

SACO, MAINE, June 10, 1872.

As to whether there has been or not a diminution of
the liquor trade under the operation of the Maine Law,
we reply, that the decrease of that traffic has been great.
In many parts of the State it has been entirely suppressed ;
and so far as we know and believe, it does not exist any-
where in the State, except covertly, as a thing under the
ban of the law.   •

OBADIAH DURGIN,

Marshal, and other City Officers.

(*From the Overseers of the Poor of Portland.*)

OFFICE OF THE OVERSEERS OF THE POOR,
PORTLAND, June 4, 1872.

If liquor shops exist in this city at all, it is with secrecy
and great caution.   The favourable effect is very evident,
particularly in the department of pauperism and crime.
While the population of the city increases, pauperism and

crime diminish, and in the department of police the number of arrests and commitments are very much less than formerly.

JOHN BRADFORD,

Chairman, and the rest of the Board.

To General Neal Dow.

PROHIBITION OF THE LIQUOR TRAFFIC.

THE one question above all others which should engage the attention of Legislators is the Prohibition of the Liquor Traffic.

If the people's representatives would enquire, " What legislation would most benefit the commonwealth, and elevate the public, socially, morally and politically?" there can be little doubt as to the answer.

The misfortune, however, is that, in many instances, conscience is not allowed to decide a matter of this kind, but self-interest; and because the liquor influence is powerful, the traffic is winked at.

It requires no small amount of moral heroism to attempt to break down the drinking usages which have been transmitted to us by our fathers, and to assail a traffic which is fostered by the State ; but, in view of the sad havoc which drink has caused, it is high time that all those who wish our country well would take a decided stand in endeavouring to suppress the monster evil of the times.

It is preposterous to throw the sanction of law around a traffic that the physician, the chemist and the physiologist have declared to be injurious. The committee appointed by the Legislature of this Province, during the session of 1853, consisting of a portion of the most enlightened members composing that House, declared in their report, as the result of a careful and thorough investigation of the whole question, that,—although impossible "to present a full estimate of the effects of the use of intoxicating drinks upon the peace, happiness, health, morality and prosperity of the people of this Province," —from police reports, coroners' reports, the reports of the British House of Commons on this very subject, and a variety of other testimony of the most incontrovertible character, "three-fourths of the misery, pauperism and crime in this Province have their origin in the use of intoxicating liquors!" And further, that "alcohol is not, as a beverage, needful for, or conducive to, the enjoyment of health, nor for the greatest ability for bodily or mental effort and length of life."

"It is to the human constitution a poison, the use of which, as a beverage, is *always* hurtful."

"It produces many and aggravates most of the diseases to which the human frame is liable."

"It tends to render diseases hereditary, and thus to deteriorate the human race."

"It weakens the understanding, stupifies the conscience and hardens the heart."

"It is the frequent cause of insanity, and produces predisposition to that disease in the offspring of those who use it."

"It occasions annually the loss of an immense amount

of property ; and is the fruitful source of domestic misery, pauperism and crime in the community."

"It powerfully *counteracts* the efficacy of *all* means for the intellectual elevation, the moral purity, the personal benefit and the public usefulness of every part of society." "It endangers the purity and permanence of our free institutions, by its corrupting and debasing influence on the public morals and mind." "It alarmingly shortens human life, induces men and women to disown God and ruin themselves," and as an incontrovertible consequence, "for men to use intoxicating drinks as a beverage, to make or to furnish it to be used by others, is morally wrong, and ought universally to be discontinued." And notwithstanding the success which has attended the efforts of temperance organizations, "in appealing to the reason, the conscience and self-interest of men, proving by incontestible evidence the injury that has resulted to individuals and the community at large, your committee are of opinion that such philosophic efforts cannot be completely successful while the Legislature *countenances, encourages, protects* and *legalizes* the pernicious traffic in alcoholic drinks. The Legislature HAS NOT taken a neutral position in this matter; its aid has been extended, and its power used as a *shield to this evil*, by which so many thousands of the people of this Province have been destroyed. The law *authorizes* the mischief, and the Government derives revenue as an *equivalent* for the legal sanction which extends to the traffic,"—*every shilling of which is wet with the tears of disconsolate female wretchedness, and stained with the life's blood of our countrymen.* " Thus the civil power of Canada, instead of serving the purpose for which it was instituted, becomes the *abettor of crime* and misery."

It may not be out of place to look at the reaction which follows licensing wrong-doing. Has it not culminated in a proverb, " Drunken Rulers?" Members of Parliament have admitted to the writer, that by endeavouring to secure the influence of the liquor sellers to assist them in their elections, their moral power became weakened, and the result was they fell an easy prey to the drink devil.

Is it not a lamentable truth, that to enter the field of politics is almost equivalent to becoming a drunkard ? Some have been so disgusted with parliamentary life that they have retired into private life; so that, in many instances, the most undesirable men are retained in office through the power of liquor and other corrupt practices.

That this sad state of things is so, the following paragraphs will testify :—

(*From the Belleville Intelligencer, Conservative.*)

" But let us go directly to the heart of the nation. We will leave mere political sin out of the question, and examine one of the roots that is the prolific parent of political sin as well as of all other sins. What do we find ? The most gifted intelligence of the nation staggering to their seats in the Legislature in the open light of day, and in the presence of the assembled wisdom of Canada—staggering from the Parliamentary saloon—

staggering from rooms where alcoholic liquors flow as freely as does the Ottawa over the Falls of the Chaudiere. Not only the talented, but the ignorant made still more debased—the sensual still more sensual—the tippler confirmed in his habit by the example given in high places. We know what vices the use of these stimulants lead to. Can we wonder, then, when we witness such scenes, if outraged justice avenge itself? Could we complain, while we wink at and justify such iniquities, if Heaven's judgments were visited upon us in their most terrible form? Can we reasonably expect, while we tolerate such outrages on our common decency, such flagrant violations of God's law, to escape the wrath of the Avengers' band?"

(From the County of Perth Herald.)

"On many occasions, during the late session, the House presented more the appearance of a drunken brothel than the Legislative Halls of a free and enlightened people. Ministers of the Crown often came to their desks in a state of beastly drunkenness, and acted more the part of drunken sots or buffoons than confidential advisers of Her Majesty's representative. And, to their shame be it said, the drunken antics of these besotted Ministers elicited applause. Has drunkenness, then, become a virtue, that men should glory in it? Can a country prosper while such a class of men have the management of its affairs? Can the approving smile of Heaven rest upon such conduct? and can we, dare we look for national blessings? What! is that man fit to be the ruler of a free, enlightened and Christian people, who is so lost to all sense of shame and decency as to make his appearance in the House fresh from the harlot's embrace, exhaling the pestiferous breath of the drunkard, and reeling from side to side as he staggers towards his seat ? Surely not. Surely it has not come to this with us. Surely the indignation of the people will at last burn as a devouring fire, and hurl such 'rulers from their present place. During the time of the Fenian raid, when as one man the youth and chivalry of the land sprung to arms in defence of their country and their flag, that man in whose hands, it may be said, these young men for the time had placed their lives, was lying *drunk*—yes, *drunk*—let the proper word be used—so drunk as to be incapable of performing any official act ; and there are more in the Cabinet like him. Merciful God ! are these the men we have to depend upon when a powerful and unscrupulous enemy threatens our very existence ? Are these the men who are entrusted with the management of our affairs ? Yes, these are the men, and they, by special bill, retain themselves in office. How long will the people keep silent ?"

THE TEMPERANCE ENTERPRISE.

"But I don't like this total abstinence." Now, all past experience proves that nothing less is an effectual remedy for the evils under which society groans. You may stop, but you cannot tame the drinking usages of society. I know there are some strange remedies resorted to in order to effect certain cures. A man was afflicted with a hypochondriac wife. Ofttimes, as the clock struck twelve, she would give him a knock with her elbow, and cry, "William, William, I'm going to dee." William bore long and patiently, but he was a poor working man, and had to toil hard all day to provide for his small family, and much required rest. At last his patience was exhausted; he thought and prayed over what he should do, and at last resolved that the next time she disturbed him he would either kill or cure her. So the good man, determining to put his resolution into practice, retired to rest; and no sooner had the clock struck twelve, than the elbow (or perpetual motion) was at ·work. As she exclaimed, "William, William, I'm going to dee," "Amen," replied the old man; "Amen, glory be to God." At which she burst into a flood of tears, and asked if he really wished her to die. The experiment, however, proved effectual, and William got peace ever after.

Total abstinence, which some despise, is a certain cure for drunkenness, and a safe preventive. Yet, notwithstanding the goodness of our cause, and the terrible evils against which we contend, there are some who won't join us. They very much resemble an obstinate deacon we have heard of, who opposed almost everything that was calculated to benefit the church with which he stood connected. No matter what scheme was advanced, he would oppose it. The minister had done all in his power to get him to work in harmony with his brother deacons; but no! he would oppose, and object, and hinder. At last the minister requested Deacon A. to pray that God would take Deacon B. home to Himself; that they had done all they could to get him to act for the good of religion, without effect, and now to please take him out of the way. "You need not mind," said the refractory deacon, "I won't go." So with some people; they are obstinate, and refuse to connect themselves with our cause. May they be led to see and to do their duty.

> "Act as in the living present,
> Heart within and God o'erhead."

No doubt there will be much to contend against, and considerable to bear in upholding the Temperance enterprise, but let us bear with one another, and work for the right.

A minister observed a marked change in the conduct of a man and his wife in his congregation. Now they were gentle, kind and loving, just as man and wife should be; but a few years before they were cross, surly and snappish. When the wife would speak, the husband would scarely answer; and when the husband broke silence, the wife would almost bite the nose off him, she was so snappish. "May I take the liberty to ask you, Mrs. Grant, how it is that you and Donald are now so pleasant with each other?" "O, minister," quoth the wife, "we hae lived unco happy since we got twa bears in the house." "Twa what?" said the minister, as he looked around, expecting every minute to be eaten alive. "O dinna misunderstand me," said the woman, "the kind o' bears I mean are these, ye ken. I bear and he forbears; and since I began to bear (and wives sometimes have a

good deal to bear off their husbands) wi' him, and he to
forbear wi' me, we hae lived unco contented and happy."
So in this enterprise; you will have much to bear and forbear the one with the other, but let nothing prevent you
from doing your duty. Poor drunkards are dying, their
children are suffering, while language cannot depict; the
misery of the inebriate's wife. Gaze upon that pale, wan
face; see that careworn and wrinkled brow; alas! the hue
of health has left her cheek; her countenance, how sad!
her eyes, once so bright, have lost much of their fire, and
are now suffused in tears. Her hair is prematurely grey;
her step is feeble; her wasted frame is but the index of
the keen anguish that fills her soul and wrings the life-
blood from her heart. That poor besotted wretch yonder,
the cause of all her grief, is her husband; and, with all
his faults, she loves him still. God pity her! She hides
within her breast a world of sorrow which she will not
reveal. God pity her! God help her!

In the evening of the day that Alice D—— arrived at
S——, a great temperance meeting was to be held in one
of the churches. Her friend, who had become enthusi-
astic in the cause, urged her to go to the meeting, which
she did, though with reluctance. The house was
crowded above and below. The preliminaries usually appertaining to such meetings having been ar-
ranged, a brief opening address was made by one of the
ministers. A reformed man then related his experience
with great effect. After he had finished there was a pause
for nearly a minute. At length a man who had been
seated far back, with his face partly turned from the

R

audience, arose slowly, and moved to the front of the stage.

A half suppressed exclamation escaped Alice, as her eye caught the well-known features of him who had once been her husband, while a quick thrill ran through her.

Then her frame trembled in accordance with her trembling heart. The face of Mr. Delaney had greatly changed since she had looked upon it. Its calm, dignified elevation had been restored—but what a difference !

"Mr. President," he began, with a broken voice, "although I had consented, at your solicitation, to address this large assembly to-night, yet I have felt so strong a reluctance to do so that it has been with the greatest difficulty that I dragged myself forward. But I passed my word and could not violate it. As to relating my experience, that I do not think upon. The past I dare not recall. Would to Heaven that ten years of my life were blotted out."

The speaker here paused a moment, although much affected. Then with a firm voice he said :

"But something must be said of my own case, or I shall fail to make that impression on your minds that I wish to produce."

Pictures of real life touch the heart with real power, while absent presentments of truth glitter coldly in the intellectual regions of the mind, and then fade from the perception like figures in a diorama.

"Your speaker once stood among the first members of the bar in a neighbouring State. Nay, more than this, he represented his country in the Assembly of Commonwealth; and more than that still, he occupied a seat in Congress for two congressional periods."

At this period the stillness of death pervaded the crowded assembly.

"And yet more than all this," he continued, his voice sinking into a low, thrilling tone, "he had a tender wife and two sweet children. But all these honours, and all those blessings, have departed from him," he continued, his voice growing deeper and louder in his efforts to control himself. "He was unworthy to retain them. His constituents threw him off because he had debased himself and disgraced them. And worse than all—she who loved him devotedly, she who had borne him two babes, was forced to abandon him and seek an asylum at her father's house.

"And why was I so changed in a few short years? What power was there to abase me so that my fellow-beings spurned me, and even the wife of my bosom turned away heart-sick from me? Alas, my friends, it was sad indulgence in mockery! A very demon, a curse changing us into a beast! But for this I were an honourable and useful representative in Congress, pursuing after my country's good, and blessed in the home circle with my wife and children. But I have not told you all; after my wife left me, I sank rapidly. A state of perfect sobriety brought me to many sober thoughts. I therefore drank more freely, and was rarely, if ever, free from the bewitching effects of intoxication. I remained in the same village several years, but I never once saw her. For two years of the time I abandoned myself to the fearful impulses of the appetite I had acquired. I had not a week of sobriety during that time, nor caught a glimpse of my children. At last I became so abandoned in my habits that my wife, urged on by her friends, filed an application for divorce. And as a cause could easily be shown why it should be granted, separation was legally declared. To complete my disgrace, at the next congressional canvass I was left off the ticket as unfit to represent my district. I left the country and State where I had lived from my boyhood up.

" Then I heard of this movement, the great temperance cause. At first I sneered, then wondered, hesitated, and finally threw myself upon the great wave that was swelling onward, in the hope of being carried by it far out of the reach of danger, and I did not hope with a vain hope. It gave me all, and certainly more than I could have dreamed of. It set me once more upon my feet— once more made a man of me.

" Three years have passed since then. Earnest devotion to my profession, and fervent prayers to Him who alone gives aid to every good resolution, have restored to me much that had been lost ; but not the richest treasure that I proved myself unworthy to retain ; not my wife and children. Ah! between myself and these, the law has laid its stern, impassable interdiction. I have no longer my children, though my heart goes out toward those dearly beloved ones with the tenderest yearnings. Pictures of our early days of wedded love are ever in my imagination. I dream of the sweet fire circle ; I ever see before me the once placid face of my Alice, as her eye

looked into my own with intelligent confidence. I feel
her arm twine around my neck—the music of her voice
is ever sounding in my ear."

Here the speaker's emotion overcame him. His utterance choked him, and he stood with bowed head and
trembling limbs. The dense stillness was broken here and
there by half stifled sobs. At this moment there was a
movement in the crowd. A single female figure, before
whom every one appeared instinctively to give way, was
passing up the aisle. This was not observed by Delaney
until she had come nearly in front of the platform on
which he stood. The movement caught his ear, and lifting his eyes they fell on Alice; for it was she that was
pressing forward. He bent toward her with sudden uplifted hands and eager eyes, and stood like a statue until
she had gained the stand and advanced quietly to his side.
For a moment they thus stood—the whole audience,
thrilled with the scene, were upon their feet and bending
forward. Then Delaney opened his arms and Alice threw
herself upon his bosom with a quick and wild gesture.
Thus for the space of a minute they stood—every one by
a singular intuition understanding the scene. One of
the ministers came forward and separated them.

" No, no," said Delaney, " you must not—you cannot
take her away from me !"

" Heaven forbid that I should do that," replied the minister. " But by your confession she is not your
wife."

" No, she is not," replied Delaney, mournfully.

"But she is now ready to renew her vows again,"

said Alice, smiling through her tears, that now rained over her face.

Before that large assembly, all standing and with few dry eyes, was said, in a broken voice, the marriage ceremony that gave Delaney and Alice to each other. As the minister, an aged man, with thin, white locks, finished the rite, he laid his hands on the two he had joined in holy bonds, and lifting up his aged eyes that streamed with drops of gladness, he said in a solemn voice :

" What God has joined together, let not rum put asunder."

" Amen !" was cried by the whole assembly, as with a single voice.

It was a bitter cold night, on the twenty-fourth of December ; the snow lay deep upon the ground, and the bright moon rode half-way up the heavens. In the high road, a short distance from a quiet village, stood the form of a human being ; his garments were by far insufficient to keep out the biting frost, his frame trembled, and his countenance bore all the fearful marks of horrid intemperance. Before him stood a cottage, elegant in its simple neatness, and as he gazed upon it, the tears rolled down his bloated cheeks as he clasped his hands in agony and exclaimed, " O thou fond home of my happier days ! beneath thy roof I was married to the idol of my soul, and within thy peaceful walls God gave me two blessed children ; under thy sacred roof peace and plenty smiled, and love and joy were mine. Six years have passed since the demon I took to my heart drove me from thy sheltering. O thou fatal cup! No! 'twas I myself who did it

But there is room upon earth for another man, and by God's help I'll be that man."

Within the only apartment of a miserable and almost broken-down hovel, sat a woman and two children, a boy and a girl. The cold wind found its entrance through a hundred crevices, and as its biting gusts swept through the room, the mother and her children crouched nearer to the few embers that still smouldered upon the hearth. The only furniture was four poor stools, a ricketty table, and a scantily-covered bed ; while in one corner, nearest to the fire-place, was a heap of straw and tattered blankets, which served as a resting place for the brother and sister. Part of a tallow candle was burning upon the table, and by its dim light one might have seen that wretched mother's countenance. It was pale and wan, and wet with tears. The faces of her children were both buried in her lap, and they seemed to sleep peacefully under her prayerful guardianship. At length the sound of footsteps upon the snow-crust struck upon the mother's ears, and hastily arousing her children, she hurried them to their lowly bed ; and hardly had they crouched away beneath the thin blankets when the door was opened, and the man whom we have already seen before that pretty cottage, entered the house. With a trembling, fearful look, the wife gazed into her husband's face, and seemed ready to crouch back from his approach, when the mark of a tear-drop upon his cheek caught her eye. Could it be, thought she, that that pearly drop was in truth a tear ? No—perhaps a snow-flake had fallen there and melted. Once or twice Thomas Wilkins seemed upon the point of speaking some word to his wife, but at length he turned slowly away and silently undressed himself, and soon after his weary limbs had touched the bed he was asleep.

Long and earnestly did Mrs. Wilkins gaze upon the features of her husband after he had fallen asleep. There was something strange in his manner—something unaccountable. Surely he had not been drinking; for his countenance had none of that vacant, wild, demoniac look that usually rested there. His features were rather sad and thoughtful than otherwise; and—O, heavens! is it possible?—a smile played about his mouth, and a sound, as if of prayer, issued from his lips while yet he slept.

A faint hope, like the misty vapour of approaching morn, flitted before the heart-broken wife. But she could not grasp it—she had no foundation for it; and with a deep groan she let the phantom pass. She went to her children and drew the clothes more closely about them; then she knelt by their side, and after imprinting on their cheeks a mother's kiss, and uttering a fervent prayer in their behalf, she sought the repose of her pillow.

Long ere the morning dawned Thomas Wilkins arose from his bed, dressed himself, and left the house. His poor wife awoke just as he was going out, and she would have called to him, but she dared not. She would have told him that she had no fuel, no bread—not anything with which to warm and feed the children; but he was gone, and she sank back upon her pillow and wept.

The light of morning came at length, but Mrs. Wilkins had not risen from her bed, nor had her children crawled from out their resting place. A sound of footsteps is heard from without, accompanied by a noise, as though a light sled was being dragged through the snow. The door opened and her husband entered. He laid upon the table a heavy wheaten loaf, a pitcher and a paper bundle, then from his pocket he took another paper parcel, and again he turned towards the door. When next he entered he bore in his arms a load of wood, and three times did he go out and return with a load of the same description. Then he bent over the fire-place, and soon a blazing fire snapped and sparkled on the hearth. As soon as this was accomplished, Thomas Wilkins bent over his children and kissed them ; then he went to the bedside of his wife, and, while some powerful emotion stirred up his soul and made his chest heave, he murmured : " Kiss me, Lizzie." Tightly that wife wound her arms about the neck of her husband, and as though the love of years were centred in that kiss, she pressed it upon his lips.

" There—no more," he uttered, as he gently laid the arm of his wife from his neck ; " these things I have brought are for you and our children," and as he spoke he left the house. Mrs. Wilkins arose from her bed, and tremblingly she examined the articles upon the table. She found the loaf, and in the pitcher she found milk ; one of the papers contained two smaller bundles—one of tea and one of sugar, while in the remaining parcel she found a nice lump of butter. " O," murmured the poor wife and mother, as she gazed upon the food thus spread out before her, " whence came these ? Can it be that Thomas has stolen them ? No, he never did that ! And then that look ! that kiss !—those kind, sweet, sweet words! O, my poor, poor heart, raise not a hope that may only fall and crush thee."

"Mother," at this moment spoke her son, who had raised himself upon his elbow, "is our father gone?" "Yes, Charles." "O, tell me, mother—did he not come and kiss me and little Abby this morning?" "Yes, yes —he did, he did!" cried the mother, as she flew to the side of her boy and wound her arms about him. "And mother," said the child in low, trembling accents, while he turned a tearful look to his parent's face, "will not father be good to us once more?" That mother could not speak; she could only press her children more fondly to her bosom, and weep a mother's tears upon them. Was Lizzie Wilkins happy as she set her children down to that morning's meal? At least a ray of sunshine was struggling to gain entrance to her bosom.

Towards the middle of the afternoon, Mr. Abel Walker, a retired sea-captain of some wealth, sat in his comfortable parlour engaged in reading, when one of his servants informed him that some one at the door wished to see him. "Tell him to come in, then," returned Walker. "But it's that miserable Wilkins, sir." "Never mind," said the captain, after a moment's hesitation, "show him in." "Poor fellow," he continued after the servant had gone, "I wonder what he wants. In truth I pity him." With a trembling step and downcast look Thomas Wilkins entered Captain Walker's parlour. "Ah, Wilkins," said the old captain, "what has brought you here?" The poor man twice attempted to speak, but his heart failed him. "Do you come for charity?" "No, sir," quickly returned Wilkins, while his eyes gleamed with a proud light. "Then sit down and out with it," said Walker, in a blunt but kind tone. "Captain Walker," commenced the poor man, as he took the proffered seat, "I have come to ask if you still own that little cottage behind the hill." "I do." "And is it occupied?" "No." "Is it engaged?" "No," returned the captain, regarding his visitor with uncommon interest; "but why do you ask?" "Captain Walker," said Wilkins, in a firm and manly tone, even though his eye glistened and his lip quivered, "I have been poor and degraded, deeply steeped in the dregs of poverty and disgrace. Everything that made life valuable I have almost lost. My wife and children have suffered—and O! God only knows how keenly. I have long wandered in the path of sin. One after another the tender cords of friendship that used to bind me to the world have snapped asunder; my name has become a by-word, and upon the earth I have been but a foul blot. But, sir, from henceforth I am a man! Up from the depth of its long grave I have dragged forth my heart, and love still has its home therein. I have sworn to touch that fatal cup no more, and in my heart there is no lie! My wife and children shall suffer no more for the sins they never committed. I have seen my old employer at the machine shop, and he has given me a situation, and is even anxious that I should come back; and, sir, he has even been kind enough to give me an order in advance for necessary articles of clothing, food, and furniture. To-morrow morning I commence work."

"And you come to see if you could have your cottage

back again to live in ?" said Captain Walker, as Wilkins
hesitated. "Yes, sir, to see if I could hire it of you,"
returned the poor man. "Wilkins, how much can you
make at your business ?" bluntly asked the old captain,
without seeming to heed the request. "My employer is
going to put me on to job-work, sir; and as soon as I get
my hand in, I can easily make from five-and-forty to fifty
shillings a week." "And how much will it take to support your family ?" "As soon as I get cleared up, I can
manage to get along with twenty shillings a week."
"Then you might be able to save nearly eighty pounds a
year." "I mean to do that, sir." A few moments Captain Walker gazed into the face of his visitor, and then
asked : "Have you pledged yourself yet to abstain from
strong drink ?" "Before God and in my heart I have ;
but one of my errands here was to get you to write me a
pledge, and have it made to my wife and children." Captain Walker sat down to his table and wrote out the temperance pledge, and then in a trembling but bold hand
Thomas Wilkins signed it.

"Wilkins," said the old man, as he took his visitor by
the hand, "I have watched well your countenance and
weighed your words. I know you speak truth. When
I bought that cottage from your creditors six years ago, I
paid them two hundred pounds for it. It has not been
harmed, and is as good as it was then. Most of the time
I have received good rent for it. Now, sir, you shall have
it for just what I paid for it, and each month you shall
pay me such a sum as you can comfortably spare until it is
all paid. I will ask you for no rent, nor for a penny of

interest. You shall have the deed of the estate, and in return I will take but a single note and mortgage, upon which you can have your own time." Thomas Wilkins tried to thank the old man for his kindness, but he only sank back into his chair and wept like a child; and while he yet sat with his face buried in his hands, the old man slipped from the room, and when at length he returned he bore in his hand a neatly covered basket.

" Come, come," the captain exclaimed, " cheer up, my friend; here are some tit-bits for your wife and children— take them home, and believe me, Wilkins, if you feel half as happy in receiving my favour as I do in bestowing it, you are happy indeed." " God will bless you for this, sir," exclaimed the kindness-stricken man. " Stick to your pledge, Wilkins, and I will take care of the rest," said the old captain, as his friend took the basket. " If you have time to-morrow, call on me, and I will arrange the papers." As Thomas Wilkins once more entered the street, his tread was light and easy, a bright light shone in every feature, and as he wended his way homeward he felt in every avenue of his soul that he was once more a man.

The gloomy shades that ushered in the night of the thirty-first of December had fallen over the snow-clad earth. Within the miserable dwelling of Mrs. Wilkins there was more of comfort than we found when we first visited her, but yet nothing had been added to the furniture of the place. For the last six days her husband had come home every evening and gone away before daylight every morning, and during that time he had drunk no intoxicating beverage, for already had his face begun to assume the stamp of its former manhood, and every word that he had spoken had been kind and affectionate. To his children he had brought new shoes and warmer clothing, and to herself he had given such things as she stood in immediate need of; but yet with this he had been taciturn and thoughtful, showing a dislike to all questions, and only speaking such words as were necessary. The poor, devoted, loving wife began to hope; and why should she not? For six years her husband had not been thus before. One week ago she dreaded his approach, but now she found herself waiting for him with all the anxiety of former years. Should all this be broken? Should this new charm be swept away? Eight o'clock came, and so did nine and ten, and yet her husband came not.

"Mother," said little Charles, just as the clock struck ten, and who seemed to have awakened from a dreamy slumber, "isn't this the last night of the old year?" "Yes, my son." "And do you know what I have been dreaming, dear mother? I dreamt that father had bought us New Year's presents, just the same as he used to do. But he won't, will he? He's too poor now!" "No, my dear boy, we shall have no other present than food; and even for that we must thank dear father. There, lay your head in my lap again." The boy laid his curly head once more in his mother's lap, and with tearful eyes she gazed upon his innocent form. The clock struck eleven! The poor wife was yet on her tireless, sleepless watch! But hardly had the sound of the last stroke died away ere the snow crust gave back the sound of a footfall, and in a moment more her husband entered. With a trembling fear she raised her eyes to his face, and a wild thrill of joy weut to her heart as she saw that all there was open and bold,—only those manly features looked more joyous, more proud than ever. "Lizzie," said he, in mild, kind accents, "I am late to-night, but business has detained me, and now I have a favour to ask of thee." "Name it, dear Thomas, and you shall not ask a second time," cried the wife, as she laid her hand confidingly upon her husband's arm. "And you will ask me no questions?" continued Wilkins. "No, I will not." "Then," continued the husband, as he bent over and imprinted a kiss upon his wife's brow, "I want you to dress our children for a walk, and you shall accompany us. The night is calm and tranquil, and the snow is well trodden. Ah! no questions! Remember your promise." Lizzie Wilkins knew not what this all meant, nor did she think or care; for anything that could please her husband she would have done with pleasure, even though it had wrenched her very heart-strings. In a short time the two children were ready; then Mrs. Wilkins put on such articles of dress as she could command, and soon they were in the road. The moon shone bright, the stars peeped down upon the earth, and they seemed to smile upon the travellers from out their twinkling eyes of light. Silently Wilkins led the way, and silently his wife and children followed. Several times the wife gazed up into her husband's countenance, but from the strange expression that rested there she could make out nothing that tended to satisfy her. At length, a slight turn in the road brought them suddenly upon the pretty white cottage where, years before, they had been so happy. They

approached the spot.   The snow in the front yard had
been shovelled away, and a path led up to the piazza.
Wilkins opened the gate—his wife tremblingly followed,
but wherefore she knew not.   Then her husband opened
the door, and in the entry they were met by the smiling
countenance of old Captain Walker, who ushered them
into the parlour, where a warm fire glowed in the grate,
and where everything looked neat and comfortable.   Mrs.
Wilkins turned her gaze upon the old man, and then upon
her husband.   Surely, in that greeting between the poor
man and the rich, there was none of that constraint which
would have been expected.   They met rather as friends
and neighbours.   What could it mean ? Hark! the clock
strikes twelve !   The old year has gone, and a new, a
bright-winged cycle is about to commence its flight over
the earth !   Thomas Wilkins took the hand of his wife
within his own, and then drawing from his bosom a paper,
he placed it in her hand, remarking as he did so : " Lizzie,
this is your husband's present for the New Year!"

Five years have passed since that happy moment.
Thomas Wilkins has cleared his pretty cottage from all
encumbrance, and a happier or a more respected family
do not exist.   And Lizzie,—that gentle, confiding wife—
as she takes that simple paper from the drawer, and gazes
again and again upon the magic pledge it bears, weeps
tears of joy anew.   Were all the wealth of the Indies
poured out in one glittering, blinding pile at her feet, and
all the honours of the world added thereto, she would not,
for the whole countless sum, give in exchange one single word
from that pledge which constituted her Husband's Present

MISCELLANEOUS.

THE SMOKY CHIMNEY.

There was an eccentric squire named Jones, who was troubled with a very smoky chimney. One evening a would-be philosopher entered (thumbs in arm-holes of his vest) and remarked, " You have got a very smoky chimney, Squire Jones." " I know that," replied the squire. "Well, I think I could remedy it," returned the would-be philosopher. "How could you do that ?" said the squire. " Well, let me see," said he, stooping down and looking up the chimney. "O, it's easy to remedy that, squire; just get a transtwistification, and place it upon the top of the chimney, and that will cause a proper vent for the smoke." " What's the word you named ?" said the squire; " I never heard such a long word in my life." "Transtwistification. You get it placed upon the top of your chimney, and I'll bet my life on it you're rid of this smoke." " Where will I get it?" said the squire. "In the village," responded the would-be philosopher. " Will it cost much ?" " No." " Well, I'll have it done." The squire drove to the village, purchased the " Transtwistification," placed it as directed, but the chimney smoked as bad as ever. Another would-be philosopher entered one day (holding up his coat tails behind): " Good day, Squire Jones; very smoky chimney, squire." "I know that." " Well, I guess I could fix that, squire." " How would you fix it ?" " Let me see." So he put his glass to his eye and said, " Well, squire, I would get a " circumbendevication " and that

S

would rectify matters. " Get what ?" asked the squire. " Get a circumbendevication, built of bricks in a slant — eh — position." " I'll have it done," replied the squire ; but it smoked as bad as ever. Shortly after a poor man entered, and meekly bid the squire "good morning." " Your chimney smokes greatly, squire." " I know that." " Well, squire, I can fix it in a few minutes." "How would you fix it ?" "Have you a broom convenient ?" he enquired, on procuring which he ascended the chimney, and *swept it* clean, when there was not a better-drawing chimney in the township. What the chimney wanted was sweeping. The soot removed, rid the squire of his smoke. So what we want to remedy the evils of intemperance is an entire Prohibitory Liquor Law to prevent the importation, manu- facture and sale of intoxicating drinks as a beverage.

A WIDOW'S ADDRESS.

At a town meeting in Pennsylvania, the question once came up, as to what number (if any) of licenses should be granted for the ensuing year ; there was a very full at- tendance, one of the magistrates presided, and on the platform were seated, amongst others, the pastor, one of his deacons and the physician. After the meeting had been called to order, one of the most respectable citizens of the borough rose and moved that the meeting petition for the same number of licenses for the ensuing year as they had on the previous. The proposition seemed to meet with almost universal favour; the president rose and was about to put the motion to the meeting, when an ob- ject arose in a distant part of the building, and all eyes were instantly turned in that direction. It was an old woman, poorly clad, whose care-worn countenance was the painful index of no light suffering, and yet there was something in the flash of her bright eye that told she had once been what she then was not. "You all know who I am," she said, addressing the president. "You once knew me mistress of one of the best estates in the borough. I once had a husband and five sons, and woman never had a kinder husband, mother never had better or more affectionate sons. But where are they now? Doctor, where are they now? In yonder burying ground there are six graves filled by that husband and those five sons, and oh! they are all drunkards' graves! Doctor, how came they to be drunkards? You would come and drink with them, and you told them that temperate drinking would do them good. Minister, what made them drunkards? You would come and drink with my husband, and my sons thought they might safely follow your example. Deacon, you sold them rum, which made them drunkards; you have now got my farm and all my property, and got it all by rum. And now," said she, "I have done my errand; I go back to the poorhouse, for that is my home; I shall never meet you again till I shall meet you at the judgment seat of Christ, where I shall meet you minister, you deacon, and you physician; where you also will meet my ruined and lost husband, and those five sons, who through your influence and example now fill drunkards' graves." The old woman sat down; perfect silence reigned till the president rose and asked, "Shall we petition the court to issue licenses to this borough for the ensuing year?" when one unbroken

"NO' made the very walls re-echo with the sound, and told the power of the old woman's eloquent appeal.

THE APOSTROPHE TO WATER.

The origin of the apostrophe was as follows :

One Paul Denton, a Methodist preacher in Texas, advertised a *Barbecue,* with better liquor than was ever furnished.   When the people were assembled, a desperado in the crowd cried out—" Mr. Paul Denton, your *Riverence* has lied.   You promised us not only a good barbecue, but better liquor.   Where is the liquor ? "

" There," answered the missionary in tones of thunder, and pointing his motionless finger at the matchless Double Spring, gushing up in two strong columns, with a sound like a shout of joy, from the bosom of the earth.   " There!" he repeated, with a look terrible as the lightning, while his enemy actually trembled on his feet; " there is the liquor which God, the Eternal, brews for all his children ! Not in the simmering still, over smoky fires choked with poisonous gases, and surrounded by the stench of sickening odours and rank corruptions, doth your Father in heaven prepare the precious essence of life, the pure cold water, but in the green glade and grassy dell, where the red deer wanders, and the child loves to play, there God brews it; and down, low down in the deepest valleys, where the fountains murmur and the rills sing ; and high up on the tall mountain tops, where the naked granite glitters like gold in the sun, where the storm-cloud broods and the thunder-storms crash ; and away far out on the wide, wild sea, where the hurricane howls music and the big waves roar the chorus, sweeps the march of God—there He brews it, that beverage of life, health-giving water. And everywhere it is a thing of beauty. Gleaming in the dew drop; singing in the summer rain; shining in the ice-gem till the trees all seem turned to living jewels—spreading a golden veil over the setting sun, or a white gauze around the midnight moon; sporting in the cataract; sleeping in the glacier; dancing in the hail-shower; folding its bright snow curtains softly about the wintry world and weaving the many-coloured iris, that seraph zone of the sky, whose warp is the rain-drop of earth, whose woof is the sunbeam of heaven, all decked with celestial flowers, by the mystic hand of refraction. Still always it is beautiful—that blessed life-water! No poison bubbles on its brink; its foam brings not madness and murder; no blood stains its liquid glass; pale widows and starving orphans weep not burning tears in its depths; no drunkard's shrieking ghost from the grave curses it in words of eternal despair!—Speak out, my friend, would you exchange it for the demon Alcohol?"

COST OF INTEMPERANCE.

In the village of M ——, containing about two thousand inhabitants, and the centre of trade for about two thousand more, there were sold, during the year 1863, 581 barrels of liquor, and 551 of ale. Let us see what could have been done with the money thus expended.

Allowing 81 barrels of the liquor to have been used for mechanical and medicinal purposes—a generous allowance, certainly—we have a balance of 500 barrels. This is equal to 15,750 gallons. Supposing one-half of this (7,875 gallons) to be sold by the gallon at only $1, and we have $7,875. Selling the remainder, which is equal to 252,000 gills, at only five cents a gill, we have the snug sum of $12,600, making in all for liquor $20,475.

With this $20,475 could have been secured—

5 Clergymen at $1,200 each........................... $6,000
1 Principal in the Academy, at......................... 1,000
3 Assistant Teachers in the Academy, at $500... 1,500
10 Teachers for Village Graded Schools, at $300... 3,000
15 Teachers for District Schools, at $200............ 3,000
2 Colporteurs for the County, at $600............... 1,200
20 Dailies for reading-room, at $10................... 200
25 Weeklies   "   "   2.................... 50
30 Monthlies   "   "   5.................. 150
20 Quarterlies   "   "   4.................. 80
Rent for Reading-room................................. 100
Clerk... 600
Fuel, lights and postage............................... 120
34 Lyceum Lectures, at $100........................... 3,400
Printers' Bills... 75

Total... $20,475

So much for the liquor. Now for the ale. In 551 barrels of ale there are 141,056 pints. This sold at five cents a pint, would amount to $705,280. As ale-drinking is considered a lower form of intemperance than wine-drinking, etc., we will put this sum in part to a lower, but none the less worthy service. We will pay a clergy-man to preach to the 160 inmates of the County alms-house, $1,000 ; 2 teachers for the children there, $250 each, $500 ; 15 poor students in the academy, $300 each, $4,500; 2 students in a theological seminary, $525, $1,050; and leave a balance of $280 in the treasury.

The writer has no great confidence in statistical argu-ments. Men will say this is guessing, and that this ill-fated village is an exception. There is no guessing about it, except in the price at which it was sold. If we are in error there, we are beyond a peradventure on the inside of the truth. As to that village being an exception, the writer, in travelling leisurely three thousand miles, de-clares that there are other places far worse.

We do well to talk about retrenchment in dress and living generally, to save expense. Add to this the ruin of *soul and body* with *estate*, and my figures ought to claim attention.

A LIQUOR DEALER'S ADVERTISEMENT.

FRIENDS AND NEIGHBOURS,—Thankful for your liberal support during the years that are past, I beg to inform you that I have on hand a very large stock of choice wines, spirits and malt liquors, which I shall as hereto-fore continue to vend, heedless of the increased number of paupers, drunkards and beggars made by the same. There are Temperance men enough in our county to care for and support them; or, if not, I cannot help it. My liquor (being good) may excite the lower classes to riot, robbery and blood, but our Legislature has provided for these things. With our substantial and enlarged jail, and a superabundance of magisterial power on every side, what have we to fear? Accidents are increased somewhat by the drinking usages of the day, but we have our coroners, and it is their duty to attend to these matters by holding inquests, making enquiries, and to see that there is no foul play. It has been said, and we are not prepared to deny it, that strong drink is the prolific source of fearful diseases, but then we are blessed with a large supply of M.D.'s in our midst; and certainly in this enlightened age we should be prepared to live and let live. You may expect it will consume a large share of your means, become a tax on your reason, a blight upon your character, and a destroyer of your peace, but what is the use of living without enjoyment? and besides, they say the Bible says "We brought nothing into the world, and it is certain we can take nothing out of it." As a consequence of the traffic, it will doubtless make many fathers fiends, wives widows, mothers cruel, children orphans, and thousands poor; but you must remember that it takes all kinds of people to make a world.

I will, therefore, "accommodate" the public. I have a family to support—the trade pays—you, my friends, encourage it. I have a character from my minister and a license from the council; my traffic is lawful; Christians countenance it. It is an easy way of getting a living; I shall therefore carry on my trade with energy, knowing that if I do not bring these evils upon you, somebody else will. I have found by past experience that my business increases in proportion to the ignorance and sensuality of the mass; it will therefore be necessary for me to use every legitimate means in my power to prevent the intellectual elevation, moral purity, social happiness, and eternal welfare of all.

In view of the coming election, I have great pleasure in intimating to my old customers and the public generally, that Messrs. Vitriol, Strychnine, Nux Vomica, Cocculus Indicus, Tobacco, Opium and others of my very esteemed friends, have kindly consented to be with us during the polling day so near at hand, by whose kindly aid I shall be enabled, with but very little expense to myself, to give free drinks to all who will oppose the passage of the by-law which will inflict such an outrage upon the freedom of the people. By close application to my business, and a devoted attachment to my principles, I hope to merit a continuance of your support.

JUDAS HEARTLESS.

WOMAN'S INFLUENCE.

AIR—*Nelly Gray.*

I fell from Wisdom's ways
In my thoughtless youthful days,
And became a poor drink-fettered slave,
Led captive, body, soul,
Under passions' strong control
I was hastening on to ruin and the grave—

Chorus—When an Angel stopped my way,
It was lovely Nelly Gray
Who persuaded me to give my drinking o'er.
Her kind words did prevail
As we wandered through the Dale,
And I'll never taste the drink any more.

Though humble is our lot,
Well furnished is our cot,
With its neatly-trimmed garden at the door :
Our children's mirth and glee
Is our sweetest minstrelsy,
And the bounteous gifts of heaven fill our store.

Chorus—When an Angel stopped my way, &c.

Ah, well it is I know
That all I have I owe
To my Nelly's timely, kindly sympathy ;
When sinking in despair
She then saved me by her care,
And I love her for the love she bore to me.

Chorus—When an Angel stopped my way, &c.

DEAR FRIENDS, DRINK NO MORE.

AIR—*Hazel Dell.*

On this Rum-curs'd earth I long have wandered,
  Weary and oppressed,
Where the dearest ties are often sundered
  In the fondest breast.
Here, 'mid scenes that oft are sad and trying,
  Sorrow's cup runs o'er,
For the bravest, choicest ones are dying—
  Dear friends, drink no more.

Chorus—All the while my watch I'm keeping
    In this vale of gore,
      For the bravest, choicest ones are dying—
    Dear friends, drink no more.

Cold and silent friends are near me sleeping,
  Where the flowers wave,
And in mournful strains are often weeping
  Loved ones round their grave.
While the gentle gales are round me sighing,
  In the lute's sad tone,
They toll the knell of Drunkards dying,
  Dearly loved and gone.

Chorus—All the while my watch I'm keeping, &c.

Come, my brethren, friends of God and mankind,
  Boldly aid the right,
Let us gather force, and, like a whirlwind,
  Drive Rum out of sight.
Come, my brave friends, never be discouraged,
  Help is near at hand ;

By the signs of the times be encouraged—
  Nobly take your stand.

Chorus—All the while my watch I'm keeping, &c.

THE DYING SON.

Air—*Lily Dale.*

To yon low cottage home, in the hawthorn's shade,
  Where the stream ripples sweetly by,
Unfriended and weary, a poor youth there came,
  In the home of his childhood to die.

Chorus—O, mother ! dear mother !
        Pray for me now ;
      For the life stream is ebbing from my poor
        lorn heart,
      And the death-dews are cold on my brow.

O, dear to my heart were the scenes of my youth,
  When my life welled in beauty and joy ;
But life's brightest hours I have squandered for naught—
  O, comfort thy poor dying boy !

      O, mother ! fond mother ! &c.

They showed me the wine-cup, with roses entwined,
  In the hands of the good and the fair ;
But I saw not the coils of the reptile beneath,
  Till its sting filled my heart with despair.

      O, mother ! kind mother ! &c.

I would I had lived all thy love to repay—
  All thy kindness, by toiling for thee:
There's but one star beaming through the darkness of
    death,
  'Tis thy holy affection for me.

        O, mother! good mother! &c.

I thought to have soothed thy declining years,
  To have ranked with the good and the brave;
But the bright sun that gilded the dawn of my youth
  Must set in the gloom of the grave.

        O, mother! good mother! &c.

www.ingramcontent.com/pod-product-compliance
Lightning Source LLC
Chambersburg PA
CBHW020944120726
47905CB00008B/2670